Praise for *Ten Indians*

"Shootings, kidnapping, hit-and-run, routine and inventive stabbings, crack overdose, fist-and-foot-fights, child neglect and abuse, a mounting toll of murder; in *Ten Indians,* the action unrolls at a thriller pace. Bell has a compelling, gut-gripping way with the violent incident . . . he builds his tightly structured narrative primarily, and most convincingly, with such wrenchingly realized moments . . . within the context of Bell's authentic obsessions—cruelty and fear as epitomized by our bizarre human invention, racism—*Ten Indians* acquires echoes and reflections of a deeper kind."

—*Los Angeles Times Book Review*

"We read not with a sense of futility, but of passionate concern. . . . While *Ten Indians* is far more intimate in scale and colloquial in language [than *All Souls' Rising*], both books demonstrate not only Bell's powerful qualities of imagination, but the research he does." —*Chicago Tribune*

"A winning novel set in the inner city . . . the working out, told partly from Devlin's viewpoint and partly, in convincing street language, from that of the drug dealers and their women, is spare and cinematic."

—*Time* magazine

"His apparently fearless depiction of black characters might be expected of Bell . . . his forays into black street slang are dead on and devoid of condescension. . . . His black characters are neither overly noble nor hopelessly cartoonish; it is sufficient to say that they simply are, and convincingly so."

—*The Washington Post*

"*Ten Indians* is taut, tense, and explosive." —*The Miami Herald*

"A fine novel, well-written and thought-provoking. . . . Bell's novel follows a complex pattern of development that often slides off into miniature morality plays as death, grief, and personal loss perform a mocking dance around Devlin's 'sanctuary.'" —*The Dallas Morning News*

"A briskly paced, street-smart and often harrowing book. . . . *Ten Indians* should impress you with its urgency and skill. Bell has taken care to make both his troubled urban aggressors and his hapless victims human and sympathetically real."

—*The Milwaukee Journal Sentinel*

"A moving, intelligent portrayal of contemporary society's most pressing questions, *Ten Indians* also happens to be a good read. Bell has honed his storytelling style, blending philosophical reflection and narrative momentum with a newfound ease. As powerful as a crisp kick to the solar plexus, *Ten Indians* may well be Madison Smartt Bell's most fiercely brilliant and haunting novel to date."

—*San Francisco Bay Guardian*

ABOUT THE AUTHOR

Madison Smartt Bell is the author of ten previous works of fiction, most recently the novel *All Souls' Rising* (available from Penguin), which was a National Book Award finalist and a finalist for the PEN/Faulkner Award for Fiction in 1995. He was recently named one of the Best Young American Novelists under 40 by *Granta*. He lives in Baltimore.

MADISON SMARTT BELL

TEN INDIANS

PENGUIN BOOKS

PENGUIN BOOKS
Published by the Penguin Group
Penguin Putnam Inc., 375 Hudson Street,
New York, New York 10014, U.S.A.
Penguin Books Ltd, 27 Wrights Lane,
London W8 5TZ, England
Penguin Books Australia Ltd, Ringwood,
Victoria, Australia
Penguin Books Canada Ltd, 10 Alcorn Avenue,
Toronto, Ontario, Canada M4V 3B2
Penguin Books (N.Z.) Ltd, 182-190 Wairau Road,
Auckland 10, New Zealand

Penguin Books Ltd, Registered Offices:
Harmondsworth, Middlesex, England

First published in the United States of America by
Pantheon Books, a division of Random House, Inc. 1996
Reprinted by arrangement with Pantheon Books, a division of Random House, Inc.
Published in Penguin Books 1997

3 5 7 9 10 8 6 4 2

Grateful acknowledgment is made to Sara Mosle
for permission to reprint an excerpt from "Annals of Childhood"
from *The New Yorker* (18 September 1995).

PUBLISHER'S NOTE
This is a work of fiction, and the characters and events
described in this book are of the author's own creation.

THE LIBRARY OF CONGRESS HAS CATALOGUED THE HARDCOVER AS FOLLOWS:
Bell, Madison Smartt.
Ten Indians / Madison Smartt Bell.
p. cm.
ISBN 0-679-44246-4 (hc.)
ISBN 0 14 02.6846 4 (pbk.)
1. Tae kwon do—Study and teaching—Maryland—Baltimore—Fiction.
2. Inner cities—Maryland—Baltimore—Fiction. 3. Violence—Maryland—Baltimore—Fiction. 4. Gangs—Maryland—Baltimore—Fiction.
5. Youth—Maryland—Baltimore—Fiction. 6. Baltimore (Md.)—Fiction. I. Title.
PS3552.E517T46 1996
813'.54—dc20 96-14357

Printed in the United States of America
Set in Bulmer
Designed by Cassandra Pappas

For my masters:

Lee Young I

Park Kyung Sik

Kim Chong Min

Son Duk Sung

For all the good people I've trained with,

too numerous to name

And in memory of

Craig Daniels

1962–1995

My firend's boyfirend died. And she was sad. I herd in the phone that she was sad . . . She lives in New Jersey he was selling drugs for 100 dollars and a man came with 50 dollars and sede if he could take a pack and he sede no. So he had a gun and shot him three times in the chest. then he died. I did not go to the funirow.

—Anonymous child quoted in
"Writing Down Secrets," by Sara Mosle

At least this will be my chance to find out if I am what I think I am or if I just hope; if I am going to do what I have taught myself is right or if I am just going to wish I were.

—William Faulkner, *The Unvanquished*

Ten Indians

TRIG

DON'T KNOW I can say how it all started, but I tell you how it almost finish up. I was walking back to the block with the rest of them when I felt something touch the side of my neck. Didn't feel like as much as a bee sting even, more like a push of somebody's finger—that all I felt. But it must of been sharper than a finger because when it pulled away, my blood came following it, shooting out of some big vein like it blasting out of a fire hose. It was a neat little dark red ray of blood and out the corner of my eye I saw it blast through the bars of the cell I was passing and even dent back the blanket somebody had tack up there to try to give his scumbag self a little privacy.

But I already covered it up with my hand by then. I wanted to feel around the edge and see what kind of a hole it was but I knew I had to just cover it over and mash down hard. It wasn't much of a hole for size, but I could feel it pressing hard back against the center of my palm. Then I fell over against the bars, and when I turned I could just see Charlie Alcorn grinning over at me as he faded back in the line, a real big grin that wrinkled up his forehead where he decided to cut his motherfuckin Aryan Nation dagger tattoo. He already handed off whatever it was he used—some kind of nail I guessed later on from the size of the hole. All he'd of had to do is pound it sideways through a scrap of wood to set it up like a push dagger. Used things like that myself from time to time. When you get done you can slide the nail back out of the wood and wash it off and it ain't nothing but just another nail.

The guys were stirring up all around me and some was yelling and then a lot of the hacks came running up and started thunking a few heads and herding people off for a lockdown, no doubt. I was already starting to feel lightheaded and I was scared too. My pulse was beating right against my hand where I was trying to keep that fountain of blood clamped down inside me somehow, and I could tell my heart was going a lot too fast. If it didn't slow down soon it wouldn't take me three minutes to bleed to death right there where I was standing on the tier. So I started thinking about breathing deeper and slower and I started trying to get myself together.

One of the hacks called over to me then and told me the gates were clear for me to walk over to the infirmary if I felt up to it. He didn't want to get too close to tell me this. The hacks been real nervous of blood these days. My eyes were about half shut and I was trying to think . . . Devlin use to tell us to think our hands be warm when he want to send energy out through the body, so what I got to do is think my hands be cold. That would bring the blood back to my heart. Right? Cold like a dead man. Devlin use to say, concentrate on your pulse so you can feel it, and it wasn't no problem to feel it the way things was now. But I couldn't laugh because it gonna make me bleed faster if I did. I thought my hand be a big block of ice just chilling down my blood and making it run slower and sure enough I could feel my heart slow down right there where I was holding it in my hand.

Then came the big slam of the tier locking down. My head cleared some and I pick up my feet and started walking. I was all alone on the tier, what it felt like. I could hear a couple hacks talking somewhere behind me and I feel the eyes of the locked-down guys in the cells to the left of me but I didn't look over at any of that. I couldn't quite make out what people was saying but I did get the idea there wasn't nobody putting out no bet that I gonna make it all the way to the infirmary.

I came to the end of the tier and the gate slid open smooth as butter. Man, I thought, I got to try this shit more often. But my heartbeat jump like a frog in my hand and I remembered I couldn't laugh.

Then I was walking down the stairs toward the bottom of the tier. My feet was cold as lead, and heavy, with the metal mesh ringing wherever I set down my shoes. I was starting to get tired. I start whispering under my breath, "Light and sweet, light and sweet," which was what I use to tell myself back when Devlin had the school, if I get tired in the middle of practice. I'd think those words and if it worked I'd start to feel like I was floating in a cloud and my arms and legs don't be so heavy no more cause the cloud stuff holds'm up like I was swimming. I don't know why sweet, though. Why would I pick that?

At the bottom of the tier was a hallway I had to go through to get to the next block. A double gate went between the two and I had to stop for the first one to close behind me before the one ahead would open. That wasn't so good. Broke my momentum. But the second gate open easy-greasy and I pick myself up and went through.

Slow. Slow now. Truth was, my mind in a big hurry to get to that infirmary if I could do it but I known I couldn't rush my body cause it speed up my heart if I do. I already been about five hundred years on this walk so far, just thinking about keeping my pulse real slow.

Not much light along this next tier but what they was kept shining over all those fine little threads of wire that crisscrossed in the air up over my head. You take a wire and tie a soap cake or a chunk of wood to it—anything for a weight—and sling it out your cell bars and across the corridor to catch on a pipe or a stanchion or something on the other side. Make an antenna for your radio or TV or whatever. I looked up and saw the wires zigzagging all the way up the tier, six or eight catwalks high above me, crossing each other like spiderwebs and catching the light like a cobweb do. Most days I wouldn't of noticed them at all but this was different. Wasn't nobody playing the TV much or listening to the radio. It was quieter than it was supposed. I ain't seen nobody but I got the idea guys listening and peeping out they cells to see me pass by.

Two more gates and I came out into a square where a couple new dudes waiting to get took to they cells. I only took a good look at one that I remember. White guy with a pale bushy beard and had on overalls like a farmer. His hands were cuffed in front and he was staring up at the tier behind me like they all do when they first come in. The tier come hulking over you like a cliff leaning out the shadows of the ceiling, all those cages stacked on cages going up and away into the dark . . . This one white dude didn't seem startled to see me come out of there—it was like he expected a thing like me to be coming out of a place like that. But when I caught his eyes I could see myself like looking in a mirror. I saw how the blood was all pumping out through my fingers and soaking through my sweats there on the right side. For the first time now I felt the blood was squelching in my shoes. Then I almost lost it but somehow I kept walking. I passed the white dude by and went through two more gates.

Five hundred years. It wasn't far now, though. But I had to go up some stairs now and I didn't like that. It was a closed stairway, all bricked in, and they might be somebody laying for you at the turn, or some nasty sex business going on you wouldn't want to have to look at it. I never liked that stairway at the best of times. It was worse now because I was so tired I just wanted to sit down, lie down, go to sleep, give up. My eyes not working right. My sight keep closing down like a shutter was turning across it, I'd see it fall across my eyes and it would go dark for about half a minute, then the shutter turn past and it was light for about as long. Roaring sound between my ears like wind blowing in a cave. Out of the roar I heard voices coming, sometimes Devlin, or Gramma Reen, or my own voice even. The voice say: Don't stop, don't stop, keep moving, break on through. Breathe. Keep walking . . . you don't need to see. Just walk. Which it appears I must of done.

I don't know how I got up the stairs exactly. Wouldn't

been nobody hiding there noway because of the lockdown. On the corridor above it was lighter and the walls were painted yellow to a tape line about my chest height. Seem like I just float on down that yellow line till I see my fist falling on the infirmary door. No sound come back to me though. That was strange. Clearwater jerk the door open and I saw his mouth come open but I didn't hear what he had to say because right then I fell over on the floor and I died.

I could look back from somewhere and I seen my body twisting and jerking on the floor. My hand come loose from my neck and the blood spraying all over the joint again until Clearwater slap his hand down over it, kneeling there beside the body and hollering for a hemostat. Didn't make no difference to me though, I was gone.

That's one way to get out of the Cut, I guess. Which was about the last smartass thought I had. Cold wind blowing behind me and driving me down a long dark hallway full of stars, and as I got more further along I started to pass a lot of people I used to know who was dead now too. They wasn't none of them smiling or happy or glad to see me like you hear about from them other bullshit artists who claim they died and then come back. It didn't look like they was gonna be no welcome party in my honor. Everybody heaven be different I guess. In mine, people didn't even look halfway pleased that I shown up. Not only that but I got the idea that they was something bigger, somebody in back of them, who wasn't too happy at all about the way I been handling myself.

But I never seen this mysterious dude. Instead, everything switched back in the other direction and I was slipping back down that hall like getting sucked feetfirst down a vacuum cleaner. Next thing I know it was three days later and I woke up lying on an infirmary cot all stuck full of needles and blood bags dripping into me and everything like that. All the AIDS guys making they usual death-rattle noise trying to suck a little wind through they pneumonia and TB and shit, and over that I could just barely make out the radio playing the news.

Rosa Parks, the radio say. Rosa Parks, the lady who kicked off the bus boycott which set my people free if that what you want to call it, been beat up and robbed in her Detroit apartment and everybody all upset and she under police protection.

Only thing I can think—what about all the others? Who bugged about them? Where they getting protection at? Shouldn't of happened to Rosa Parks. Shouldn't happened to Gramma Reen. Shouldn't happen to any old ladies or anybody at all. But I knew in the time it took me to think it probably two or three old ladies get they neck broke over whatever they might have in they purse.

What it is. I ain't know if I can change nothing. Nobody bringing those dead folks back. But I figure I might better try. Shine what little light I can. Maybe I can turn my heaven into a friendlier place, come time I got to go there and stay. Like Devlin would say it—clean your own house.

Only I wasn't in the mood to hear all Devlin sayings run in my head. Out of all them dead people Devlin the one I was the maddest at. Because the others, they didn't have much choice the way I seen it. But you, Devlin, you were free to choose. You been to college, got a good-money job, house in a nice neighborhood. You were white. People cared for you. So why did you go and waste yourself and leave the ones that loved you all alone like I left mine? Yeah, you a stone fool to do like you did, Devlin, you dumb motherfucker, I like to drag you back and kill you all over again just to show you what a dumb motherfucker you are. You just thrown yourself away. Nobody made you—you did it for nothing. It was stupid and reckless. It didn't get you nothing. Got nobody nothing but misery. It—what was the worst thing I could say to Devlin?—it was unnecessary. UNNECESSARY! You hear what I say you sonofabitch?

Which of course he didn't, but Clearwater did, cause it appears I was shouting out loud, along with crying and all that shit. Clearwater just raise a big hallelujah and come over and start talking about what a miracle it was I woke up at all, when the hacks wouldn't ship me out to a regular hospital and all they had to work on me here was staples and tape and shit like that. Probably true for what it was worth.

Then I calmed down, and Clearwater calmed down, and I closed my eyes and made like I was asleep. But I was still hearing the AIDS guys fighting to breathe, and I was thinking over one thing and another, Devlin and the others, and Rosa Parks, and things I'd be having to do myself after however long it took me to get able to stand up off of this bed. Deal with Charlie Alcorn somehow, that was one thing.

But who knows how you suppose to live your life? All I known was I definitely fucked up the first time I tried it. Might be I had as many lives coming to me as a cat, but I still thought I better play this next one like it gonna be my last.

10

IT WAS cold enough that Devlin could just see his breath whirling ahead of him as he huffed up the crown of the hill, his rubber soles slapping the asphalt just beyond the concrete edge of the storm drain. The leaves had begun to turn as well, so there was a Japanese maple charged a rich blood red in a nearby yard, though it was in shadow now, with the sun so low in the west behind Devlin as he ran. Twilight, but ahead of him and sixty feet above, the leaves of the old sycamores were shot through with a sundown brilliance, so that they glistened like gold foil, moving lightly, all together, on the wind like water, foam on the crest of a wave of darkness.

Later he thought that was one thing wrong; he shouldn't have been looking up, because once he saw the car, the time had already passed for him to throw himself out of the way. He jumped or hopped straight up instead, just enough for his feet to clear the ground, a reflex, not a thought. The first impact he felt was the heels of his palms skidding across the warm hood, while the brakes began to howl, and he saw a featureless shadow of his own reflection on the windshield glass. A skein of frost was on the edges of the windshield and underneath two faces swimming, passenger and driver, mouths and eyes dark holes through them. A flash of sunlight from the glass and Devlin was rolling sideways, scarcely aware of his fingers clawing, spun by some torque of the collision that flipped him up and over the curb and landed him on the strip of grass between the sidewalk and the storm drain.

The car, a black Camaro, hovered a few yards past, its engine coughing and grumbling in the cold. Devlin saw cottony puffs of steam bouncing out of the rusted tailpipe. He was instantly aware that he had not been killed, but it seemed impossible he was not badly hurt. The ground was cool, damp, not yet frozen, but the slam across his back had winded him. Apart from that, he felt no pain. He sat up cautiously; his legs drew up automatically with the movement. Not broken, then. His astonishment still could not quite come through. The Camaro coughed and trembled; its brake lights pulsed red. A windshield wiper stuck out at a wrenched angle from the near side. In the sideview mirror, Devlin saw a face turned to inspect him: teardrop sunglasses, and a cigarette hanging from the lip. He put his fists on the ground and pushed himself up. As he reached his feet, the face rolled out of the mirror, the brake lights winked, and the car backfired softly as it shot away from him down the hill.

"Son of a bitch!" Devlin said out loud, but with no real

heat. His whole being had begun to sing with endorphins and adrenaline. Now he realized he had not attended to the license number. That frost still on the windshield . . . the car must belong to someone who lived nearby, more than likely across York Road, given the make, and the attitude. But to hell with it, really. They were just scared. As for blame, Devlin had been running in the roadway, his head in the clouds. He wore a dark denim jacket over a sweatshirt, a couple of strips of reflective silver tape above the pockets his only concession to safety precautions. The Camaro'd had no lights on—the best he could remember that flashed impression of its nose shoveling toward him—but it couldn't have been going as fast as it seemed, else Devlin would never have got to his feet.

A couple of other cars whizzed past and down the hill to the Charles Street stoplight. Devlin looked down at his left hand, which clutched a strip of wiper-blade rubber. He must have snatched at the wiper as he was being tossed clear of the car. Yes, and his palm was bleeding from light scratches here and there. He let the rubber drop into the gutter, then thought again and crouched with a slight effort, retrieved it and stuck it into his jacket pocket. He stood up. There was a knotting sensation in the meat of his left upper thigh, no worse than a bad charley horse really. Perhaps the bumper had struck him there.

He was actually already walking away from the whole thing, and with scarcely as much as a limp. A few steps down from the hill's low peak, he glanced back and saw that the Camaro's angle would have been as blind as his own when he came running up the far side. So. The cold air he gulped tasted fresh to him as springwater, and his heart was beating vigorously, his sweat was fresh. It was a straight shot down the gentle slope to the corner of his street. Oddly, no one was out on the sidewalks or in the yards, no dog-walkers, bicyclists, other joggers. The falling sunlight came striated through the limbs of the old trees, tiger-striping the leaf-littered lawns. Evening birdsong was very grateful in Devlin's ear, that moment upon him, its presence sweet. With the catch in his thigh no more than an accent on his mood, he picked up his pace and began to jog.

"WHAT HAPPENED?" Alice said, frowning slightly as Devlin walked in the kitchen door. She was standing at the stove, stirring grated cheese into a sauce.

"What happened where?"

Alice licked a fleck of cheese from her finger, pointed at his pants leg. "Looks like you've been rolling on the ground."

Devlin glanced down, and noticed for the first time the smudge and tear of the fabric over the sore spot on his leg; he was rubbed all over with grass stains too. Absently he scratched at the back of his head, and his hand came away full of scraps of dead leaves.

"Took a tumble," he said, and with scarcely a flicker of hesitation, "Stepped on my shoelace—that's what it must have been." The evasion seemed necessary to him, though he didn't know why. From deeper in the house came the thrum of music, Michelle tuned into MTV. Alice nodded abstractedly at her saucepan, and Devlin was moved to hug her from behind, to lift her slightly from under her breasts, but she was distracted, shifting her hips away from him, air-kissing vaguely in his direction.

"Why don't you go and get cleaned up? Dinner's soon."

"Right." Devlin snapped his fingers and walked through the dining room, the living room, stuck his head into the den. Michelle was propped on couch cushions, her legs drawn up, a math book open across her knees. Music and light pulsed from the television, washing her in fluorescent colors.

"Hey, Shell . . ." Devlin hadn't seen her that day, since she got home from school. He lowered a couple of blinds and turned on a floor lamp; he stopped himself from nagging her about reading in poor light. "What're you up to?"

Michelle pinched her nose for a parody robotic accent: "Find the derivative." She shook back her long chestnut hair and spoke normally. "Want to help?"

"I'm a liberal arts major," Devlin said. "Useless to you."

He looked at her with the mixture of pleasure and fear he often felt. She was seventeen and very pretty, his only child, looking up at him now with a faintly ironic smile on her full mouth, patient with his interruption. Her green eyes were dilated to spheres of black, from the dim light probably. On the TV screen, Janet Jackson stood in a line of dancers with her hands on her hips, squatting, jerking upright, snapping her head angrily from side to side.

"Talking to yourself there, Dad?"

Devlin caught his lips moving over the secret: *I was hit by a car and I walked away from it.* Keeping his silence, he felt a flush of euphoria swell from his heels to the roots of his hair. The room seemed to glow with a hyper-real luminance. On the screen, the music changed, some band Devlin had never heard of. Michelle dropped her head so that her hair swung down, and scribbled something on her math pad.

"Um . . . I guess I need to finish this."

In the upstairs bathroom, water slammed on the enamel of the tub, waiting to run hot. Sweat had turned clammy inside Devlin's shirt. He stripped off his clothes and stuffed them in a hamper. A glimpse of his body in the bathroom mirror rather pleased him, how it was intact, unbroken. Raising a foot to the edge of the tub, he probed the edges of the bruise on his thigh. A hot soak would have done it good, but there wasn't time. He pulled the valve on the faucet and stepped into the shower.

Alice's voice came floating up the stairs as he was toweling off. "Mike . . . five minutes till it's ready?" Devlin dressed quickly and went down to supper at the kitchen table: baked chicken and potatoes, beans in the homemade cheese sauce. Michelle had changed her clothes, he noticed, ready to go out. Devlin ate with sincere appetite; everything seemed unusually satisfactory: the food, his glass of wine, the warm kitchen and warm presence of his wife and daughter, all burnished bright by his clash with the Camaro. It was pleasant also to imagine their surprise if he told them now. He held the secret to him with a little smile.

Michelle pushed back her plate and stood, smoothing her hands down her tight-jeaned hips and arching her back with the graceful laziness of a well-fed cat.

"We have ice cream," Alice said.

"No thanks," said Michelle. "I gotta run."

"Where're you going?" Devlin said.

"The movies," Michelle said, and with an air of resignation. "With Holly and Amber. And Mark and Ricky."

"I didn't ask," Devlin said, with a pushing motion of his palms.

"You didn't have to," Michelle said. Her tone braked just short of sarcasm. "I've made a full disclosure." Her pupils were still very wide, even in the bright light of the kitchen.

"Check," Devlin said. "Have fun."

"I won't be late." Michelle's hair whirled, fanning out a faint citrus scent as she moved to the door. In a moment the sound of her car's motor cranking came back from the driveway.

"Who's Ricky?" Devlin said. He stood up and carried a couple of plates to the sink, aware that his bruised leg had stiffened while he sat at dinner. Through the window over the sink he could see Michelle leaning across the passenger seat of her secondhand Corolla, fishing for something in the glove compartment.

"You've met him," Alice said. "He played in the band at that party at the Taylors'. . . . he plays bass." She set a stack of plates on the drainboard beside him.

"God," Devlin said, rolling rubber gloves onto his hands. "He wears a nose-ring, doesn't he? Makes him look like Porky Pig."

"What's the difference?" Alice said. "A nose-ring here, a nose-ring there. . . . He's a harmless kid. Don't be a cop."

"For the love of—" Devlin stopped himself; he captured the surge of anger like a balloon, punctured it, and let the irritation hiss away. No use to squander the good mood he'd returned in. "Dinner was great."

"Glad to hear it," Alice said.

His retreat was tacitly acknowledged. She put some leftovers into the refrigerator. Devlin squirted soap into a pan. Beyond the window, Michelle sat up and the glove-compartment light winked out. Scouring a pot, Devlin watched her back around the corner of the house and out of view. Sure, he reminded himself, she'd earned that car, which was less flashy, less expensive, than what many of her classmates drove. They'd agreed to let her out on school nights, so long as she kept up her work. A little freedom . . . this time next year she'd be away at school. She was a National Merit finalist and the counselors said she'd be a shoo-in for the college of her choice. All was well. Indeed she'd never given them any worry. Still, Devlin was perhaps perversely pleased that she usually ran in large loose groups instead of going with just one boy.

"You're quiet tonight," Alice said.

But of course, Devlin thought, secrets lose their power when they're told. It was still possible that he might tell her now what happened, enjoy her sympathy and concern, but it would certainly seem peculiar to have waited this long, and somehow he needed it all to himself, this thrill of his survival. Instead of speaking he turned toward her and kissed her on the mouth, holding his wet hands behind his back. This time she let her mouth relax and kissed him back.

"Just wondering . . ." she said when he drew away, "what you were thinking."

Again Devlin faced his indistinct reflection in the windowpanes over the sink. "Not worth a penny," he said. "I'm just fine."

WEEKDAY MORNINGS at six-thirty, Devlin got up and drank some coffee, ate an apple, or sometimes a roll, while

Alice sat at the kitchen table still yawning in her bathrobe, for she went to work a couple of hours later than he. He scraped the frost from his windshield with his comb, started the car, and drove south into downtown Baltimore, to park in the underground garage near his office building on Redwood Street. In the lobby he bought another coffee—in a Styrofoam cup, decaf this time for the sake of his blood pressure—and rose in the elevator to the ninth floor. In his office he debriefed his answering machine, sat down in one of the fatly stuffed recliners, and began.

His patients were children from three to eighteen whose families were well-to-do or well-insured, and often both. They came from the same social stratum to which Devlin and his wife belonged: educated, professional folk. Some of the children went to Glendale School with Michelle, though Devlin excused himself from treating her close friends. Most were children of divorce or multiple divorces, veterans of kaleidoscopic rotations of parents, stepparents, siblings, and relations. All day long, Devlin listened to their voices, combining, recombining. Increasingly, they frightened him.

Fifteen-year-old Julian slumped on the office's leather couch, slapping his knees together, then spreading them rudely wide. He'd spent two years at one of the local private prep schools and this fall refused to return; his mother, whose work as a dress designer frequently took her out of town, had passed this problem along to Devlin.

"You want to take your sunglasses off?" Devlin reached toward the cord of the window blind.

Julian wore wire sunglasses with perfectly round black lenses which he never consented to remove. His hair was crewcut at the back and sides, with a flip in the front carefully sculpted with mousse. On his left bicep was a blue-inked tattoo roughly the size of a paperback book jacket, depicting the Marlboro Man. "Nah, man, I don't wanna."

"Whatever." Devlin dropped the blind cord, which swung against the large double pane with a plastic click. Outside, a siren was winding down Greene Street; the rooftops were pinkening in the dawn. Devlin took his own sunglasses from his shirt pocket, put them on. "Better?"

Julian snickered. "Doc, you're a trip." He yawned and returned to his previous theme. "Anyway, you know, like, she can't *make* me go."

"Well, I guess maybe there're some laws on the subject," Devlin said.

"Really?" Julian's tone was of abstract interest. His IQ, for what it was worth, was unusually high.

"So I've been told," Devlin said. "Legally, you're supposed to go to school, I think. Till you graduate, or turn sixteen."

"You mean somebody's going to come after me with a big net or something."

"Right," Devlin said. "Like a dogcatcher."

"Man, you're funny," Julian said, with no hint of amusement. "I could home-school. Like that thing, you know, that Calvert sends out, to army brats and kids overseas."

"It's supposed to be a good program," Devlin said. "Were you planning to check it out?"

"Hey," Julian said, "what've those guys got under there?"

"I can't tell what you're looking at," Devlin said. "The sunglasses, remember?"

"Those dolls . . . there." Julian flipped a limp hand toward a bookcase opposite him. On a middle shelf were several cloth dolls dressed to resemble modern adults, or children.

"What've they got underneath those clothes—like, little dicks and pussies and stuff? You know, for, like, the little kids to play with?"

"Guttermouth," Devlin said. "You're shocking me. Go home and wash your mouth out with soap."

"Well, do they?"

"Why don't you look?" Devlin said. "I wouldn't stop you."

Julian raised his hand again, let it fall limp to the edge of the couch. "Head games, man, these stupid shrink head games . . ."

"Were you talking about home-schooling?"

"Sure, come on, but what's the point? I mean, I'm supposed to finish *high school* so I can get into *college,* and I'm supposed to go to *college* so I can go to, I dunno, *law school* or something, and then . . . like, where does it all end up?"

"Beats me," Devlin said.

"Yeah. Like screw it, you know? There's not really any dogcatcher, man. They can't make me go."

"Well, maybe they won't," Devlin said, slight stress on the *won't.* "Julian, do you want somebody to make you go?"

Julian was suddenly suspicious. "Crazy, man, why should I want that?"

When Julian was done, Devlin shook a couple of Tums from the large canister in his desk drawer, chewed them slowly and washed them down with juice from the small office refrigerator while he wrote up his notes.

Half an hour later a new patient arrived, Rachel Weintraub, five years old: sleep disturbances, violent tantrums, biting. Her parents were six months divorced and there was joint custody, so that Rachel spent a week with Mom, (who'd recently returned to work and was preoccupied with Rachel's one-year-old brother), then a week with Daddy, who commuted to Washington, where he was sometimes obliged to stay late, in pursuit of the affair that had originally broken the marriage. Rachel had initially been referred by a teacher at the kindergarten of Moorgate School, which she apparently had entered with the force of a tornado.

Given her record of symptoms, Rachel herself seemed shockingly meek. Devlin invited her into the playroom next to his office. Alice and Michelle had helped him decorate and arrange the area so that it resembled a nursery school or pediatrician's waiting room less than a cross between an upscale toy store and a magician's cave from a children's book; lighting produced much of this effect. The contents were routine for such a place: an assortment of dolls, stuffed animals, and puppets, some miniaturized domestic furniture that could be arranged and rearranged, toy guns and toy soldiers, a drawing table with art supplies, a tent, an oversized chess set arranged on a checkered rug, and various other attractions. Rachel stood at the edge of the room, looking. Whenever some particular item caught her eye, she would quickly glance back to Devlin to estimate his reaction. All the while she kept two fingers thrust so deeply into her mouth that her knuckles glistened with saliva. Her hair was light blond, the consistency of spun sugar, and fell in loose tangling curls almost to her waist. That hair would be a lot of work for someone, Devlin thought.

"Red dress you have there," Devlin said, pointing at the patterned jumper Rachel wore.

The girl pulled her fingers from her mouth and gave him what he could only describe as a black look. There was no movement of her features really, it was purely a change of color.

"How does it feel to you?" Devlin said. "Red."

"*Don't say that,*" she told him. "You're not supposed to."

"Sorry," Devlin said. "Why not?"

"Because," Rachel said, definitively. She wiped her fingers carefully in a fold of her jumper, then crossed the room and touched a purple velour dragon on a middle shelf. "This is *not* Barney," she said.

"Certainly not," Devlin said. "You're absolutely right about that."

Rachel carried the dragon through Devlin's office to the waiting room. Her mother's jacket and a shopping bag were on a chair, but the lady herself was absent for some reason; perhaps she'd gone to phone the baby-sitter. With no visible reaction, Rachel came back into the playroom.

"Do you like Barney?" Devlin said.

"I have Barney." Rachel dropped the dragon on the carpeted floor. "At my dad's." She set the toe of her saddle shoe on the dragon's tail. Experimentally she shifted her weight forward.

"It doesn't hurt him," she said, looking quizzically at Devlin. "He doesn't feel that."

"No?"

Rachel covered the dragon's foot with her shoe and mashed down harder. "Mom takes pills to keep her happy," she said.

"That's nice," said Devlin. "I hope they work."

"Barney's not a real dinosaur," Rachel said. She set her foot on the ridges of the dragon's back. "Real dinosaurs aren't pretty. You wouldn't *say* they were."

"Depends on the dinosaur," Devlin said.

"*No,*" Rachel said. "You wouldn't."

"All right," Devlin said. "I guess I better not."

"Real dinosaurs don't get cold or hungry," Rachel informed him. "It doesn't matter a bit to them."

"I don't understand how that could be possible," Devlin said.

"Because they're *petrified,* silly!" Rachel jumped on the dragon with both feet, then lost her balance and skittered off to the side. "For a million thousand years."

"Oh," Devlin said. "I see."

After Rachel, he left the building, ostensibly for lunch. For half an hour he wandered a several-block area in the neighborhood of his office. There were a couple of pawnshops here and he went in, browsing among cheap jewelry and secondhand musical instruments and guns and battered stereo equipment. The pawnbrokers regarded him with a certain suspicion for his aimless lingering.

At length, Devlin went into a small cafeteria and deliberately bought bad food, a soggy salad with iceberg lettuce, browning at the edges. He sat at a small, ill-balanced table near a window. Across the street hulked his office building, all dull chrome and dark glass; he stared at it with a degree of disaffection while picking at his food. Although the neighborhood was overshadowed by a large state hospital, Devlin's practice was now exclusively private, had been so for almost ten years. His former association with the hospital still won him the odd referral, and meanwhile his reputation had expanded on its own. The practice was lucrative enough that he might have afforded to work considerably less hours than he did, and that was a thought with some attractions, because of late it seemed to require a certain gray determination for him to rise and face his day. He was still as effective as he ever had been, he believed. Still, he might thin his list of patients easily enough by failing to replace the ones who, one way or another, left his care.

What then? What to do with sudden windfalls of free time? Devlin felt a dull shortage of inspiration. He ate about half of his salad, chewing it like hay, drank a carton of orange juice, and went back to his office.

Then there was Kirk, an anxious and aggressive twelve-year-old in glasses, who for his last few sessions had wanted to do nothing but play chess. Kirk spent much of his free time reading chess books and never failed to trounce Devlin soundly, though the games seemed very stressful for him no matter their result. Sitting crosslegged before the chessboard rug, Devlin felt the boy's tension as an ache in his own back, though usually he was quite comfortable playing with the children on the floor. Kirk always played in a bitter silence, with a grand master's air of concentration; Devlin was looking forward to his moving on to a new phase.

After Kirk came Brittany, who picked up one of the dolls from the shelf and held it on her lap while she sat in a recliner, stroking it as if it were a cat.

"How's it going?" Devlin said.

"*Cosi, cosi,*" said Brittany. At *her* private school, she was learning Italian.

"But I'm an Irishman," Devlin said. "You could always try Gaelic."

Brittany gave him a weak smile for this weak jest. She had a shallow broad face with wide cheekbones. Her hair was cut to the length of her earlobes, and heavily hennaed. Today she wore a flower-print babydoll dress with black combat boots; the hems of white socks peeked over the boot tops. With it all went an air of world-weariness which should have been an affectation in a girl of seventeen. "New earrings?" Devlin said.

"Who's counting?" Brittany dropped a hand from the doll in her lap and began fidgeting with the lever of the reclining chair, popping out the footrest, then snapping it back. Both her ears were pierced as many as ten or fifteen times. She wore dangles from her lobes, then studs that grew progressively smaller as they climbed the curved cartilage of her ear. The upper piercings, which were inflamed and looked extremely painful, reminded Devlin of ritual mutilation. Common enough, though, among his clientele. He was waiting for somebody to swagger in with a wooden disc distending the lower lip in the manner of New Guinea tribes, or African-style full-facial scarification, or stacks of concentric gold rings elongating the neck.

"How's home?" Devlin said. "How's school? Or you pick something."

Brittany stretched out her boots on the footrest and sat back, studying the doll—it was the mother doll she'd chosen, or the one the children often tended to identify as the mother. Devlin put a hand in his pocket and felt along the muscle of his upper thigh. The bruise from the Camaro had flowered into a hematoma, a multicolored bloom of spongy blood-drenched tissue with a lump in the center the size of a dried lima bean. The bean itself was spookily insensitive.

Devlin touched it gingerly through the cloth of his pocket, then curled his fingers away from the area.

"I got my IUD taken out," Brittany said. "That's news."

"I'd say so," Devlin said. "Does this mean you want to get pregnant?"

"No *way,*" said Brittany. She held up the doll by a hank of its yarn hair and looked past it at Devlin, as if to mock whatever symbolism he might search out in this behavior. "I just don't want to have any more sex."

"I see," said Devlin. "Forever?"

"For a while." Brittany put the doll facedown in her lap and stroked it.

"Well," said Devlin. "It seems you've thought it through."

"There's condoms, anyway," she said. "You know, the guy really should wear a rubber now—safe sex."

"This too sounds like a mature thought," said Devlin, suddenly unutterably depressed. He sat in silence, fingering the edges of his bruise. Brittany clicked down the footrest and leaned forward, looking at him with new concentration. Her eyes were brown.

"Tell me something, Mike," she said. "Did anybody ever kill theirself on you? You know, one of . . ."

". . . my patients?" Devlin said. "Yes."

"What did you think when it happened?"

"Think?" Devlin said. "I blamed myself. And I felt bad for a long time. Guilty." He cleared his throat. "Betrayed too, for that matter. I'd thought we had an understanding."

"Hey, you know I would never do that," Brittany said. "I'm not trying to send you some message here or anything. Do you get that?"

"I get it," Devlin said. He knew that Brittany wasn't suicidal. She didn't even meet his definition of "disturbed." A year before, at age sixteen, she'd finished off a reasonably typical teenage power struggle with her parents by going off without permission to follow the Lollapalooza tour—where, in fact, she'd had a quite lucrative job managing some concession. Her parents had responded by having her committed to a mental hospital on her return. Brittany had emerged from that experience no more angry or paranoid than Devlin would have expected of any sane person under such circumstances. She had even kept up with her class in school in spite of the ten weeks she'd lost in the bin.

Yet her parents (undivorced for once) were obsessed with the notion that she was crazy, or drug-addicted, or both. For his part, Devlin thought she needed a friend more than a shrink. He believed what she told him about drugs: sometimes a joint, some drinking at parties. She'd tried Ecstasy once at a rave but didn't like how it made her feel. That was all. But two weeks previously her mother had asked for a meeting with Devlin—unusual in itself because neither parent was much inclined to become involved with Brittany's treatment. Mom's mission turned out to be to learn if Devlin could arrange for Brittany to be put on a urinalysis program. No, Devlin had said. She doesn't need urinalysis. She needs love. Tough love, the mother said, tonguing the buzzword with a certain assurance. Devlin remained silent for a moment. The woman before him was not intentionally cruel, not even extraordinarily neglectful, yet he had come to the conclusion that just as some people are temperamentally unfit to have a dog, so Brittany's parents were thoroughly unsuited to have children. No, he told her finally, just ordinary love.

"I believe you," he said to Brittany, and she let herself relax, raising her boots to the footrest and drawing up her knees.

"Thanks," said Brittany. "Thanks, Mike." She held the doll near her face and looked at it seriously. "Who was it, your one that died? Guy or a girl?"

"I can't tell you," Devlin said. "You know that."

"Yeah," Brittany said. She shrugged against the nubby fabric of the chair. "Sorry. But, you know, I've never even thought of it? I mean, not seriously. If you're feeling sorry for yourself, that's one thing . . . but that's not real." She put the doll back on the shelf and looked at it from a distance, at all the dolls together, lifeless there. "I know I'll be all right in the end," she said. "I just have to get through this time." She looked at Devlin with ordinary interest; she didn't really need him to agree.

I'm forty-six, Devlin thought of saying. *In another forty-six years, I'll be dead. I've got through quite a lot of time already.* He held his tongue.

IN THE BACK-ROOM OFFICE of Ryu's Tae Kwon Do, Devlin set his foot on the edge of the desk and rolled back the loose white cloth of his uniform trousers to display the elaborate blood-etched flower of his bruise. Master Ryu, who was roughly Devlin's age but didn't look it, leaned across the desk and squinted. Beyond the office's glass window, students milled around the floor, waiting for the five-o'clock class to begin.

"Urrgggh," said Master Ryu, a low growling sound common to him, and uninterpretable. Devlin waited. "You can be exorcising," Master Ryu said.

Devlin took his foot from the desk and shook out his leg. The bruise was not painful when he moved; he only felt a tightness there, and he thought that a workout would help his bloodstream begin to wash it away; besides, he needed it for other reasons.

"Mee-shell," Master Ryu pronounced. "She no come school?"

Devlin shrugged—an unmartial thing to do. Michelle was, he supposed, suffering from post–black-belt slump; she'd passed the test the previous spring but fallen off since then. Not uncommon, though from time to time it bothered him.

"It's better if I don't make her go," he said. "She's at that stage—whatever I say, she pulls the other way." He forced a laugh, in which the master joined.

"So," said Master Ryu, "when you starting downtown school?"

"Still looking for space," Devlin said warily. He had been dancing around this subject for some weeks with the master, who wanted him to open a new branch of the school deeper into the city, but Devlin was shy of the idea for different reasons: the responsibility, the extra time involved. Master Ryu gave him a penetrating look, but Devlin did not volunteer anything more. He composed his face into a perfect blank, bowed to the master, and left the room.

A second-degree black belt, Devlin was the ranking student on the floor. He called the class to attention as Master Ryu walked in, and gave the commands to bow, to kneel for meditation, but this afternoon his mind would not come clear. The problem of the new school kept pricking through to him, piercing the invisible sphere he tried to form around himself in meditation, which sealed this daily hour of pain and sweat hermetically away from the rest of his life. Finally he gave up and clapped his hands for the class to rise. In unison they bowed to Master Ryu, then Devlin led the warm-up, stretching.

He drove himself through basics hard, punching, blocking, kicking, working himself toward a breathless sweat, toward mental vacancy, he hoped, though his thoughts still nagged at him: the new school, and behind it something else, something indeterminate. Basics done, the class split into groups, and it was Devlin's task to teach the intermediate belts their new form, which left too much room for his mind to wander. He rolled the issue of the new school into a ball and blasted it away from himself with an imaginary roundhouse kick, but instantly the other thing lunged at him from behind it: the face of Talia Crawford as he'd last seen her, seven years before, smiling, optimistic, and utterly deceitful. She'd be twenty-two this year if she had lived, and Devlin had been so confident that she would live and prosper. Talia had outwitted everyone—teachers, parents, shrink, all. Her grades were up, her social life improving, the scars on her inner wrists faded to scarcely noticeable spidery white lines. She kept her last appointment with Devlin, attended rehearsal of a school play in which she'd won a significant role, went home and finished all her assignments for the next school day, then climbed into a warm bathtub and executed herself by sealing a blue plastic grocery bag around her head with duct tape. What horrified Devlin most was the combination: that wish for comfort, relaxing in warm water, and then the vicious gangland cruelty of her self-murder. There had been no note, no nothing.

Devlin's concentration was completely broken. He

made two mistakes in the form he was teaching, and Master Ryu punished him with twenty-five push-ups, bare knuckles on the hardwood floor, for which Devlin was grateful. When he got up, his head had shifted, a constricted gray knot without content now, and that was some relief.

Paddle drill. Outside the large glass windows of the room, the light was falling, the sky gone dark; automatic streetlights had snapped on above the parking lot. Master Ryu stood offering a red paddle-shaped target, held at a slight angle just above waist height. Devlin hit it with an instep roundhouse, not really hard, a rangefinding kick; he spun through and away and ran back to the end of the line. The rhythm of kicks drummed out ahead of him, *smack, smack, smack.* When it came his turn again, Devlin could release himself completely, so that the paddle broke free of the holder's hand and fluttered up in a graceful arc to rebound from the ceiling tiles and drop like a shot bird. Stooping to retrieve the target, Master Ryu smiled approvingly, and Devlin was where he had wanted to arrive, aware of nothing but the heat of his muscles, the flash of energy, and the shock of contact from high roundhouse kicks, three-sixties, wheel kicks with a jump or adding a punch, then combinations—the rotary motion of a roundhouse followed through with a spinning hook or wheel or crescent. Following through, Devlin drilled like a tornado. The side of his foot lashed against the paddle with a gunshot crack, and he let out a spontaneous catlike yowling cry as he spun out.

"Put that away," Master Ryu said gutturally. Devlin breathed deeply into the *chi* center a couple of inches below his navel, refreshing this area so it glowed like a hot coal under a bellows. All his clothing was limp with sweat. Fifteen minutes of paddle drill would wring you out completely, like a sponge.

"Full equipment," said Master Ryu, and Devlin automatically trotted to his gym bag. Because of the bruise, and his mental uneasiness, he'd explicitly decided not to fight tonight, but the momentum of the practice carried him irresistibly past that decision, so that despite any misgivings, he was putting on groin cup and shin pads and arm pads and chest protector and foam helmet. Biting down on his mouthguard, he stood to face his first opponent, both of them somewhat comically swollen with all this padded body armor. Devlin wondered for a second if a direct hit might shatter the lima-bean bull's-eye of his bruise and send a blood clot racing to his brain or heart to end all his distractions and worries permanently, but it was necessary not to think of that, not to think of anything.

"*Charyet. . . . Kunye,*" said Master Ryu. Opponents bowed all down the line. *"Si chak!"*

Devlin sparred warily with lower belts, conserving his energy very carefully. His age worked against him now; he could no longer fight many rounds without tiring, or sustain a constant hail of attacks. But he could block, keep covered up, keep breathing while he watched for the opening where one clean combination could be made to count for everything. In the blackening glass of the windows, the palely reflected figures of the fighters moved like wraiths.

In his fourth and final round, Devlin faced Jhun Cho, an unusually burly Korean youth who was pumping for his first-degree black-belt test in two months' time. He was somewhat less than overjoyed to be meeting this opponent so late in the practice, when he was tiring and his breath had gone almost completely ragged. Devlin himself was something under average height for a white American, but since much of his length was in his legs he was accustomed to fending off attackers with side kicks. This tactic would not work well on Jhun, who both outreached and outweighed him somewhat.

"Charyet. . . . Kunye. Si chak!"

Devlin moved in quickly, sliding step, his knee rising for a first attack, but Jhun spun faster with a mule kick, thrusting his heel into Devlin's upper thigh. Devlin grunted with annoyance, though luckily it was the unhurt leg. He'd have a bruise to match the other, and a hitch in his stride for the rest of the fight. He moved in and hit Jhun's chest protector with a roundhouse, but the new knot in his leg cut into his speed and the kick was not strong enough to penetrate. He changed up and faked toward the body, then went to the head with the same leg, but another back kick from Jhun caught him solidly under the sternum, sending him staggering back with the wind hissing out of him. He could just contain Jhun's follow-up, punching once weakly as Jhun rushed in, then clinching for a moment before he rolled away.

Jhun changed up, then switched back again, bouncing on his toes, more confident now, and Devlin was quite definitely discouraged. He had to work to conceal the fresh limp, and his *chi* center felt shattered, empty and cold. Time seemed to be passing with excruciating lethargy. Devlin held his hands close to him, taking shots on his forearm pads, spending as little effort as he could and hoping to recover. Under this kind of pressure he tended to fire side kicks like a robot, but now he was too slow, or Jhun was too close, so that the kicks were jammed. It seemed the round would never end. Devlin had to do something, anything—win himself some breathing room. He spun inside, his shoulders jarring Jhun back slightly, and—before he thought—his leg came up, following through the turn with a crescent kick that caught Jhun squarely on the side of his padded helmet.

A stun. Devlin had time to switch stance and find his range for a million-dollar side kick that hit Jhun middle-target and knocked him reeling back toward the wall. A couple of students sitting crosslegged on the floor shifted away to avoid him.

"Break," cried Master Ryu. He directed them both into the center of the ring. *"Sook!"* Jhun's face was unreadable, but he no longer seemed much inclined to charge. Devlin tiptoed around him for another twenty seconds before the master stopped the fight. He and Jhun bowed to each other, then fell on each other's necks in a brief embrace.

DEVLIN HEADED home in his steamed-up car, pumping sweat and adrenaline, humming a little under his breath. The match with Jhun had served its purpose, purging him, and he might sustain the feeling of carefree emptiness for a little longer, before he must reenter the doors of his life. He stopped at a shotgun bar on Loch Raven and sucked down a bottle of beer quickly, for his thirst, then ordered another, with a shot of whiskey. Customers were grouped loosely around the rectangular bar which occupied the center of the room, most drinking from long-necked bottles. Devlin, who was unknown in this venue, eavesdropped idly on their conversations. The walls were mirrored, so he could watch himself watching the barmaid, who was rather pretty, a woman in her middle forties, trim in jeans and a man's dress shirt, her face just slightly lined from the habit of pleasant expressions. On a television screen fixed to a high bracket in the corner, the electronic red ball of a keno game bounced slowly. In the mirror beyond the double counters of the bar, Devlin's face was a mask of shadow; he could still savor the feeling of being a stranger to himself.

He had cooled down completely by the time he returned to the car, so that he no longer fogged the windshield glass. Some soreness from his workout reached him now, and he felt the catch in his other leg where Jhun's kick had landed, but at the same time the drinks he'd had relaxed him, their warmth fanning out and circulating through his limbs. He drove slowly and attentively, while the radio broadcast some inoffensive pop song from the rear speakers of the car. Half entranced, but still sufficiently alert, Devlin mouthed the lyrics as the car floated down the night-lit street. The tune ended, there came a weather bulletin predicting heavy frost, and then a plug for an organization seeking volunteers to work with abused children in the inner city—some sort of buddy-big-brother thing, and *call this number.* Devlin thought, with his customary ironic detachment, that these would be quite a different class of victims from the ones that he was paid to help, if help it was. On the radio began another song, with a stronger ring of authenticity, faint sound of calluses sliding on the strings of an acoustic guitar, and a woman's voice, mournful and low. Devlin began crying uncontrollably, tears that felt the size of coins spurting from his eyes. He barely had the presence of mind to pull the car to the side of the road and slam it into park. Slumping forward over the wheel, he went on weeping violently, and after a few minutes he began laughing through his sobs, for the inexplicable strangeness of it all, and this thought, with the laughter, brought more tears. At last he sat back, swallowing and gasping in cold air. The radio annoyed him now; he flicked it off, then dragged his sleeve across his nose. There was a sharpish pain in his sinuses, like an ice cream headache. He fell back in the seat and rested, listening to the car tick as it cooled, and thought, *I can't just do nothing, I cannot do nothing . . .*

A FRIDAY EVENING, Devlin cooked ambitiously, making a flank steak roulade, French vegetables, and a fancy salad. Everything turned out as he had intended, winning the slightly startled admiration of Alice and Michelle when they came to the table. Tonight all three of them were in good humor with each other, and Devlin could enjoy a pleasant sense of the fitness of things that persisted when dinner was done and he began to wash the dishes.

Michelle swung through the kitchen on her way out to a Halloween party. Devlin was just slightly spooked by her; she'd made up her face in solid black and stuck her long hair down into a dark turtleneck so that her head was sleek and narrow as a seal's. Behind the black pancake surface her eyes looked merry at his surprise.

"Good Lord," said Devlin. "A burglarette."

Michelle laughed and moved in to give him a sticky black kiss. She didn't smell of citrus now, but something musky, like burning rope, or cedar. Was it the face paint? She laughed again, moving toward the door, and Devlin waved her out, dismissively, a shoo.

He finished the dishes and shucked off his gloves. Alice called from the den as he went up the stairs.

"Ready to start the movie?"

She'd rented them a video—cocooning time. Devlin hesitated, halfway up the steps.

"I'll just be a minute."

At the head of the stairs he turned into Michelle's room, thinking he was looking for cold cream to wipe off the black lipstick smudge on his cheek, though of course he could have used Alice's. Or soap and water. Pushing the door softly to behind him, he inhaled deeply, a faint trace of the cedary smell. She'd left the window open despite the cold, both the upper and lower sashes slightly ajar. Clicking his tongue, Devlin moved to close and latch it. He turned and looked around the room, uncertain.

The ambience was somewhat similar to the therapeutic playroom at his office, not too surprising since Michelle had helped with those arrangements. Michelle was atypically neat; her bed was made, and arranged with cushions and various stuffed animals from her childhood. Devlin found these latter touching and a little sad; many of his teenage clients also clung to such souvenirs. The art on the walls bore witness to mutating taste. There was the inevitable silver unicorn mincing through a fluorescent faery glade. A full-length poster of a ratty-looking rock star who'd blown his head off with a shotgun not too long before. Since this event, Devlin rather wished that Michelle would take the poster down, but he could think of no way to mention the subject that wouldn't make him look like an utter fool. On the opposite wall hung a framed print of a painting by Odilon Redon . . . sign that Michelle's likes were shifting slightly toward the higher-brow.

Devlin moved across the carpet to her desk, where a screen-saver glowing on her small PC seemed to beckon him. He was aware of his effort to make no sound with his steps. He snapped on the cantilevered lamp and sat down in her chair. On the blotter were some handwritten notes for an English paper. A redheaded troll, dressed in a black and silver punk-rock costume, gazed up at him with its glass eyes. There was a little brass incense burner, supporting a cone of ash, and beside it a small brass-bound lock box, cheaply made to resemble a pirate chest with its curved top. Devlin reached for this, hesitated, then drew it to him across the blotter.

The lock, naturally, was a joke. Devlin straightened out a paper clip and popped it. There was a velvet-lined tray in the top, divided into two compartments, holding some gold jewelry and freshwater pearl earrings. Devlin lifted out the tray. Underneath were a prayer wheel of birth-control pills with about half the pellets punched out, a pack of Zigzag cigarette papers, a small metal hash pipe, and a Ziploc bag of expensive-looking gold-colored marijuana.

Devlin prickled. His fear was unspecific. Brittany's voice arose in the space between his ears, mentioning something about condoms. He opened the bag of dope and sniffed—that cedar smell, almost a taste, went directly to the back of his throat. He folded one of the cigarette papers and shook a modest amount of the dope into the crease. It had been ten years at least since he'd rolled a joint, and it came out a little lopsided. He bent the paper with Michelle's notes on it and blew the leftover crumbs back into the bag and rolled it up and put everything back into the box and shut it. No way to lock it with the paper clip, but it seemed probable to Devlin that she would simply turn the key in the lock without checking first to see if the box were open—why should she check? Thus he would not be caught.

He sat, rolling the joint back and forth in the circle of lamplight. As a matter of fact, he had never been caught. He had begun smoking marijuana in high school himself and continued through college and for a few years afterward, then drifted away from it like most of his friends at that time. In his high school days, alcohol had also been very easy to obtain, and Devlin, who grew up in rural West Virginia, had often driven long distances late at night under the influence of both. After his fashion, he had been very circumspect, but the fact that he had come to no harm must be credited to whatever god looks after fools and little children. This thought did not much reassure him now. He was not comfortable telling himself that it was "different with a daughter," and his feeling that the world was an infinitely more dangerous place now than then struck him as . . . subjective.

"Mike?"

Devlin smoothly palmed the joint and looked up toward the door, wiping his expression scrupulously blank. A knack that returned to him out of nowhere, like riding a bicycle, or picking a lock. Alice had arrived in the doorway, soundlessly in stocking feet, and stood there looking at him with a slight ironic smile. It bothered Devlin that he hadn't heard the door open. His heart slammed like a teenager's—not quite caught, but close.

"What are you poking around in here for?"

"I wasn't *poking* . . ." Devlin swiveled in Michelle's desk chair, looked blandly up at his wife.

She had Michelle's coloring, the wide full mouth, and the same chestnut hair in a shorter cut, barely grazing her shoulders. She was six years younger than he and looked still more youthful. They were lucky in this way, Devlin thought, but then so were most of the people they knew, all fit and fresh-faced and healthy, as if they'd live forever. A headachey-looking vertical crease appeared in the center of Alice's forehead.

"Cat got your tongue?" she said. "You know she hates to feel like she's snooped on."

Devlin felt a flash of irritation. "Well, hell, I never even—" He caught himself, seeing the skin tighten over the fine bones of her face as she set herself. She gave better than she got in household quarrels, and Devlin didn't want a fight tonight. The thought that he was lying did not affect him.

"She left the window open," he said meekly, and stood up, slipping the joint into his pants pocket as he moved. "I just came in to close it."

Of course that didn't explain why he'd be sitting at her desk, but Alice seemed willing to accept it. Her face relaxed, and now her eyes looked only tired. Stepping carefully so as not to break the joint in his pocket, Devlin put his hands on her shoulders and dug into the tightened muscles there, massaging.

"Ahh . . ." Alice said. "Come on, let's watch the movie."

She took his elbow and Devlin went with her down the stairs, his free hand in his pocket, cupping the joint against his bruise.

The film was some sort of period piece, based on a turn-of-the-century novel, or perhaps the life of a turn-of-the-century novelist? Devlin had a little trouble concentrating. The movie had been Alice's pick; he might have been happier with some simpleminded thriller, if not Bruce Lee or Jackie Chan. The subtleties of the cinematography seemed ineffective on the TV screen. But, after all, there was no need for much attention. Devlin let the streams of cultivated talk flow over him, watched the shifting of the pixilated colors. Narrative wallpaper. Alice leaned into him comfortably on the couch, her head aligned with the television. Devlin fidgeted with a lock of her hair, began absently fondling her earlobe.

"Tickles," she said and touched his hand with her own forefinger to make him stop.

After about an hour, Alice declared an intermission and went to the kitchen to make popcorn. Devlin remained on the couch for a moment. The patch of his side where she had rested felt suddenly cool. The frozen television screen displayed the face of an English actress, an overbred-looking, watery blonde who had recently become very popular among discriminating moviegoers. Her lips were parted and her weak chin tucked, locked by pause mode in the mid-expression of some delicate nuance of emotion.

Devlin yawned and went to the kitchen, where Alice was tending the popcorn machine. Butter-free and exquisitely healthy—Devlin had given it to her, to the house, the preceding Christmas.

"What?" Alice said, surprising him. Had he been staring? When he didn't answer, she went over and sat down at a chair across the kitchen table from him. For a moment they both watched the popcorn whizzing around the yellow-tinted cannister of the machine. The burst kernels made a sound somewhere between a pock and a whisper as they rebounded.

"How was everything down at the shop?" Alice looked at him directly, her beautiful deep eyes so like Michelle's.

Devlin shrugged. "Another day at the orphans' picnic."

Alice clicked her tongue at him; she disapproved of such cynicism. Her gaze turned back to the popcorn machine, now trickling off its last few pops. She might have sympathized with his stirrings of professional unease, Devlin thought with a slight flare of irritation, except that she was too pragmatic. If you don't like what you're doing, Alice would say, do something else. She herself had been a psychiatric social worker for a number of years, but shifted to a strictly administrative post when she became exhausted by dealing with an endless succession of hopelessly self-destructive lunatics. So if she did say what Devlin imagined she would say, she would be quite right. She had already put her own money where her mouth was.

After twenty years of marriage, a great number of possible conversations became fundamentally redundant. Alice would disapprove of this notion too—which seemed a good reason for Devlin to keep it to himself. He had been holding his tongue a lot lately, not with an effort of restraint, but with a sort of fond possessiveness. Alice was pouring the popcorn into a flowered ceramic bowl. She smiled at him, beckoned. There was no discontent between them. Their quiet was a kind of calm.

Devlin returned with her to the den. He put his hand

into his pocket and curled his fingers around the joint again to protect it from his movement. His knuckles grazed painlessly against the bruise. Two secrets. Why did he want to keep them? He wondered idly about Michelle, less with concern than curiosity. Not where she was or what she was doing, but what she might be thinking and feeling. What would it feel like, Devlin wondered, not to already know exactly what would happen?

THE LEAVES had all fallen on the median of Broadway, and the stripped limbs of the small unhealthy-looking trees bowed and whined in the wind, which came in short sharp gusts that would make an umbrella useless. Devlin tightened the string of his sweatshirt hood. A fine misty rain whipped on and off his face with the wind; it was very cold and stung like ice. He had consciously dressed down for the occasion. Jeans with fat-laced sneakers, sweatshirt under leather jacket—that was the uniform in these precincts, and with his hands in his pockets and his head turtled back inside the sweatshirt, Devlin wouldn't be taken, at a distance, for white. Or at least, that thought reassured him, though he was worried about his car. He'd come shopping for space for Master Ryu's downtown school, down here where commercial space was surely going begging. The Kae (as the Korean community loan fund called itself) wouldn't spring for much rent, and Devlin was damned if he'd sink his own money into the venture, dubious about it as he already felt. But he was doing it. So it appeared. No, he wasn't definitely doing it. He was giving it a look.

He turned on Eager Street and walked east. Incongruously, there were a good many late-model cars parked along this block, many flashier and more expensive than Devlin's little Saab, and he felt slightly more confident that he might find his own vehicle intact when he returned to it. He passed a liquor store, a derelict building sheathed in plywood, a bar, a hairdresser, a liquor store, a derelict building whose doors and windows were gaping, smoke-stained holes, a convenience store, a liquor store. Despite the foul weather, there were a great many young black men milling around on the street, smoking extra-long cigarettes and drinking out of paper bags, sometimes shouting or amusing each other with menacing gestures or mock assaults. No one seemed particularly to notice Devlin, who walked briskly, keeping his head down.

At the next corner he turned and went south. As he came out of the side street's windbreak, the rain swung into his face again. Devlin rehearsed the directions he'd had from Mr. Spetakis on the telephone: corner convenience store, the Parrot Bar, a surplus store, and next to that the storefront he'd come to check out. The gates were closed and massively padlocked, with mesh so fine that Devlin couldn't see into the darkened interior. Under the gates, the filthy plate glass was cracked and crisscrossed with silver duct tape. Evidently Spetakis had not yet arrived.

Devlin snuck a look at his watch. Nervous about finding the place with no delays, he'd come almost fifteen minutes early. He stepped back from the gates and looked first one way on the street and then the other. The soft leather of his tennis shoes seemed to be porous enough that his feet were getting wet. The bars, on the whole, seemed not worth chancing. Devlin went into a convenience store and bought a can of malt liquor and asked for a pack of matches also. The Plexiglas between him and the cash register was so thick that he had to shout to make himself heard. It was a Korean store, and Devlin grinned secretly at the suitability of that, as his paper sack rotated toward him on the Plexiglas turntable.

He walked down to the next corner, sipping from the bag, a gesture that would improve his camouflage, he thought. There was a shattered playground, streaked with mud, with the metal stubs of an uprooted swing set and huge coiled springs from which the rocking animals had been ripped. The only intact piece of equipment was a jungle gym made of four-by-fours and metal pipe. Around its base was a large trash heap: papers and rags and many half-pint liquor bottles, and a sodden, single-bed mattress.

Devlin swung onto the jungle gym and climbed to the top. He felt somewhat more secure here, though he also suspected the feeling was delusional. The wind abated, and the rain slackened off. Devlin heard a horn blowing, and a couple of distant shouts. He found the matches at the bottom of the bag, took out the joint he'd swiped from Michelle, and lit it.

Time took on a curious elasticity. Devlin stared down at a wet alley cat that picked through the litter beneath the jungle gym, hunching its damp shoulders. There was a dead pigeon there with the trash, but the cat didn't seem to connect with it. The roach burned against his fingers and Devlin started. He stubbed it out on the pipe and flicked the remains down onto the trash pile. Absurd to be busted for a joint down here, though not perhaps very likely either. The rainswept cement, the trash itself, the orangish tiger stripes of the wretched cat, all seemed brighter, more vividly present than before. Devlin's beer tasted flat and metallic now; he didn't much want to finish it but his mouth was cottony and dry. He was so stoned, in fact, that he could barely remember his own name. The thought of his daughter smoking this stuff bewildered him. Evidently it was two-hit shit —he'd been a fool to smoke the whole thing.

It seemed he'd forgotten Mr. Spetakis for what must have been hours. He snatched at his wrist to look at his watch and discovered that only ten minutes had passed. It was clearing now, with slanting rays of sunlight pouring down from a rent in the clouds. Devlin shivered, and dropped his can onto the trash pile—contributing to the community spirit, he thought. He climbed down and walked back toward the storefront in a fog of unfocused paranoia.

The Parrot Bar's blacked-out glass door swung open as he approached; there was a blast of music and two men came out shouting at each other, shoving. Devlin's reactions were molasses-slow; he seemed to be aware of this event for aeons, during which his legs continued to carry him toward it. At last he stopped and drew back, but the two men had separated, one going around the corner in the opposite direction from the other. The bar door swung shut on its pressure hinge, cutting off the music sharply. A small white pickup truck was idling by the curb, and as Devlin began walking that way again, the truck shut off, and the driver stepped out to greet him.

Spetakis was a large and rather soft-appearing man, exuding a winey smell which was not unpleasant. He introduced himself as "Georges," giving the name the French pronunciation. His hand was soft and rather moist when Devlin shook it. He hauled an enormous brass ring of keys from his pocket and began undoing the padlocks on the gates. The door behind them was lockless, a hole through the metal frame where the cylinder had been. Spetakis smiled at Devlin, displaying a gold front tooth with a heart cut out to show the white enamel. The gates pulled away with a rusty scrape, and they went in.

"So," said Spetakis, his gold tooth winking in the dim interior. "So you are the man of karate."

"Yes," Devlin said. His tongue felt thick and slow. "Tae Kwon Do," he added, automatically. The Koreans were particular about such things.

"You do not carry the knife or the gun."

"No," Devlin said. It seemed to cost him a profound effort to utter these monosyllables. But Spetakis, nodding approvingly, seemed satisfied with his reply.

Focus, Devlin told himself. With an effort of concentration on the business at hand, he could bring himself down enough to function. Mr. Spetakis manipulated a light switch back and forth several times—dust on the contacts, he explained. Fluorescent lights flickered on overhead. The space was long, rather narrow, but wide enough for four practitioners to stand abreast. A partition at the side walled off three cubicles that might be used as dressing rooms. Devlin went to the closets in the rear and flushed the toilets and turned the water on and off. The pipes belched a little rust from disuse, but the plumbing appeared to be operational.

All in all, it looked better than he'd been expecting. The space would not require much in the way of remodeling or repair. The partitions could serve as they presently stood.

There was some shelving to be removed from the walls, a modest amount of debris to be cleared. The torn and grimy linoleum on the floor could be covered with mats easily enough.

Devlin felt an odd rush of confidence: momentum. The thing was possible, and why not? His risk was nil; Ryu and the Kae would support the operation. If it went well, Devlin would even be compensated for his time—at nothing like the rate he pulled at his practice, but . . . He might think of it as a different kind of opportunity.

So he told Spetakis that he thought the place would do, but, aware that his judgment might well be impaired, he also said he'd have to postpone the formal closure of the deal to another day. Spetakis didn't seem concerned by the delay. He relocked the gates across the storefront and they shook hands again beside the little truck. Devlin mentioned something about repairing the front window and promised to phone by the following Monday.

Hands in pockets, he turned the corner of Eager Street. The clouds had parted further, rolling eastward in a bulging, bruiselike mass, and from the west, fresh light poured over the buildings and the street, clear and cold and brilliant. Devlin clutched for a moment, anxious that he'd forgotten to ask Spetakis about the heat, or the missing front door lock, but then he recalled the deal was open still, the problem had been anticipated; he was maintaining. The afternoon light rushed down as the rain had earlier, carving the buildings sharply from the shadows, throwing the people on the street into electric relief. The wind rose, lifting scraps of colored paper into swirls like autumn leaves, and Devlin's mood lifted with them into a kind of exaltation.

His steps began to roll in time to the mega-bass pounding from a cruising car on his right. There was laughter, and a child ran out of a store pursuing a rubber ball with blue stars on it, then picked it up and carried it inside. Devlin keyed into a young woman pushing a candy-striped stroller a few paces ahead of him, slender and long-legged and walking with an antelope grace. Her hair was done in long thin braids, caught at the nape of her neck with a gold pin. Devlin overtook her and looked back to see her face. Her forehead was high and she held her chin up, and Devlin saw a flash of her teeth in the dark skin. Foggily he remembered it wouldn't be wise to stare.

Slam of a car door and a voice shouting right in Devlin's ear it seemed. "Ima KILL you, nigga!" He snapped to the front, fists rising reflexively to cover his face. Someone crashed into him, dressed much as he, in leather and sweatshirt, but with a black face and black shades. Devlin regained his balance and moved toward the wall. A second man, larger, swung back the flap of his oversized field jacket and reached into his waistband, shouting still, his face twisted and spraying spittle. Leather jacket ducked, his hooded head tucked into his elbows, and dodged around the girl with the stroller, while several sulphurous flashes sprouted from the shadows inside the green field jacket. Devlin heard a sound like a string of firecrackers lit together. Leather jacket was sprinting toward the corner; he vaulted between the shoulders of two women coming the other way, scattering their groceries. But the shooter only stood, his arms hanging down, the pistol swinging just below the zipper of his field jacket. He was a big man, knotty-looking and thick through the chest, with reddish hair cut very short and a light-skinned puffy face, pock-marked with old acne scars. He stood for a long moment as if paralyzed, then someone snatched him into a car which raced away with its tires crying.

Now Devlin looked at the girl, who had fallen on her back with her head slightly raised against a building wall. The shots had blown her several yards backward from the stroller. Her short jacket had come open and her orange rayon top welled with a dark pulsing stain which was also spreading underneath her body. Devlin knelt over her, stretched out his hand. Someone nearby was screaming, crying hysterically. As for Devlin, he could feel nothing. He was reaching for a pulse or a breath but there would be neither, and in the end he drew back his hand without touching the girl at all. The whites of her eyes showed under the long still lashes, and there was blood coming through her teeth.

Now Devlin felt the eyes on him and he straightened and backed away. A circle of onlookers closed, leaving the stroller outside. A siren was howling northbound on Broadway. Devlin took another few steps back and looked at the infant in the stroller. Somehow he thought it was a boy, and maybe five or six months old. He had forgotten how to estimate the age of babies. The child's skin was very black and glossy, with a big forehead and brows that seemed knitted together. He was not crying, or moving at all, only his eyes moved slightly as he looked about himself, very soberly. His eyes seemed to fix on Devlin, who remembered reading somewhere that such a silence was an adaptive response for infants under terrible stress. Keep silent and hope for the predators to pass you by. Indeed, no one was paying any attention to the baby at all. Devlin heard doors of a police car banging, static on a radio. The voice seemed to reach him from outside, a long way distant: *I cannot do nothing.* He took hold of the stroller's rubberized handles and began to push it in the direction of his car.

9

SHARMANE

So we sitting out front of the house, just me'n my homegirl Tamara, and Gramma Reenie. Me'n Tamara had pulled out some chairs so we can sit and hang our feet out over that green metal rail that run our whole block of the Poe Homes. Gramma Reen, she just sat down there on the door sill. Her little knees poking up through that green dress, no bigger'n a bird legs. Me'n Tamara, chill, smoking a Kool, not really waiting on Jaynette so far but every now and then looking down the block to see if she might be getting there, pushing that stroller up from the bus stop, with Froggy laying back in there chuckling and sucking his fat little fingers. Or asleep, I hoped. Cause we going out that night, Jaynette and me'n Tamara and . . . whoever. Hook up with D-Trak or Gyp and Mud-dog or whoever Trig could spare off that crack corner. Gramma Reen was set to watch the baby. We'd find some club and dance the crazies out. Jaynette had not hardly been nowhere since the baby. Trig did like her to stay in but like Tamara would tell Jaynette, "He aintcha *hus*band, yo—aintcha daddy neither." Which Jaynette would just only give her cow smile, eyes rolling white to the side. They didn't even live together . . . and Trig ain't claimed that baby. It did look like him.

Some white people came driving down in a Volvo—lost. You get a few like that every day, looking for the Poe House it ownself, which it's right there at the end of our block. They missed it. Drove down the next block and pulled a buttonhook and came back up and missed it again. Here came the car cruising by real slow, like maybe they looking for Trig instead . . . but they didn't seem the kind to want to cop. It was a green Volvo—minty colored, and the window came partway down on the passenger side. White woman behind it look like maybe she working up the nerve to ask directions.

So Tamara yell out, "Looking for the Poe House? There it is!" And she pointed. "They close up now, though. After hours."

Inside the Volvo, the man and the woman look at each other confused, then he back it up half a block and into a parking place. Out they get, make sure the car is locked up a few hundred times ("Whyn't they just boot it," Tamara say). They go down, scoping nervous all around theyself, and start reading the plaque screwed into the pale rosy brick of that little house Poe was supposed to of lived at. I been in there one time myself—it ain't nothing. Two rooms down and one on top and none of'm bigger than a closet. Poe Homes nicer, where we stay.

I leaned out over the rail to see if Jaynette might be coming along. The white dude had back out into the street and aiming a camera at the woman, who was standing in front of the Poe House still scoping nervous up and down the street. Who turned the corner was Odell—Freon as he like to call himself since he got back from California. White dude snap the picture quick and both them start hustling to they car. It made me laugh . . . anybody being scared of Freon.

Here come Freon stomping along in new-looking blond Timberlands he must of stole, and his hood rolled back on his sweatshirt, hanging back over his leather jacket. His short fat dreads sticking up like rubber studs on one of them balls that bounce all crazy. Just when he get up to us that Volvo whooshes by and we can hear the power locks going down—*schlonk!* Then Tamara make a mean noise back in her throat, thinking now we be stuck with Freon all night probably.

"Whatchoo know, O-*dell*," Tamara say.

Freon pull up. He got a sack in his hand and a blue bandanna hanging out the back of his loose loose jeans. Which was bullshit, Trig said, and everybody. We didn't have no Crips'n Bloods in Baltimore then. Didn't need it, didn't want it. But since Freon had went to L.A. he try to come on like a big gangbanger.

"Now, baby," he say. "You know they call me Freon cause I so cool that—"

"—cause you freeze onto people till they can't shake you loose," Tamara say.

"Bee-*atch*," Freon said, or he start to say it.

"I doan wanna hear yo nasty," Gramma Reen say, but soft. "Take it on down the street if that how you gots to talk." But she stood up then herself and went inside the house and shut the door.

She could still shame Freon—you know, Odell. But it seem like she getting tired—already tired before that day.

"Aw, Sharmane," Freon say to me, hang-dog sorta. "I got a forty." He rolled back the sack from the bottleneck and passed it to me.

"Think we wanna suck yo spit?" Tamara said. But she took some too, when I passed it.

It was windy, a little cool, had rained earlier that afternoon. Across the street the trash and the weeds in the vacant lots was still slick from the rain, and shiny. But it was sunny then. The rain clouds all rip open and drifting away past the dome of the B&O roundhouse down on Pratt Street. Red sunlight striping lowdown over the stoved roofs and burned-out windowframes of them little two-story shells other side of the block. Empty right now, though at night they be people crawl in there to smoke they rocks. Freon beer was strong, some kinda malt liquor. I felt a little sad, just restless maybe, like I wanted to move, do something. Let Jaynette show up already. The wind was moving in the tall weeds sprouted from the trashpiles, moving those straw-color weed tops together in kinda a sad way. I was thinking how Gramma Reen, when we was kids, she make us clean up the other side the block too, pick up the bottles and rags. Now we didn't do it no more. But we still kept our side nice.

So I lit myself a Kool.

"Let me get one," Freon said.

Tamara spit out over the rail, made her mouth disgusted. She what Gramma Reen call *lamp-black,* shiny rich-color like oil. Sharp face and a sharp tongue and don't take nothing off nobody, I mean to tell you. But I passed Freon the pack. We *was* drinking his beer, you know.

Freon screw the cig in his face, start feeling himself all over for a match I guess. I held out my lighter to him but he keep on groping hisself. Hike up his sweatshirt looking for his pocket . . .

"You wanna show us yo skinny little johnson?" Tamara say.

Right there it was already, what he want us to see, sticking out the waistband of his jeans. Butt-end of a pistol, Dick Tracy style. Tamara jerk her head away. Freon grinning. I couldn't think what he need with that thing.

"That go off on you, you wish you found a different place to stick it," Tamara say.

"Oh," Freon say, Kool wagging in the corner of his mouth, still not lit. "It on safety. See?"

That gun still look big, laying there in Freon's big yellow hand. Look just like Dick Tracy gun except it made of some greeny plastic. So it pass a metal detector—I heard this from Trig.

"Put that thing up, Freon." I made my voice tight and hard. "Quit fooling."

Freon grinning. He stuck the pistol back in his pants. Took the lighter from me finally, fired his smoke. He scratching up under the scar on his neck where he say he got stab one time in L.A.—got a mole cut off more like it, what Tamara say. He hand me the lighter back, blow one smoke ring through another. Look like he ready to brag a new brag.

But here came Trig idling down the street, the black

Lexus purring like a cat. New leather smell just pouring out when he open the window, and the bass pounding from some rap, out the big speaker he got in the trunk. Then Trig shut the music down.

"Ladies," he say. Voice smooth like wine.

When Trig bend his finger, Freon go bouncing over there just like a puppy dog. Lean down to the window and listen real close to whatever Trig want to say in his ear. Then he straighten up and walk back toward us, feeling up his pants to make sure that gun ain't drop out on the street.

I seen Trig leaning back on the leather seat, thumbing a call on his car phone. Sunglasses wrapped round his head that tight you can't see nothing of his eyes. Gyp get out the passenger side, slap the door shut. And Trig go sliding down the street, still on the phone, that car just humming.

Gyp put a hand on the green rail, vaulted hisself over.

"Don't break yo neck," I say. But I was smiling.

"What up, cuz," Freon say. He just keep coming with that *cuz* shit all the time. Fact of it, Gyp and Freon *was* cousins some way. But Gyp didn't say nothing to Freon.

"Hello, young lovelies." Gyp drop a hand on my shoulder, maybe halfway down the neck of my shirt.

I shook him off. Gyp just laugh, twirl around with a break step. He come around holding up his palm, thumb folded over a blunt he was cupping.

"Nuh-uh," I say. "Not now." I didn't want to fire up so close to Gramma Reen.

Gyp palm the blunt away into his belly pocket. "So when?"

"We got to wait for Jaynette," I say.

Only what come around the corner then was a Channel

13 news truck. Making it on two wheels, almost. Unlucky number, what it was. And it was like I known already, before I ever seen it come.

It was almost dark by then, couldn't hardly see over to those vacant lots no more. The camera lights came shining down all over Poe Homes like it was a raid. Then come a truck from another station, then some cops. Wasn't no raid though. Cops wasn't wearing they flak jackets, didn't have they battering ram. This time they just come with questions. Then out step the man reporter from the one station and the woman reporter from the other station, and it was microphones in everbody face and everbody jabbering at once and not nobody making no sense. Gyp done a fast fade somehow cause he wasn't there no more when the cameras start to rolling. But Freon, he still stuck there blinking in the lights.

Keisha was in that second truck and it was her finally got the story out, except she was crying and screaming and shit to where it took her longer than it might of. Which of course looked good on the TV later, and they kept on running it for half the next week. She was hollering that she tried to call, she had tried to call. But our phone was broke, which we knew. Call about what? It was Keisha Jaynette gone to see over there on Eager Street, but Keisha didn't see it happen. Come out finally though, Jaynette had got shot in some kind of crossfire, but the strange part, part that brought the cameras, was the baby was gone too. Not shot, but just . . . nowhere. Froggy. Disappeared. Like he just had hop off on his own.

But it was like it couldn't get through to me. All the voices asking questions was in some language I didn't know, and the lights had blinded me, or something. I was alone underneath that cone of white light like somebody drop me down a well. Some way I was thinking, you know, how nobody live long enough to get ugly round here noway . . . But the one thing I did see clear was Gramma Reenie opening up the door, that good gumbo smell of her cooking steaming out behind her. How she did stand there with her hand raised up to the throat of that spotty green housedress, and I could see her heart beating through the fingers of that hand.

BULLETS DIDN'T HAPPEN to hit Jaynette in her face so she still look something like herself, once undertaker got through fixing her right. All trick out in her best red dress which was shiny and stood out real strong against the white satin lining of that coffin. Trig had *thrown* money at that funeral—he did that. Gramma Reen had not thought much of burying in a red dress. But I was for it, and Trig backed me underhand—it was her favorite. She had on too that red lip gloss she love so well. I taken it to the funeral home myself—found it in her purse, which nobody stole when they stole Froggy. She look pretty with it on, and her hair just so.

But Jaynette didn't look like she was sleeping, no. She looked dead as meat.

Gramma Reen want her brought to the house, the night before . . . for sitting up with. I didn't much like it but she deserved her way I thought, since we won about the dress. Jaynette laying there right in the room where the TV was at. In Gramma Reenie's old times I guess they'd had candles but we just sat up by the TV light, only the colors changing cause the sound was off. I had picked up the room, put all Froggy's toys in a box. His crib was in there. The beads he'd play with. Sometimes they'd show a snap of him on the TV. Have you seen this baby? There on the screen go Freon looking foolish, and me looking like my head on Mars, and there go Keisha crying and screaming, from two days before, but no sound now. There go Gramma Reenie with her lip zipped tight, just letters under her, spelling out IRENE PACKER, cause she didn't have nothing to say to them. And I didn't neither, and Trig was keeping his head down solid, so TV didn't have too much of a distress family to put on.

They was people come by, a whole lot at first. Trig float through with the main part of the crowd, them wraparounds still tight to the sides of his head. I had thought he might stay, even though he had his own place on the other side of the project these last two three years. When he left to go home, I had an idea what the shades was covering. Him and Jaynette was like that, yo, no matter what he didn't say. And you don't crawl off and hide only when you hurt.

Then some the other guys from the block, and neighbors, and church friends of Gramma Reen. We had the hugging and crying and all. People with the papers kept trying to get in cause of Froggy. Good time to have your phone be broke was what I say, and don't let's hurry fixing it. By eleven o'clock news everbody was gone. Tamara offered herself to sit up with me but I told her to go home.

All that time me'n Jaynette been girls together, going to school, skipping school, tasting that first beer and weed, starting to look at the guys more closer. We was like sisters, though she not any blood kin, and I didn't remember no time without Jaynette cause we was just the same age. Jaynette just only a baby down the block and her daddy disappeared like mine did, and my momma too. But Jaynette's momma, she died of an o.d. Then Gramma Reen took Jaynette in to raise.

I looked across the room at Gramma Reen, red and blue TV light waving on her face. Thought, *Don't you want to go and lay down or something?* but I would of wasted my breath to say it. She was that still she looked asleep but I known she wasn't. I tried to think if I was her—that would make Jaynette different. Not somebody just shot into your life outa somebody dick just swinging on through, but the one you chose yourself.

I wanted to cry but I couldn't do it. It was getting out from behind my own eyes made me feel that way. And somehow what I saw was me'n Jaynette as little kids going up and down the other side of the street with big trash bags, bottles and cans going in one sack and rags and paper in the other. We would feel proud when we got done, to see how it looked nice. And Gramma Reenie sitting in her porch chair smiling.

Cause we knew Gramma Reen would always be there. My momma Estelle I don't hardly remember. She gone off with some man to Chicago, they say, when I was not but two or something. And not a word back from her since that day. Trig, now he remember her better. Still, she not but sixteen when she have Trig. And that man, Trig daddy, he was killed in the Nam. Which mess Estelle up, so Gramma Reen say, that she never did get over it. About my daddy, well, who can say? I ain't met the motherfucka to this day, that I know of. All I can tell is they ain't been no stay-with-you type of man in this family since Grampa Packer died, and I don't hardly remember him neither. But Gramma Reenie, she say he was solid. Come up from Georgia to work in that steel, and held that job *down* for thirty-some years.

My mind traveled so, time went by and I didn't know it. The TV now putting out nothing but static. It did make Jaynette look ghostly, those colors washing over that still still face. I went and opened the door and looked outside. In one the shells across the street a match or a lighter struck and held—somebody firing a crack pipe. Maybe this be the night they burn down the whole street . . . but it was a too-wet night for that, with the wind blowing a few stray raindrops by. The trash heaps in the vacant lot was just wet and soggy down under the weeds. I thought about Froggy, wondering if he was somewhere warm and dry and thinking more than likely he wasn't. Cause I didn't expect to see Froggy no more, unless on the side of a milk carton.

I lit me a Kool but I couldn't smoke it. Mouth was too dry. Or something.

Indoors, Gramma Reenie's eyes drop shut, and she was breathing easy in her chair. I known if I ask her to go to bed she wouldn't, and it was no use to wake her. So I left her resting there and went and laid down myself. Couldn't sleep for nothing all that night, but then I must of dozed enough to dream, cause it seem like I'm talking to Jaynette all about everthing that happen, and it wasn't till I wash my face next morning I remembered she was dead.

THE SERVICE was held at that storefront church Gramma Reen went to since she live in Poe Homes. Not much of a place, just a railroad room through the building with folding chairs set up in rows, and a cross-shape window cut in the street door. I had not hardly set foot there since I was little, only for funerals I guess.

We had the crying and screaming and holy rolling. Prayers was offered up for Froggy too, wherever he might be, and that we'd get him back. Yeah, and *hope in one hand and spit in the other, see which one fills up first,* like Gramma Reen would sometimes say, but not in church.

There was some uncles and aunts I didn't hardly ever see, come from New York and Philly to brace up Gramma Reen. Me, I sat between Tamara and Keisha, only Keisha was nodding till she didn't even know where she was at. Ought not to come to a funeral that way. But since she move over to Eager Street, Boxcar have her strung out pretty far on that smack. No sign of Boxcar himself though, not at the church. I didn't like it Keisha would come so high, no matter how she hurting over Jaynette. But still we give her a ride to the cemetery, me and Tamara with Gyp driving his car. And Freon too, he tag along.

Greenmount Cemetery was the burying. Gramma Reen and Grampa Packer been paying on they patch up there since 1965. How them old folks like to do, own they grave before they ever own a house. The rain had pass on over and the day was sunny, cold and bright. More people showed up at the graveside. Some from Eager Street—Boxcar was there, and Stuttz and a few others from Candyman crew.

I didn't much like to watch'm sliding Jaynette into the ground, covering her over with that dirt. That grave was partway up hill where you overlooked the city, and my eyes kept slipping off down south, over the cemetery wall, to where the Super-max raise up like some castle in a horror movie, all circled around with razor-ribbon and gun towers. I felt Gyp keep looking that way too—Gyp already done himself a bit down at the Cut, but Super-max scare everbody.

I more'n ready to leave that place when they once got the dirt all shoveled in, but they was some wanted to hang around hugging and talking. Keisha had come up out of her nod, she was all crying again now and wiping her nose on one shoulder or another. I saw Gramma Reenie walk over slow and lay a wreath of flowers on that mound of raw dirt. She stood still there for a minute till my uncle Oscar down from Philly came over then and led her to his car. And I felt old, old, watching them go. Like I had already lived through all the years that Jaynette never would.

It was Stuttz took my mind off that, Stuttz jabbering something at Trig who was still locked down in his wraparounds, lost in a loose black suit. We all known Stuttz from around, from school, he was just kind of a fool like Freon, though a few years older. Wasn't no trouble between us and Candyman crew at that time, and plenty them come over to Jaynette funeral—it was nearby to Eager Street anyhow. I saw Rebo and Clayvon and some others I guess. Stuttz was the last of the Eager Street guys to be hanging around the graveyard—Boxcar was just leading Keisha down the hill toward the cars—and it seem like he hanging back for some reason.

"I'ma-I'ma-I'm *sssszzzzorry,*" he spit out. Stuttz have that name not cause he stutter all the time, but sometime when he get excited.

He nervous now, I could tell, fooling around with his leather jacket collar, running the zipper up and down. Trig was not hardly listening to him, already starting to turn away, but Stuttz put a hand out and pull him back. That caught me up, cause you don't lay a hand on Trig for nothing.

Trig whip back, thrown off the hand with a jerk of his shoulder. Then Stuttz spoke up clear like he sometimes can. "No, man," he said. "I mean, I'm *sorry* . . ."

He stopped there, but I could hear what he was getting at, not that he felt bad for Trig but that he felt bad for having something to do with it. My ear swung around like a satellite dish. And Freon, who was standing by, start trying to get closer.

"It was l-l-l-l-like . . ." Then Stuttz came clear again. "It was a accident, man, you see, I was—" But Trig saw Freon edging in and he turn his back to cut him out.

Then I couldn't hear no more what Stuttz was saying. Freon was nearer, with his ears fanned out, and I guessed maybe he could still hear something. What I could tell by looking was Stuttz not giving up all what Trig wanted him to. Trig stick him in the chest with a stiff hand, and Trig mouth pull away from his teeth when he ax the question, but Stuttz broke away from him and went scrambling down the hill through the gravestones, shoulders hunching up thin through that leather. And Trig shook his head and went stalking off toward his car.

I once called his name, but he didn't want to hear me. Trig my brother, my half-brother, and sometime he be so sweet with me, and always he look after me or try the best he can. But they times it ain't safe to touch him with a stick, and this was one. He got in the Lexus, alone, and drove away.

The horn on Gyp car blew, that silver Honda. Tamara had leaned across Gyp to blow it. We was about the last to leave by this time. Freon and me walk on down, wind whistling in our ears. It seem colder than when we got there cause the sun was gone behind a cloud. I looked back once when we got in the car, and seen a gull flying over the top of the hill, blown in from the harbor I guess it was.

It was me and Freon in the backseat and me still wondering if he had catch more of what it was Stuttz had to tell than I did. If I axed him, got it out of him right then, things might of come out different. But maybe I didn't want Freon to think he knew nothing I needed to hear about. I figured I would get it out of Trig anyhow, in the long run. Or maybe it was I just didn't feel like talking.

Gyp took a right and then another one, cruising along the outside of the cemetery wall. I don't really know why, cause it wasn't our way home. Probably he just wanted to check they action down that way. He made the next turn, headed south now, where the graveyard wall get high, almost two stories there on the right-hand side of the car. Feel like driving alongside of the Super-max jail, no razor ribbon but that wall the same square-cut brown stone.

I just as happy to be in a car, not walking. They some bad-looking guys just standing there against the wall, like always, drinking out they paper sacks and staring a dead stare through you. Sometime Candyman crew would be slanging down this way, but I didn't see nobody I knew. Except for Stuttz, walking along by himself about half a block along, hands in his pockets and his head bowed down.

Gyp was peeping, checking the scene, not looking for anything special, just seeing what they was. Then Freon let his window down, first an inch or so and then all the way.

He was bringing in the cold and I just starting to tell him to roll it up when I seen we was coming up on Stuttz.

"Yo!" say Freon. "Head up, cuz!" Stuttz turn toward the car, not a yard away.

The sound came first, like a rag ripping but a whole lot louder, and something stung me on the back of my neck. And not till then did I see that plastic pistol, bouncing in Freon yellow hands. Stuttz lying against the wall, hands crushed into his side and blood leaking out through the fingers. Freon stick his head out the window and holler out loud as he can, *"Poe Homes! Poe Homes!"* And Gyp is yelling, "What the *fuck,*" and he mash the gas and off we fly around the next corner with the tires bunched up and screaming.

It was fire up the tailpipe the next few blocks. Gyp was clean through the JFX overpass before he could make himself slow down. But then he driving easy-easy. I look out the back window and didn't see nobody following. No siren, no nothing. Something gripe the back of my neck and I reach in my collar and picked it out, the brass end of a bullet that had flew in there and burnt me.

Gyp looked back over his shoulder and say one word to Freon: "Fool." Then he raise Trig on the phone and tell him to be over to his place, Gyp's, as fast as he can make it. And they wasn't nobody said nothing else before we got there.

Gyp live over there on Lexington, highrise just above that Martin Luther King highway, but he ain't drive straight to the building—parked a couple blocks up Fremont instead. Right away he's cleaning out the car, the phone, snap-out tape deck, tapes, and anything else he might want to hang on to. When he pulled the bass speaker out the trunk I known he wasn't counting on coming back to that car at all.

Gyp was smoking. And I could read his mind like a thought balloon on the funny page: *I ain't going back to the Cut over this one.*

I thought a minute, and I shown Gyp that shell casing, lying there in the palm of my hand. Gyp whip around on Freon.

"Nigga, you clean them things outa my car. And I mean you better find'm *all.*"

Freon done like he was told—digging under the cushions and under the seats. I didn't see the gun nowhere, he must of stuck it back down his pants. When he got done he held out the shells to Gyp like a little kid hoping for a pat on the head. Gyp just shove that speaker into his hands for him to carry, and Gyp lock the car up and we started walking on down.

Gyp building, we used to kid him he live there cause it remind him of the Cut. They got these outside walkways all the way up the north side and they covered over with storm fence on a pipe scaffold, so you can't throw nothing down I guess. And the south side empty, windows all sealed up. But people still live on the north side.

Lexus pulling up front about the time we get there. Trig jump out.

"What went down, yo?"

"We better get in first," Gyp say, tight-mouth.

Then Tamara give a little smile and about one quarter of a wave and she high-stepping back down the street toward Poe Homes. But I was holding this box of tapes I didn't quite know what to do with so I went inside with the rest of them.

Got this little security shack you hafta pass to go in the building, but it ain't nobody there but a rentacop, and him half asleep. Didn't pay us no mind. The elevator was broke so we walked up, six flights. And walked that catwalk to Gyp's door, storm fence throwing diamond shadow lines across us all. It do feel something like a cell block, what I hear. I'd moved somewhere else if I was Gyp.

But Gyp place nice inside, it is. Got the digital stereo and the big-screen TV and the leather chairs and couch and high-tech lamps and shit. Well, I been up there plenty times. I tried the bed, you know.

"What happen, yo?" Trig say again.

"What happen?" Gyp say. "Like we driving down the east wall of the graveyard, right?"

Freon standing in the middle of the room still holding that bass woofer like he don't know what to do with it.

"We cruising." Gyp point to Freon. "Fool nigga roll down the window, start busting on Stuttz right out the backseat of my car."

"Shit," Trig say. "Kill him?"

"Look like it to me," Gyp say. "We didn't wait to find out for sure."

Freon set that speaker down in the middle of the rug, then he straighten back up kinda slow and shaky. I felt sorry for him, he look so small.

"Don't let me forget this part," Gyp say. "He yell out our address a few times, after he empty his gun."

Trig made a kind of a spitting sound. "Who heard him? Anybody make your car?"

"Don't know," Gyp say. "They was some cats on the corner like they always is. I'm set to give up the car, yo. Call it in stole, whatever."

Trig step over to Freon, yanked that pistol out from

under his shirt tail. He sniff the barrel, shot that empty clip out in his palm. Pitch the pistol in the corner and he take hold of Freon stubbly little dreads and pull him close.

"Why, ma'fucka? Tell me why."

"For Jaynette." Freon voice came out squeaky, he swallowed once and make it low. "For Poe Homes, for us. For you, Trig . . ."

"The fuck you think you talking about?"

"Ain't Stuttz shot her?" Freon voice cracked again.

All of a sudden Trig let go Freon hair and he sat down on the edge of that leather couch. Take off his wraparounds and fold them up in his long brown hands. Such a long time it seemed since I saw Trig's eyes, and they was red and tired.

"Odell, you dumbshit," Trig say. "Stuttz ain't the one shooting. He the one getting shot *at*."

Freon pulling flies outa his mouth—me too, I guess. I seen Freon Adam's apple pump, under that scar he lie about.

"Well, who done the shooting then?" Gyp say.

"Stuttz ain't told me," Trig say. "Sound like he won't be telling nobody now."

Then it seemed like I been there long enough, and heard as much as I needed to. I set that box of tapes down on Gyp's glass end table and I eased on out the door. They wasn't paying me no attention noway.

It felt cold, so cold outside that door, though the wind had died down and the sun come back. I went to the east end of the catwalk and hung on the fence, cold wire cutting into my hands. I could see over the cars buzzing up and down the MLK highway, and past that over to the Lexington Market, people walking the outdoor mall, the size of bugs. Seem like I was froze for a while to that fence.

Then they wasn't nothing to do but walk the few blocks home. Halfway, I remembered that shell still stuck to the palm of my hand, so I thrown it down a storm drain. Like Trig would want me to do.

Some guy standing on the sidewalk time I got back, squinting up at our house number. Coulda been anybody from the block—jeans and leather and his face turtled back in a sweatshirt hood. Except when I got up close I seen it was a white guy.

"Looking for the Poe house?" I say. "It down the end of the block."

"No, excuse me," white dude say. "Is this Irene Packer's house?"

Reporter, I thought then. "What if it is?"

"Do you know if she's home?"

"I don't know," I say. "I know she don't want to be bothered with you—been more than enough of y'all hanging around."

"Oh," white dude say. "I'm not with the press."

He roll back the hood of his sweatshirt so I can see him better. Kind of a hawky face, black hair a little long in the back, and with some gray streaks in it, just a couple. Deep eyes looking at me deep, like he trying to read some small print off the back side of my brain.

Then he must of make up his mind about something, cause he step off the curb and unlock a car which is parked right there. Bends in low and up he come with a baby. This baby is quiet and look natural, comfortable, riding on this white dude hip, only this a black baby, and it's Froggy.

I reached out, and Froggy came to me so quick. He molded onto me like babies will do, like warm wet clay, wet mouth nuzzling the cloth of my coat. I guess I must of said his name. I closed my eyes, and it all came out, all those last few days came out of me. When I looked again, white dude was gone.

8

Bright bitter sunlight poured from the cloudless sky over McDonogh Street, the slope rising up the hulk of the Hopkins hospital a few blocks to the south. Shadows of the eastside row houses stretched darkly across the littered pavement to the western sidewalk, where Devlin stood within the folded gates of his new Tae Kwon Do school, twisting a new cylinder into the frame of the glass door. All up and down the street was the scrape and clash of other gratings as different businesses began to open: newsstand, a hairdresser, the bars. Only the Korean convenience store had been open already for hours when he arrived on the block; there Devlin had bought the cup of astringent black coffee that now steamed beside his feet, through the siphole bitten in the plastic lid of the container. Since it was Saturday morning, there was not much motor traffic on the street, though a few idlers were beginning to pass by on foot, some pausing for a moment for a glance at Devlin's newly brightened storefront.

He tightened the set screw on the cylinder and straightened up to try one of the two keys that had been furnished with it. The dead bolt shot, a little stiffly, and retracted when he reversed the turn of the key. Devlin stooped for his coffee, raised it to sip, letting the door drift shut. On the glass were appliquéd the letters RYU'S TAE KWON DO—DOWNTOWN, along with some characters in *han gul,* then the times of the classes, and his own name followed by the title: INSTRUCTOR. Inside, the long rectangular space shone starkly under the fluorescents: fresh paint, mirrors lining one wall, the floor resurfaced with red and yellow mats in alternating stripes. Though not particularly handy, Devlin had done much of the work himself, hiring some fixer-uppers who sometimes did odd jobs at his own house to complete whatever was beyond him. White men, they'd been uneasy in this neighborhood, but had not refused the work.

Devlin smiled and sipped his coffee; there was some thrill in this project after all, despite his manifold reservations. Something new. A car door banged, startling him slightly. A green Corolla, like Michelle's—with a slight shock Devlin saw that it *was* Michelle. She came toward him smiling, flipping her hair back. A light gym bag swung from her shoulder.

"What are you doing down here?" Devlin said.

"Morning class, right?" Michelle said, pausing before him. Was it sarcasm flavoring her smile? "Didn't you want me to practice more?"

"Yes, but it's not till eleven," Devlin said. "Besides . . ."

"I know," Michelle said. "I'll warm up first."

She remembered to bow before crossing the threshold, to the flags hanging at the far end of the room; that pleased Devlin, though he was disturbed to see her here. He watched her now as through the glass of an aquarium, casting about and then homing in on the dressing room. Besides, he'd meant to say, there might not be much of a class; it was his opening day and so far he had no students here. Why couldn't she go to Ryu's main branch on the north side, that safe, more or less suburban neighborhood? But the truth was he was glad to see her anywhere. She had been very scarce with him these last two weeks, since . . . Devlin shrugged and went inside to change.

HE'D STILL BEEN very stoned when he arrived home with the baby he'd rescued from Eager Street, but the high was blunted, heavier now, had lost the ebullience of its first phase. Under the spotlight that played across his driveway, he sat in the idling car, where the radio played softly, jazz. The child had gone to sleep in the seat beside him, though somewhat awkwardly lap-belted in. He could see Alice at the kitchen window, her head lowered over the sink; she had not yet looked up to notice his arrival. With a sluggish feeling of apprehension Devlin shut off the car and gathered the sleeping baby to his shoulder and went into the house.

For the first few minutes, nothing unusual seemed to happen, and Devlin even believed that somehow he might carry it off, though just *where* he would carry it began dimly to trouble him. The baby stirred, snuffled against his neck under his jacket collar. Alice turned from the sink, laying lettuce leaves into a colander. When she first noticed the infant clinging to Devlin, she smiled reflexively, shook the water from her hands, and reached out her arms. Devlin accomplished the transfer without waking the baby, who lay with his slack lips slightly parted and his whole body molding to the blue cotton cloth that covered Alice's breasts. Briefly it all seemed very natural, right, even, but Devlin saw that Alice's eyes were scanning past him, toward the door—after all, this baby couldn't have materialized here all by itself. Could it?

Michelle came into the kitchen, carrying multicolored handfuls of what looked like old leotards. "Mom, I—" She took in the baby and froze. "Where'd you get that?"

Alice's smile was quizzical, crooked on one side. "Ask your father."

"I found him," Devlin said, as Michelle turned his way. It didn't sound as convincing as he'd have liked. Somehow the irresistibility of his action seemed to be losing its momentum.

"You, like, just found him and brought him home?" Michelle said.

"Yeah," Devlin said. "You might say that." Alice's smile had withered, he noticed; feathery lines drew down the corners of her eyes.

"Dad, hey, it's got to belong to somebody, don't you think?" Michelle said. "Like, you wouldn't even let me keep a *cat*."

Devlin decided he didn't like her tone. "That's different. Besides, I'm allergic to cats."

"I'll say it's different." Michelle squinted at the infant. "But what if I'm allergic to little nigger babies?"

Devlin's hand flashed out and slapped her; he hadn't known what the hand would do. Michelle's face went sideways in a whirl of hair; next Devlin heard her feet slamming up the stairs, the door to her room banging shut. The baby had begun crying in a loud outraged voice.

"Terrific, Mike." Alice thrust the bundle at him at her arms' length. "Here, you take care of it." When Devlin had accepted the baby, she stalked out of the kitchen.

There'd been a grubby quilted diaper bag attached to the stroller, and now Devlin brought it into the house, hooked over his elbow as he carried the baby. He groped in the bag now and found a bottle full of some dark liquid. Still the baby was vigorously howling. Flexing the nipple, he squeezed a drop onto his fingertip and tasted: Coke. Not the most wholesome choice, perhaps, but the baby quieted instantly when Devlin put the nipple to his lips. Both his hands came up to grasp the bottle, as from old habit.

"Ah," Devlin said aloud. "You control the food supply." His voice seemed dreadfully hollow, echoed by a silence from upstairs. At the far end of the house he could faintly hear the television.

He found Pampers and wipes in the diaper bag too, and cleaned and changed the baby while it nursed. Yes, it was enough like riding a bicycle . . . Done, the baby dropped the bottle and stretched his hands to be picked up. Devlin brought him to his shoulder. The limpet-like way the infant attached to him could not soothe him as much as it had done at first. On the counter, a glistening pool of water had collected beneath the lettuce in the strainer. The leotards Michelle had dropped lay on the speckled linoleum like a snarl of tricolor spaghetti. A tear in one had frayed around the edges; Devlin stared at it with a stupefied unbreakable attention.

"Mike?" Alice's voice called from across the house.

Devlin looked at the fingers of his renegade hand, which now felt numb to him. Whether he'd hit her hard or not he couldn't tell.

"Mike!—I think you're on the news."

The baby was leaning back, fumbling with Devlin's earlobe. He hitched him up and walked into the den. Alice's face was grimly set; she wouldn't look at him directly. The television displayed the crime scene, marked off now with yellow police tape, and empty except for a patch of bloodstained concrete soaking up the glaring lights. Then a yearbook photo of the murdered girl. Then a reporter posed against the sawhorses of a police barrier, retailing the story of what she called a suspected kidnapping.

Alice's face softened slightly; she reached across and touched his shoulder. "I . . . My *God,* Mike." More concern in her voice than anger. She flipped her hand toward the television. "Okay, I see . . . but I still don't get it."

Devlin was silent. That he'd been stoned half out of his mind at the time did not at the moment strike him as an acceptable explanation. He'd set the baby on the carpeted floor of the den; he noticed that the child was able to sit up. The colors flashing from the television seemed to appeal to him.

Alice picked up the remote and zapped down the volume on the set, then turned to give Devlin a straight look. "How was it you got into this?" she said. "I mean, do you think you could walk me through it?"

Devlin rolled the back of his head on the couch cushion and closed his eyes: hot pulses. What took form against his eyelids was the muzzle flash emerging from the cave of the green field jacket. No, not that part.

"I came up there . . ." Devlin opened his eyes, tried to

focus. The baby dropped to all-fours and crawled toward the television, staring at the unfolding colors of a weather map.

"It was right when the girl was shot," Devlin said. "There was a crowd. Nobody was minding the baby."

"So you just *took* him?" Alice said. Hair switched her shoulders as she shook her head.

"What was I supposed to do?" Devlin said. "Walk on by?"

"I suppose that would be the usual response," Alice said, glancing down at her curled knees.

"That or stand there rubbernecking." Briefly, Devlin felt a little clearer; he felt he might have scored a point.

"Better that than . . . what? Kidnapping? Baby-stealing? I'm fairly sure it's some sort of felony."

"Look," Devlin said, "I wasn't thinking in legal terms. I saw the mother was stone dead. Do you suppose this kid has a father in the picture? He was there by himself. Nobody was even *looking* at him."

"You know this," Alice said, with an edge of sarcasm. "You're somehow familiar with these relationships."

Devlin's sense of clarity deserted him. He could feel the bud of a headache beginning to open, directly behind his right eye. "You might have made the same deduction. You know what it's like."

Alice didn't move or change expression, but Devlin could see, just from her eyes, that he'd stabbed into her old reservoir of pain. Unfair. If Alice hadn't seen it all, she'd seen more of it than he ever had: an endless march of injured children, beaten, raped, tortured, and abandoned. The social machinery intended to protect them from further harm was hamstrung by its own checks and balances, too cumbersome to do most people much permanent good. Nevertheless, Alice had served ten years in the front line. She had gone to the neighborhoods and the homes and looked the victims and perps in the eye. When finally she had seen enough, she made her retreat to administration. If Devlin wanted to be a real pig bastard, he might now accuse her of sticking her head in the sand.

"I think . . ." But Devlin was having trouble thinking. He could remember the sensation of his hands closing over the grips of the stroller, but not any cognitive process associated with the deed. "It felt like an impulse," he said. "I think I must have wanted to take some kind of direct action. For once." *Didn't you ever feel that way?* Unfair to say it, but still the unspoken sentence lay heavily between them.

He stretched out his open hands and flexed the fingers slightly. Alice took the one nearest her, the left, and studied it for a moment as if it were a completely unfamiliar object. Then she shook her head again, sharply, and let Devlin's hand drop back against the couch cushions.

"Now what?" Alice said. "Hope you have an impulse that tells you what to do next? This is serious, Mike. You're going to have to do something." Her face drained of expression, as if by an effort of will, and she turned toward the television: stutter of a cheaply made ad for a local car lot.

"I know," Devlin said. The baby had crawled back to the low-standing coffee table and pulled himself up by its edge. His small, serious face was a flinty black. Alice reached across the table and twiddled her fingers at him. Devlin rose and went upstairs.

Outside his daughter's room he hesitated, then tapped on the door and pushed it inward. Michelle was on her bed, knees drawn up, her back in a cushion-crammed corner, not reading or listening to music or doing anything else at all. Steam knocked in the pipes of her radiator but otherwise it was quite silent.

"Shell," Devlin said.

The girl looked up at him, cool and neutral.

"I'm sorry."

"I made you do it." Her tone was flat. She thumbed back her hair from the side of her face, and Devlin searched her cheek for a red spot or a bruise, but nothing seemed obvious, not from where he stood in the doorway.

"It didn't even hurt, you know," Michelle said finally. "I mean, you've hit me twice as hard at practice."

"It's not the same," Devlin said.

"I guess not," Michelle said. "Like—I don't know why I said that. I don't use that word—even think it. The whole thing is just *weird.*"

"Sure," Devlin said, without conviction. "It's all right."

Michelle nodded and lowered her eyes to her knees again. Devlin stepped backward through the doorway and closed the door behind him. It no longer seemed to matter, the ugly word she'd used; the thing that couldn't be taken back was what he'd done.

"I'M NOT MAD AT YOU," Alice advised him the next morning. "I just don't understand it."

Devlin nodded, noncommittal, unloading goods from a dawn-patrol shop: newspaper, formula, rice cereal, a spare plastic bottle, a few jars of Gerber, and more Pampers and wipes.

"Men in their forties do strange things, sometimes,"

Alice said. "They have odd *impulses*—to quote a friend. They may exhibit aberrant behavior."

"So I've been told," Devlin said. He clicked a cabinet shut on the baby food.

"Only, why this? Why not buy a sports car?" Alice said. "Have an affair—not that I'm asking you to have an affair. There's all sorts of stupid things you could do. But kidnapping?"

"It didn't appear to me in that light while I was doing it." Devlin opened the refrigerator and dumped some apples and oranges into a bin. "I thought you said you didn't understand it. Sounds like you've got me diagnosed."

"I don't understand it—I wonder if you do. There has to be more behind it than what you're telling me."

Devlin closed the bin and stood up, still partially shielded by the open refrigerator door.

"Shut that, would you please? Before the milk goes bad?"

Devlin complied. Now that everything had been put away, it was more difficult for him to keep his back turned to the conversation.

"Mike." She waited for him to look at her. "Did you want another baby? Is that it?"

Did you? Devlin didn't say it. Alice's voice had assumed a tone of professional solicitude. Devlin felt annoyed by that: after all, he wasn't one of her clients. "Diagnosis complete," he said, pacing a doglike circle on the kitchen floor while he studied the wallpaper. "Hemorrhage of the male-midlife-crisis-biological-clock."

"Hilarious," said Alice.

Devlin stole a glance at her; she was not amused. He

paced. "I didn't do it to get a baby," he said. "That's not the point."

Alice's neatly rounded nails clicked on the edge of her coffee cup. "I wish you'd tell me what *is* the point."

Half-turned from the open door of the refrigerator, Devlin held her level gaze. It wasn't baby-envy, no. Nor was he inclined to write it off to some aberration of his middle-aged hormones . . . though who could say for sure? Devlin stopped at the counter by the sink and poured himself half a cup of coffee, staring through the window at a yellow-beaked starling rocked on a windblown branch of a small maple tree. When the bird had flown, he dropped his head and spoke into the sink.

"If you were ever to really *register* what you read in the newspaper," Devlin said, "you would run screaming into the street."

"Jesus," Alice said. "That is not a reasonable response to the situation."

"Best I can do," Devlin said.

"So what am *I* supposed to do?" Alice said. The tendons of her neck stiffened with anger. "Call the police?"

"I suppose that would be one of your options," Devlin said, shrink-tone.

"Fine," Alice said. She jumped up and slapped her chair against the table. "Just *fine.* There's nothing to say—I won't say anything. Let's not talk about it."

Devlin nodded, leaving his head lowered. He couldn't think of anything else to do.

"I'm going out," Alice said. "I'm going out—I'll be gone all day. I might go somewhere and have lunch with a friend. I might go to the mall or a movie or a museum or *anywhere* the people are sane. Because it looks like the lunatics are running *this* asylum."

A wail from the living room interrupted her, and she got up abruptly from the table. "There," she said, jerking her coat from the pegs by the kitchen door. "*You* figure it out. It's your baby."

IT WAS SUNDAY. Alice kept her promise to stay gone. Michelle slept late, then left the house without greeting Devlin, then stayed gone. He spent the day tending the baby, flipping desultorily through the newspaper, watching patches of TV. There were never more than five or ten minutes of uninterrupted time—he had forgotten about that.

But the baby was not what you'd call fussy. Froggy; his nickname had been revealed on the TV the night before. When he needed food or some other attention, he'd utter one loudly sustained cry, and then wait with an air of patience for response. He seemed good-natured, on the whole, and happy enough to be where he was.

Devlin took off the crawler the baby'd been wearing and took it to the basement to wash. He turned up the thermostat and let Froggy ramble around on the living room rug, wearing nothing but a diaper. The nickname, Devlin decided, was not so inappropriate. Froggy stood bandy-legged, smiling and pleased with himself, whenever he managed to pull himself upright on a table's edge or chair seat, and the way the slack skin of his stomach inflated and relaxed really did suggest a frog.

That evening, with a marked absence of conversation, Devlin and his family watched the news. On the screen, the histrionics of the previous day were repeated, with small variations. A young woman identified as Keisha Raines wailed hysterically. The grandmother or great-grandmother, Irene Packer, somehow absorbed the shock into her wizened face.

"I feel like an unwed mother," Devlin cracked at the supper table. No one laughed. If he'd intended to reopen the subject for discussion, the effort was not a success. He knew from past experience that Alice was quite capable of sticking to her plan to say nothing more about it all. It was not exactly the silent treatment; she would speak to him on other topics, though stiffly. She would answer direct questions. She carried on the usual dinner conversation with Michelle, who seemed ordinary, unaffected, yet looked everywhere but into Devlin's eyes.

Froggy woke up at ten P.M., loaded for bear. Devlin fed him a meal of Gerber plum slop, which he seemed to much enjoy. After he had cleaned the walls and floor and Froggy's arms and legs and garments, Devlin put some dry rice into the empty baby-food jar to make a sort of rolling rattle for Froggy to chase around the living room rug. Michelle brought down a couple of stuffed animals, then retired wordlessly from the room. With a sort of jujitsu proficiency, she had somehow managed to avoid all eye contact with Devlin during this brief encounter.

Froggy seemed friendlier than ever, favoring Devlin with many toothless smiles. They played for two hours, then Devlin bathed him in the kitchen sink. Down the hall he could hear Michelle and Alice talking in Michelle's room: murmur, the odd burst of laughter (was it strained?), and again a low serious murmuring, unintelligible through the door. Another time, Devlin would have felt reassured to hear them so; tonight it sent him a twinge of paranoia.

Around one in the morning the baby finally went to sleep in a nest Devlin had fashioned in the seat of an armchair. Devlin considered going upstairs, to Alice's silent form curled away from him, withdrawn to the farthest edge of the double bed. Anger makes a lumpy pillow, and Devlin was frustrated by having no reason to be angry with her; whatever doghouse he'd got into was of his own construction. At any rate, it would be better to stay near his charge. He started out sleeping on the couch, then shifted his blanket to the floor when his back ached enough to wake him. Froggy cried twice in the night for his bottle and went quickly back to sleep once fed and changed. He was, as Alice might have said, an easy baby.

Monday morning Devlin called to cancel his appointments. He was rather groggy from the interruptions of the night, but so accustomed to early rising he could not go back to sleep after six. Alice and Michelle shot off to work and school, and while Froggy slept in, Devlin skimmed the morning paper. The Metro section carried an in-depth report on the dead girl and her family. Jaynette. Devlin flinched inwardly at the discovery of her name, remembering her quick light step, flashes of gold at her throat and wrists, just for that one instant . . . Jaynette herself had been adopted, said the newspaper, taken in by this grandmotherly person, Irene Packer. The house was not some crack den, evidently, but a place where children were loved, desired. Mourned. At odd intervals during the day, Devlin returned to the article and the photo spread. The old woman's wrinkled face lifted up toward a dignified resolution that abashed him somehow. In West Virginia, he had known such women; they had cared for him when he was small.

That evening the same clips ran on the news as before. The missing infant was still being sought. Devlin tried no jokes at supper. His wife and natural child said nothing to reproach him.

By Tuesday, the effects of his sleep deprivation had taken on a slightly psychotic quality. When Michelle was newborn, Devlin had always been hit faster and harder by sleep loss than his wife. Now he could feel himself getting goofy.

That morning he was awakened by a touch, and opened his eyes to see Alice perched on the edge of the couch, smoothing his forehead as one might with a feverish child. She was dressed for work, and the fresh-washed smell of her gave Devlin a wistful pang.

"There's something you want," Alice said, as she stood up. Her tone was gentler than he'd heard the last two days, her brown eyes affectionate and concerned for him. "You need to figure out what it is." Devlin slept again as she left the room, and woke up punchy in the full morning light, unsure if what she'd said had come in dream.

Again he canceled his appointments, but he had to handle a couple of crisis calls over the phone, without fully trusting his judgment because of his altered state. Froggy became restive, seeming to resent Devlin's distraction by the phone. Somehow a few hours passed. Devlin walked him up and down the floor to calm him, until the baby slept. Outdoors, the wind blew a thin sleety rain against the panes of the front windows. Devlin lay on the couch, still holding the baby, opening his shirt so that their skins could warm each other. He slept too.

At waking, early in the afternoon, he felt considerably more lucid; fatigue had drained from his mind and settled in his bones. He gave Froggy a bottle, changed him, played with him for an hour on the floor. But somehow the decision had made itself while they were sleeping; they were only marking time.

Outside, the rain had stopped at least temporarily, and colorless skylight leached through gray-marbled clouds. Devlin packed the new supplies he'd bought into the diaper bag, loaded Froggy into the car and drove downtown. Strange to be giving the baby up; stranger still to have taken him in the first place, maybe. What could he have possibly been thinking? These silent past few days at home, he'd experimented with various rationalizations. Certainly it was a bit too simple to blame it all on a cannabis aberration. He'd had some unthought-through notion that Froggy would be better off. A child could get lost in the maze of social services as absolutely as he could be lost to the street. Devlin knew that from both sides of his desk. So did Alice—even better. It was a puzzle for a child to find a safe haven anywhere nowadays.

Devlin was talking to himself as he drove, responding to an inaudible interrogator. *I saw the baby—the baby was in jeopardy. So I picked the baby up. Now tell me why that doesn't make sense?* He knew the answers but they weren't persuasive; they left the heart of the matter unaddressed. Had he gone crazy? Devlin answered no, though he knew full well there wasn't a doctor on earth properly qualified to treat himself. Alice was right—there was something he wanted, but it didn't really bother him not knowing what it was. On the contrary, he felt younger, fresher, in that uncertainty, his sense of possibility restored.

The paper had not quoted the exact address but he knew it was a project near the Poe House, in the slums a couple of miles across downtown from the neighborhood Devlin had selected to open the new school. Exactly where the Poe House was he couldn't quite remember; he thought he'd somehow missed a sign in turning westward into the grid of narrow streets, and all the project buildings looked too much alike.

The rain had started up again, and the windshield wipers flicked to and fro with a slightly irritating whir. From the fogged interior, visibility was poor. Froggy had gone back to sleep, lulled by their syrupy motion over the wet streets. Devlin parked and got out and locked the car.

With the rain, there seemed to be no one on the street. He walked to the nearest corner and turned east, looking for some landmark to orient himself. There was Lexington Market, on the far side of the highway. Devlin reversed his direction; he didn't want to be more than a few seconds out of sight of Froggy and the car. A burst of wind drove the rain across a vacant lot into the side of his face; he gathered the hood of his sweatshirt tighter and flipped his leather collar up. He became aware of someone behind him, fifteen paces back at about five o'clock and holding his speed instead of overtaking. Deliberately, Devlin relaxed himself, so that he could move quickly if need be. He measured the distance to his car, which was again in view.

The man behind him moved within range of a low voice. "I got tens and twenties, yo—"

"No." Devlin took one hand from his pocket and made a cutting motion toward the ground. "I'm just walking."

The man came nearer, not quite abreast and still not close enough for Devlin to feel menaced. He was tall, light-skinned, and wearing a faded denim jacket. Under the hood Devlin could make out a longish nose with the groove of a two-inch scar beside it, over the cheekbone. He spoke without turning his head Devlin's way.

"Keep walking on through, then—cause you make business be bad. Cause you white, yo, people gone think you a cop."

Devlin cut another quick glance; the other was also giving him a sidelong eye. The recommendation didn't seem unfriendly. Devlin stopped.

"Actually," he said, "I was looking for the Poe House."

That night, he let the television inform his family of the new development. No one remarked on it aloud, though Alice gave him a guarded look that might have been relief. *I feel like an unwed mother who's given up her baby for adoption,* Devlin thought of saying over supper, but he kept this witticism to himself.

FROM THAT DAY till this, he'd spent long hours away from the house, playing catch-up at his practice and hurling himself into refurbishments at the McDonogh Street storefront. Things at home seemed to be drifting back toward normal, the best he could determine. He and Alice were speaking again, taking up where they'd left off before the Froggy episode, which seemed to have been excised from their common history, surgically removed. Nothing to say about it. Devlin still did not know what to say. It left a sort of seam between them, a scar he hoped would pale invisibly with time.

Michelle, meanwhile, had held herself courteously aloof. This morning was the first time she'd voluntarily sought his company . . . if that was what she was doing in fact. Devlin shook his head as he changed into his uniform. He was happier not thinking about it really, and martial arts did free him from thinking any thoughts like that.

When he walked barefoot onto the floor, Michelle was stretching on the mats. With no apparent effort she'd dropped into a full split. Devlin gave an inward moan of envy; he'd need surgery for flexibility like that. He stretched for a couple of minutes himself, then clapped his hands. They meditated, kneeling before the flags, then began a hard, fast basics. Halfway through, Devlin felt his personality melting from him and was glad enough to see it go.

"*Koryo*," he said, calling Michelle to attention, then studying her for a moment before he gave the order to begin. Through the triangular frame of her paired arc-hands, her eyes were aware of him but neutral, concentrated on some point well beyond. Her personality had vanished also. She was good.

"Si chak!"

Michelle snapped a knifehand block to the left, then the double side kicks. Devlin watched with his instructor's eye but there was nothing to find fault with. Her form had the crispness that only Asian students usually achieved—there was something burly about the way most white people did the movements. And *Koryo*, with its swallowtail grace, was perfect to show off her strengths. She got a lot more power than was typical for a woman, as well.

Devlin was pleased and a little annoyed. She had no

right to look that good after a several-month defection, that fairly typical post–black-belt trough. But it bothered Devlin because Tae Kwon Do was something you had to keep up. He'd coaxed her into martial arts to begin with out of concern for her safety—over Alice's objection that there were many dangers in the world a side kick wouldn't stop, Alice's wondering how much of an advantage it would be for Michelle to be able to beat up all her boyfriends . . .

She stood now where she'd begun, in *junbi* position. Koryo was a taxing form, but it had given her only a glow; she was not breathless. Devlin thought of paying her some compliment but decided not to. The hardcore Korean instructors only dealt in criticisms; you deduced that they were satisfied if they said nothing to you at all.

He bowed to her. "Watch me on *Kum Gan.*"

Michelle bowed in her turn and stepped to the side. Devlin began the form. His joints felt a little rusty. Refurbishing the new space had left him little time the last couple of weeks for practice at the northside school. His wind was all right, and he had snap, but the whole effort felt less graceful than it should have.

He finished and returned to attention, raising an eyebrow toward Michelle. She dropped her head and paced, thinking.

"A bit wobbly in the crane stances?" she said.

Devlin relaxed and began wandering over the striped mats, going over the form in his head again. The ball of Michelle's foot snapped crisply against his uniform collar, bringing him sharply back from his abstraction.

"Some dads play tennis," Michelle said, already spinning to the right: a high reverse crescent kick. Devlin snatched his head sideways and felt the breeze go by. Torque carried her through with a roundhouse kick and Devlin backed off from that one too, following her heel with a push of his palm that might have sent her off balance but didn't quite. She was there with an impatient block when he moved in with a short punch . . . but not quite ready with a counterattack. Devlin got away from her and circled, his back to the street door. He made a fake lunge and drew a back kick with it, only it wasn't a back kick but a 360-degree roundhouse; Devlin stopped her toe about three inches from the corner of his jaw. Michelle's turn to whirl away, recovering. Then she let down and pointed to the door.

"Customers?"

Devlin turned. Two young blades of the neighborhood were at the door, slapping palms against the glass and squinting into the interior. He turned the key he'd left in the cylinder and let them in.

"Whussup?" said the slighter one. "This place new here, yo."

"Right." Devlin nodded. "Opening day." He noticed they were more expensively dressed than he'd have expected, and had identical artful haircuts: shaved up the back and sides to a circlet of hair like a skullcap on top. Each had a zigzag lightning bolt razor-cut into the stubble above the left ear. One was lean and lively looking, the other heavyset and somewhat overweight.

"What're your names?" Devlin said.

"Boxcar," said the heavier one. He flipped his hand toward the other. "Kool-whip."

Devlin watched their eyes tracking, past Michelle over

the mats and mirrors to the flags, the leatherbound heavy bag hanging from a chain, back to Michelle, and lingering.

"What all can you do?" Kool-whip said.

"Shell," said Devlin. "Demo?"

Michelle turned her back to them and took a couple of lazy, disinterested paces toward the heavy bag. She put her right foot on an imaginary step about three feet off the floor and lofted into the air; her left heel thrust out and drove into the bag, which collapsed at the middle and shuddered on the rattling links of its chain. Michelle landed in a cat stance with her fists up and vibrated for an instant, like a tuning fork, before wandering away with a hint of an insouciant swagger.

"Yo," Boxcar said. "How much do it cost?"

THE SCHOOL MUSHROOMED, faster than Devlin would have thought possible. Boxcar and Kool-whip brought in friends: young men of approximately their age with similar taste in clothes and hairstyle, down to the razor-cut lightning bolt. Clayvon, Rebo, Butch, a fast kid who was known as Bigfoot. Money, surprisingly, didn't seem to be a problem for these guys, though Devlin had prepared a sliding scale, anticipating that it would. The alternative pricing structure was necessary only for some of the kids mothers brought in to the children's class Devlin organized separately, and for a couple of older men, in their forties, who held low-paying jobs with the city. But the youngbloods Devlin came to consider his cadre always looked flush enough—which pleased Master Ryu, among other things, as he reckoned the receipts at the northside school.

It was strictly a man's game down on McDonogh Street, except for the children's class. Wives and girlfriends did stop by to watch, lugging groceries, pushing strollers. Devlin made it clear that women were welcome: the sign on the door advertised women's self-defense, and there was Michelle to prove it possible. Some of the women were regular enough as spectators for Devlin to find some folding chairs for them to sit in. He learned a few of their names: Keisha, Yolanda, Weez . . . but none of them ever suited up; they'd only giggle and duck their heads at the suggestion. And it would be hard to picture Keisha joining in, with her three-foot lacquered hairdo in the shape of a Babylonian ziggurat, or Weez, with her elaborately painted fifteen-inch-long fingernails that curved like ram's horns to cage her hands.

But the guys, the cadre, they were keen. And regular, five afternoons a week and solid on Saturday morning (though the array of hangovers was sometimes a dispiriting spectacle then). And Devlin matched their dedication, rushing crosstown from his practice around three o'clock each afternoon, converging on McDonogh Street with Michelle, who'd be driving down from school. Though Devlin wished, for her own safety, that she'd attend the northside school instead, it was nice to have the time with her. The ritual structure of Tae Kwon Do absolved whatever difficulty there might have been between them—so long, at least, as they were within the walls of the system. With only mild trepidation, Devlin presented her with her own key to the place.

Fast learners, these guys, at least for anything physical. Though in some ways they grew up too fast (fathers by fifteen or sixteen, convicts at eighteen or twenty), their bodies still had young advantages. They stretched out quickly for the high kicks, had enviable stamina, and adequate concentration for the most part. The most common difficulty was too much tension, a muscular rigidity that slowed them down and burned their energy too fast. A couple of them were overmuscled (Clayvon, Rebo, Butch), a condition Devlin had not yet learned to associate with longish stays in prison.

As for discipline, it was good enough. The guys had seen a lot of kung-fu movies, which appeared to help them adapt to Oriental courtesies. One unfortunate incident, in which both Clayvon and Bigfoot had wound up puking on the mats, had taught everyone that the Parrot Bar had best be visited only *after* practice.

The prickliest moment came just a few days in, when Devlin was teaching elementary basics: front stance, low block, high block. He'd just given the about-face command when a mechanical chirping sounded from the dressing rooms. Butch jumped out of his stance and trotted toward the noise, but Devlin's voice caught him up before he reached the door.

"Hold it! Don't break ranks."

Butch turned and stared in disbelief. "I got a phone call, yo."

"You call me *sir,*" Devlin reminded him. "And you don't take phone calls in the middle of practice. Get back in line."

The beeper rang again and stopped, and Butch started across the mats toward Devlin, hips rolling street-style under his white uniform.

"*Charyet!*" Devlin snapped.

Butch kept coming, but the others came to attention and stood facing forward, arms at their sides. Except for Michelle, who'd swung away from her position in the first rank and now stood facing the others—a slight breach of protocol perhaps, but Devlin thought it a wise precaution. Butch came to a halt a pace or two away, and Devlin willed himself to relax. Mentally he reviewed techniques that would be quickly, painfully incapacitating: chestnut fist to the ribs or cheekbone, knifehand to the philtrum . . . Butch towered over him—Devlin was so short that any of them might have towered over him, even Boxcar. He had never shown them anything spectacular; following the example of his own masters, he kept all such cards well up his sleeve.

In the silence of the room he could hear two cars swishing past on the street, the brief blare of a radio, and a distant shout. Another beeper rang in the dressing room, and was joined by a third. Rebo, who'd done a stretch in the Marines, started laughing and as quickly suppressed it, still holding himself at attention, but Devlin could feel the tension drain, and Butch too had relaxed and let his considerable weight shift backward.

"Twenty pushups," Devlin said, allowing himself a slight smile as he turned away. "On your fists. And turn those things off before you come to class."

Later, when it was almost dark, Michelle stepped through the door of the school onto the street, with Devlin a pace behind her. She helped him drag the gates together, then turned automatically and put her back to the wall, looking watchfully both ways along the sidewalk while Devlin busied himself with the padlocks. He liked that, her reflexive precautions, guard up.

"That was a little hairy, huh?" Michelle paused to smile

and nod at a middle-aged woman trudging by, shoulders drawn down with groceries like a yoke. Then a glance back at Devlin. "Butch?"

"Yeah . . ." Devlin yanked on a padlock's tongue to confirm it was secure, then straightened. "Could have been." The sky was an inky blue and held a brightening crescent moon. He noticed some large indistinguishable bird, perhaps a crow, dropping behind the roof line of the houses across the street. "Worry you?"

"No way!" Michelle said brightly, tossing her hair back, pulling a knit hat down over it. Devlin liked that too, it made her nondescript. Up the street, the door to the Parrot Bar had begun to swing more frequently, chopping up the driving beat of the music from inside. A number of his cadre students would be in there now, no doubt—Devlin figured they had earned a drink or two.

"You were cool, Dad."

"Really."

"Oh, definitely. You were . . . what's the word?"

"Inscrutable."

"That's it."

"Well, just don't tell your mother."

Michelle laughed, and Devlin linked his arm with hers quite naturally, walking her to her car.

FIVE O'CLOCK a week or so later and the school had broken up for the day. The guys were stretching, cooling down, some standing in their sweat-soaked uniforms near the street door, chatting with the girlfriends. Butch and Boxcar watched themselves soberly in the mirror, practicing *Tae Guk Il Jang* for the promotion test that would be coming up quite soon. Loud slaps of impact throbbed in the room as Bigfoot blasted the heavy bag with a brisk series of roundhouse kicks. Devlin watched him for a minute—amazing, the power he could get, so soon. Air oofed from the bag's seams with every stroke.

Someone was at the door, a group of two or three, new people. Devlin sent Kool-whip down to answer questions, watched approvingly as the boy bowed to the newcomers, then offered them a handshake. The civilizing influence had begun to gain. Devlin bowed to the flags himself and went into the back to change.

When he came back onto the floor in his street clothes, something had changed. It wasn't a silence really; people were talking as they had been before. But there was a new edginess, a shift in attention, like the moment before you actually *smell* the smoke. Bigfoot was still sending kicks into the bag, but he'd rotated around to face the door while he continued, and Butch and Boxcar were covering the newcomers from the mirror.

There were two men, but Devlin's notice automatically went to the one in the black leather jacket, Western-cut, adorned with foot-long fringes. He wore black wraparound sunglasses, though by now it was almost completely dark outside. He stood not quite as if he owned the place but as if he'd always own a five-foot radius around wherever he might happen to be standing at any given time. Devlin was quick to home in on this effect, which was something many martial artists sought to achieve.

"Michael Devlin," he said, walking toward them. In the black sunglasses his reflected features warped and ran away. "I'm the instructor here."

"Trig," said the man in the fringed jacket, and flipped a

hand toward the man at his left, who was lighter skinned, sharp-featured, with a scar on the left cheekbone, and wore a denim jacket with a sweatshirt hood hanging down the back. "D-Trak."

Devlin nodded and turned toward the woman who stood to Trig's right holding the rubber grips of a stroller. She had one of those complex conical hairdos, ornamented with a swirl of gold wire like a flavor ribbon in a Dairy Dip ice cream cone.

"Sharmane," Trig said, and took off the sunglasses. Devlin was startled by the absence of the *whaddayoulookingat-mofo* stare he'd been half-consciously expecting. Instead, Trig's eyes were full of a sadly tolerant resignation; they were almost the eyes of an old man.

"This my son," Trig said, but Devlin had already knelt beside the stroller. The small black hand came out and wrapped around his finger.

"This Froggy." Trig appeared to clear his throat.

DEVLIN HAD no good notion if they knew who he was or not. D-Trak, the one with the scar, had seen him at the Poe Homes, but not with Froggy, and D-Trak might not be likely to match the Devlin in street clothes and hoody with the Devlin in the Tae Kwon Do outfit. The same context problem made it hard for Devlin to be quite sure he recognized Sharmane, who'd changed her hairstyle radically from the day he'd handed Froggy over . . . if she *was* the same person after all.

Either way, they were back next afternoon, and with their friends. The school's size doubled almost at a jump.

Trig, Gyp, D-Trak, Mud-dog, and the kid named Odell who called himself Freon. Also, and somewhat to Devlin's surprise, Sharmane and another young woman named Tamara. He wondered if this switch in the balance might tempt some of the Eager Street girls to join in, but it didn't seem to. However, Trig and Sharmane evolved some loose arrangement with Keisha, who would entertain Froggy in his stroller while the two of them were practicing. Or one of the other Eager Street girls would watch him when Keisha had the nods, if he had not been left back home with the woman they called Gramma Reen.

It was odd for Devlin, having Froggy around that way. Absurd to think that the child would remember him, but he seemed comfortable in his presence. There would be a sort of physical memory, possibly, of smell and touch, general sensation. Froggy was happy in Devlin's hands the time or two he picked him up—it was Devlin who felt uneasy about it. After all, he never handled the other women's children. And the pose might spark a memory . . . in Sharmane. Instead it was Michelle who resolved his need to touch, fussing over Froggy like any teenage girl gone baby-crazy. She played with him on the mats before and after she changed for practice, or sometimes during breaks between different movements of the class. She even brought him little trinkets, odds and ends from the drugstore or from home. Devlin thought of quips he might have made—about her "allergy"—but held his tongue.

No mention of the situation's strangeness ever passed between them. Devlin hardly wanted to bring it up; too much else would surface with it: the argument, the slap. Sometimes he wondered if she even knew. She'd avoided him so studiously the few days he'd kept Froggy, and from a distance babies of that age look much alike. Then again, she might be playing with him, a game of *you don't know I know.* Same game Devlin was playing with her about the contents of her treasure chest. No harm . . . he thought there was no harm. From time to time he felt uneasy, though, watching Froggy clinging to Michelle's shirt or uniform top, swatting at the long black tails of her belt. Or maybe it was his uncomfortable sense of Trig's attention on the pair of them, before or after practice, Trig's eyes examining them from the secrecy of the wraparounds.

Once Trig was dressed to work out, though, his attention never wavered. Unsheathed of the sunglasses, his eyes emptied out like eyes of a carved idol; by the time he stood up from the opening meditation he'd have a perfect laser stare that went through Devlin, the flags, the wall. He was good, too, good enough that Devlin quizzed him about any prior training he might have had, but Trig was coy, owning to no more than maybe a class or two at some Y, some street stuff naturally, a trick or two showed him by friends . . .

The new guys from Poe Homes put an edge on things, for the old cadre. The class became more serious, almost grim. No more loose talk, no joking during breaks, nothing but completely sober concentration. Only Tamara and Sharmane would sometimes break ranks, pointing and giggling at each other—comic relief that Devlin grew to appreciate. Otherwise discipline was almost too good, reminding him of the way strangers faced each other at tournaments more than a bunch of students sharing a home school.

But this taut atmosphere did make for rapid progress.

Within four weeks, Devlin let them all go up for their first test together. Master Ryu came down from the northside school for the grading, signifying his approval of the new operation with resonant grunts half in Korean, half in his pidgin English. Everyone passed the test for yellow belt, and Trig and Kool-whip made a double grade.

NEXT CLASS, there was the usual self-conscious strutting, fondling of the stiff new colored belts and sidelong glances in the mirrors. No sense of a let-down, though, none that Devlin could detect, and that was strange, because the aftermath of testing usually left things rather more relaxed. Maybe sparring was the issue—they'd free spar now for the first time.

"Face each other," Devlin said, some fifteen minutes before the end of class. Two lines formed.

"Charyet. Kunye."

The two lines bowed in unison.

"Fighting stance—"

The howl of *kyai*'s clove the room; fists raised, half crouched, they were all trembling with anticipation. Only Trig seemed both controlled and relaxed, open hand hovering low above his bent front knee.

Devlin sighed. "Relax more," he said. "Breathe . . . go slow. Control. Technique. No contact."

Safety equipment, the padded body armor, was on order but had not yet arrived. Devlin wanted to break them in on no-contact fighting anyway. "No contact," he repeated. *"Si chak!"*

He circled the paired fighters, watching, mostly looking

at Michelle at first, who was matched with Bigfoot. She was doing one of the things that she did best: not getting hit. Bigfoot was agile as well as strong; they complemented one another's grace, and Michelle led him like a dancer, keeping it light, now and then stroking in a kick or a punch to show she could. Devlin was mesmerized, relieved. Then came a shout and a grunt and someone was down.

"Break!" Devlin shouted. *"Charyet!"*

Freon lay sideways on the mats, and Boxcar stood glowering over him, fists clenched tight. "Kneel down," Devlin said to Boxcar. "Face the wall."

Freon's hands were wrapped around his umbilical area. The blood had drained out of his face, turning his gold complexion sallow. A shot low in the abdomen, Devlin surmised, or more likely the groin. But with no prompting, Freon rose to his knees and then stood up.

"Jump on your heels," Devlin said, and watched as color faded back into the boy's face. "Maybe you should sit one out."

Freon shook his head. His stubby dreadlocks woggled with the motion. "Uh-uh," he said. "I'm down with this."

"All right, then." Devlin turned to Boxcar, thought once, then twice, and let him rejoin the line as well.

Everyone changed opponents. Boxcar was paired with Trig this time, and Devlin knew Trig could handle himself—supposing Boxcar was really out for trouble, which he didn't know for sure. He watched Freon, making sure he'd be all right. Younger than many of the others, he was enthusiastic but awkward to match. When he sparred he kept hurdling too far forward, leading with his head. Better not to leave himself so open. At times it had seemed to Devlin that some of the Eager Street guys didn't much care for Freon, as if some of that queer tension focused there. But he was matched with D-Trak for now, and both of them were taking it easy enough.

Devlin turned to Trig, who was fun to watch, relaxed and confident, completely outclassing his opponent. Boxcar was burly, and moved like a boxer, still hooking his punches. His kicks were low, from poor flexibility; it might have been that circumstance that had brought Freon down. He couldn't touch Trig, who understood how to move and who outreached him. But Boxcar tried, just the same, hurling himself forward with a heavy muscley punch. Trig skimmed off to the side, set up, and popped him full in the face with an instep roundhouse kick.

Boxcar went over backward, nose spouting blood. Trig swung away, expressionless, and knelt to face his blank self in the mirrors, without waiting for Devlin to tell him to do it. *Jesus!* Devlin thought, or he might have whispered it under his breath. It hadn't been a full-power kick, but he saw it must have been intentional. Devlin darted across the floor to Boxcar and knelt beside him.

"Pinch your nose there at the bridge." Devlin demonstrated. "All right, I don't think it's broken. Try sitting up. And pinch here at the back of your neck. That's it, yeah. You'll be okay."

Boxcar sneezed and someone, Keisha, scurried across the room with a wad of tissues. However, the bleeding had already almost stopped. It wasn't serious . . . not quite, not yet. Devlin stood up, let Keisha dab Boxcar's face. His head was humming.

"Face each other," he said.

The lines formed mutely. Devlin moved Rebo one place over and stepped into the spot he'd occupied, opposite Trig. For an instant he looked into his face, before the bow. Trig's eyes were washed stone empty. Devlin felt his own were needle sharp.

"Si chak!"

He wouldn't look into Trig's eyes again; it was rare for anyone to hit you with his face. You paid attention to the hips and shoulders because whatever came would start from there. There wouldn't be time to think about it. So Devlin interrupted Trig's first exploratory roundhouse kick, stopped the shin with his left fist snapping on the ridge of bone and at the same time drove the middle knuckle of his right fist into the soft, fleshy area at the top of Trig's foot. Trig flinched when he stepped down on the lamed leg and was open long enough for Devlin to pick his knee up high and drive his heel into his solar plexus. Trig reeled back quite some distance, slapped off the wall, and slid down onto the mats.

It had taken possibly fifteen seconds. Devlin skipped across the floor, almost panicked, but he felt a puff of air when he held a finger under Trig's nose, and the closed eyelids were fluttering. The others had all stopped their bouts spontaneously and stood around, looking on.

"All right," Devlin said. "Bring water from the bathroom, wake him up."

The Eager Street girls had ceased their conversations and it was quiet enough to hear the heat pipes ticking behind the wallboard. Froggy burbled, crawling after a clear plastic ball with a bell inside it, and both the jingle and his voice were strikingly loud. Trig spluttered when water spilled from a paper cup struck his cheek and lips. He sat up, bowing over his sore midsection. Then he stood.

Devlin led them through the most punishing set of finishing basics he could devise, multiple kicks and punches with no break, interrupted by sets of pushups, situps, leg lifts. He kept it going a little past the breaking point, till their edge was blunted and their wind was gone. When he judged it was done well enough, he sat them down cross-legged in their ranks and told them all to close their eyes.

"Listen," he said, pacing a red stripe of mat at the head of the room. "From today, here's how it goes. First excessive contact—no more fighting for the rest of the night. Second time excessive contact—suspension for two weeks, no practice. If there comes a third time—expelled. Permanently. You will never come to this school again."

Devlin stopped and faced the group, feet slightly spread, in line with the yin-yang symbol of the Korean flag. They were very still, all of them, except for the heaving of their breath. Sweat was still pouring down their faces; their white uniforms had grayed with it. Sweat rivulets licked at the dried blood marks that tracked Boxcar's upper lip. Devlin looked at Trig, who behind his closed eyes seemed as contemplative as the others, more or less at peace. He lowered his voice, to make them reach for it.

"I don't know what kind of hassles you might have with each other out on the street. Outside of here, I don't need to know it. It isn't my problem. What happens here is all that matters. It's a closed system."

Devlin paused, breathing. He himself was exhausted from the punishing drills they'd finished with. It seemed that a collective sigh went around the room.

"I drop the rest of my life at the door, every day when I walk in. If you want to make it in here, you're going to have to learn that too."

IT WAS fully dark when they left the school, and a few pinpoints of snow were spinning down from the indistinguishable sky. According to routine, Devlin locked up while Michelle watched the street, then he walked her to her car. She looked up at him across the curve of the roof once she'd opened the door.

"What if you'd killed him?"

Devlin noticed the fine dots of snow that clung to the fuzz of her hat, melting there. Her face was lit by diamonds of light spilled through the gated window of the liquor store opposite.

"He'd be dead."

Michelle frowned and dropped her eyes.

"I had to do something," Devlin said. "You know that."

"Yeah," Michelle said. "And don't tell Mom."

"Shell . . ." Devlin said. "You could always go back northside. To Master Ryu."

Michelle looked up at him again. "Is that what you want?"

"I don't know," Devlin said.

"Me neither," said Michelle, as she ducked into the car. "Well, see you at home, I guess."

Devlin gave the roof of the car a pat as it pulled away, as if it were a horse. The taillights went shrinking down the street and he stood for a moment longer, idly flipping the lever of the parking meter. The wind twisted, drilling the fine snowflakes into his eyes. When he turned toward his own car he saw Trig waiting a few yards from him, the wind fluttering the long black leather fringes of his jacket.

"Buy you a drink," Trig said. He jerked his thumb toward the Parrot Bar, a few doors down.

Devlin considered. "All right. Thanks."

THE BAR was thick with menthol smoke, with the thud of bass and the repetitive thrusts of some rapper's voice grunting out of the jukebox. A dust-blunted disco ball hung overhead, motionless, with red and blue shafts of light playing from its fractured mirrors. There were red leatherette booths along one side of the room and more of the same at the back. Trig and Devlin stood at the bar, haunches half-raised onto stools. Occasionally a door swung at the rear of the place, onto an alley, it looked like. Must be locked on the outside, Devlin guessed, because people went out that way but none came in.

"Always looking out, ain't you?" Trig said. "Eyes in the back of y'head, yo."

"Sure," Devlin said. "Don't you?"

Trig snorted. "It cool here, man, I watch yo back." He cocked an eyebrow above the wraparounds, glancing at the bar.

Devlin asked for any kind of beer, though he wouldn't have minded something stronger. Trig got them two cans of malt liquor. The music changed to something much the same as before, thrusting like rough sex. Devlin watched the barmaid with a sort of appalled fascination. She clawed the buttons of the register with the enameled ends of eight-inch nails on her right hand. On her left hand the nails were an elaborate helix trapping the fingers entirely, just like Weez's, but somehow the nails themselves could clutch two cans of beer.

Trig drank and wiped his upper lip. "What it is," he said. "You done like you had to. Which is what I done, too, like."

He turned from Devlin, facing away from the counter. Devlin sipped his can of Colt 45 and followed Trig's roving gaze. Others familiar from the school had established themselves throughout the bar. One booth accommodated Keisha, Weez, and Tamara, Keisha with her head thrown back against the quilted leatherette, the whites of her eyes showing. In another booth were Kool-whip, Bigfoot, and Boxcar, drinking Hennessy from miniature balloon glasses. Further down the bar sat Gyp and Mud-dog, and at the farthest end was D-Trak, engaged in some emphatic conversation with Clayvon, the heel of his hand slapping the countertop at the stress points. There were plenty of other people, too, that Devlin didn't recognize. The back door clapped with one of their departures.

"Freon," Trig said. "You know, Odell?"

Devlin sipped his beer and nodded. Freon was nowhere in sight.

"Seems like they might have something against him," Devlin said. "The guys around here, you know."

"Ah," Trig said, dismissively, revolving to face Devlin again. "Nothing for sure. Just . . . a feeling maybe. Thassall." He cleared his throat. "Freon just a kid, yo, he do got some dumb ideas. Yeah. But come down to it, he my homeboy, you know. I got to look out for him, same like Candyman spose to look after all this Eager Street crew."

This last name was completely unfamiliar, or almost; Devlin might have heard it mentioned in a passing conversation but he had no face to match. He drank from his can, then rolled his head to loosen the stiffening muscles in his shoulders.

"You don't know Candyman," Trig said. "Yeah, he keeping his head down for now." Trig smiled a little wistfully at his reflection in the mirror above the top-shelf bottles; the barmaid took the smile as hers and returned it with a wink. Trig looked back at Devlin. "What it is," he said. "Don't matter how much a fool Freon—I see my boy get beat down, I got to drop the one done it. You know?"

"Outside of the school, maybe," Devlin said. "Outside, you do what you think you have to. That's you, right? Inside, it's another matter. No beatdowns are going to happen in our school."

"I hear you," Trig said. He drank. "Yo—I respect what you done. You got y'own thing to take care of."

"It's not just mine," Devlin said. "It's yours, too. Boxcar's. Freon's. Everybody gets a piece."

"What it is," Trig said.

"It's sanctuary," Devlin said. "It's not like the rest of the world. It's a place where things make sense. Everything happens for reasons you know, or if you don't know you can learn them, and if there's a problem there's a way to solve it. You don't have to bring any trouble in, and you don't have to take any trouble out. That's what it means. Sanctuary."

Devlin stopped talking, and the music stopped, a general whir of conversation swelling up to fill the gap. The back door flashed again, through the smoke. This was it, his substitute for nothing. He didn't know for sure if Trig was listening.

Trig took off the sunglasses. There were the eyes again,

surprising, sympathetic, interested. "I hear you," Trig said. "I'm down with that."

"Good," said Devlin. "I better go. Thanks for the beer." He shook Trig's hand and left the bar.

THERE WERE no more problems at the school for the next few days. Michelle turned out as usual . . . no mention of the thought she might switch. Discipline was generally quite tight, attendance regular—except for D-Trak, who didn't show. Devlin changed the sparring routine to single bouts, one pair fighting at a time, to make sure he always knew what was going on. The practice was so trouble-free that on the fourth day he let them go back to sparring all at once. Still no explosion came. But the tension had not lessened. It was worse.

On the fifth day, Devlin called the group to attention; they bowed to the flags, he bowed to them.

"Where's D-Trak," he said to the class at large. No one spoke or shifted position; they stood straight, focusing each on some abstract point as he'd tried to teach them. Only the murmur of the girls' conversation stopped, in the back.

"What happened to D-Trak?" Devlin said. "Anybody know?"

"He's dead," Trig said suddenly. He plucked at his left sleeve, which seemed to cling to some brownish stain, seeping at the shoulder. "Somebody shot him. Outside of here. Like you said, *sir.*"

If Devlin was staggered it did not show; he remained planted on the mat, face set. Trig had not turned his head or shifted his gaze; the laser stare passed over Devlin's shoulder and through the wall and on toward some unavailable horizon.

"*Anjo,*" Devlin said at length. "*Mun yom.*"

When they had knelt for meditation, Devlin bowed and left the floor. He went into the dressing room, hesitated for a heartbeat, and then began feeling the mounds of glossy tracksuits and sweats and fly jeans and jackets, not much disarranging them but only squeezing to the core. The little cubes of beepers were quite easy to identify, and so were the rectilinear forms of guns.

He stood back, tips of his fingers tingling. It seemed to him that he had known this all along but had not been aware of it till now. He left the dressing room and returned, cat-footed, to the floor. They knelt, all of them motionless, concentrated, eyes half-lidded or entirely closed. He'd leave them so a little longer, let them consider D-Trak, themselves. The orderliness of the kneeling rows was very calming, like ranks of white tombstones in a graveyard. Only the Poe Homes people were distinguished by the stickily clinging stains on each of their sleeves, at the left shoulder. Devlin thought that soon he'd know about that too; the knowledge was on its way to him but had not quite arrived.

7

CLAYVON

BOXCAR AND Kool-whip was the first to find Devlin's place, when it just open. What it was, seem like a good idea to Kool-whip, specially him, cause of him doing a hard bit down at the Cut which he just got cut loose of a few months before. Lapped over with Gyp from Poe Homes down there, but that wasn't why, cause they wasn't no trouble with us and them then. Wasn't no *us* over here and *them* over there, like you'd think about it—like it did get to be later. Cause we had different turf so far as slanging drugs, clear across town from each other, and we all known each other anyway, from school and other places, like going to the same clubs at night, and even I used to jump hoops with D-Trak. When I was younger, still in school. There was Keisha married to Boxcar and they kids and everything. We was all cool with each other like that.

What Candyman say, cause he older than anybody, when he was hitting the bricks as a kid, if something jump off then it was fists and feet. Count more that way if you big and strong, fast on you feet with a good punch, yo. Then, time I come along, everybody all gone to guns. Make no difference what muscle you got to throw when you can just jerk a sawed-off or whip out yo nine and light niggaz up. No difference I never got no growth, even half the height of D-Trak, yo, so I'm not gone be playing no basketball for no college or pro team neither. Cause I can make the same money slanging rocks on Eager Street, like Candyman say, and don't have to pay no taxes.

Cept then Kool-whip pointed it out, they run you down to the Cut they gone grab yo gats away. You back to whatever you know how to do with yo hands and yo feet and yo brains if you got any. Which Kool-whip did say, niggaz down the Cut (white ma'fuckas too) been already spending a whole lot of time on the iron pile, like ten or fifteen years maybe, so you might come to find out you had some catching up to do.

Not that I was planning to go to the Cut, yo . . . I ain't down with that serious jailing. But like Candyman say, ain't nobody *plan* on going. You just end up. But Candyman wasn't giving out no advice right at this time because he was taking himself a vacation up in Brooklyn to wait and see when this hassle over Jaynette being dead all gonna be blowed over.

So that's how all us come to Devlin's school, there to begin with. And it wasn't like what I would of been expecting. Not like the movies or the kung fu on TV where you stare in a candle flame and mumble some Chinese type of shit and next minute you jumping all around like Spider-man or somebody. No, it was work the body, yo, and it did hurt. First couple weeks I couldn't hardly get out the bed in the morning cause I'm so shot and sore in the legs with all this stretching for the kicks. Plus which they was more rules than the army, what Rebo say, and he been in the Marines so he know.

Rebo down with it though, and the rest of us too. Something *to* all them rules beside bullshit, yo. Like this beeper thing, it make me mad at first, the same as Butch, like, *Whuffo you in my face with this turn-off-yo-beeper?* Then I got to see where it was kind of like an advantage they was one place in the world where that beeper was *never* gone ring.

Like with them rules and shit, at first you be fumbling around and fucking up all the time, every time you make a move you trip on a rule somewhere—like the army again, what Rebo say. After while though, come to where the rules just natural to you and you don't even think about'm no more. Then I could chill, at Tae Kwon Do, like I couldn't do nowheres else, and the reason was them rules stood between me and whatever might be on the way to mess with my mind. Like outside, you might be chill with yo chick, yo drink, yo weed or rock or whatever, but then you know, fuck it, the beeper goes. Or something.

It pop up in my head, what if *school*-school had felt like that? I mighta got down to really learn some shit. Anyway I was down now to learn what Devlin had to teach. And it felt good . . . till Trig shown up of course.

It ought not to bothered me, maybe, cause they hadn't yet been no problem with Trig or his crew. But we none of us liked it how he'd strut in there. Cause wasn't it our thing? But Trig himself, he learned so fast, like he just floated up over us to the top. Like him on the street with his Lexus and his locs. Nobody said nothing, it was just a tense feeling. But it come over me in my place I was trying keep clear in my mind, like at the start of class when we would all get down for this *mun yom* meditation thing, it would be Trig getting up under my skin, or I'd start thinking about how Stuttz got shot and what the winos and the junkies down by the wall had been saying.

Then all the Poe Homes crew went and tested at the same time as us for that yellow belt. Was that right, when we was there first? And Trig jumped himself all the way over to orange too. And *then* Devlin let us all loose to free fight.

It was me matched up with D-Trak that day, which he outweighed me and outreached me by about two feet. Devlin had this rap that size don't *have* to matter, which might be true if you can jump in the air and do a backflip and sling around all this Bruce Lee type of shit while you screaming like a cat with rabies. But for me all I had was my little roundhouse kick and side kick and straight punch to go with my new yellow belt. D-Trak didn't have no more'n that, except the height and reach. He banged on me some but I didn't get knocked down or get my nose half broke like Boxcar did. But D-Trak was getting me kind of stressed.

I coulda handled it though. I would of. I was down with what Devlin said, like you leave your outside problems at the door. Only it was all kind of shit feeding into that place that Devlin didn't know about. Like for one thing Sharmane wasn't happy at all about how Devlin's girl would make over that baby of Trig's. She said one thing to Weez about it, "Do you see him look at that white bitch?" Which Weez passed along to me later on up in her crib where we was getting happy. *Him* meaning Trig of course. So I told her, I didn't catch him looking at Michelle one special way or another. Can't tell behind his locs what he looking at no way and when Trig change to practice he don't seem like he look at nobody after that.

But I watched him then . . . yo, it might of been something to it. This pretty white girl holding up his baby, and Jaynette was dead. And Sharmane, who would mostly take care of the kid, she was only his sister. I didn't need Weez to tell me what Sharmane might be thinking, like, *I wanna claw this white bitch eyes out only I know she could beat me down.* That why Sharmane start training with us, cause she don't want to be weak next to Michelle. There was one thing Devlin didn't know.

I would tease Weezie about Tamara and Sharmane, them getting tougher'n her, like didn't she want to come out and train with us so she wouldn't be weak beside them. And she would just laugh, she say, *You gone look after me, Clayvon.* Which make me feel good. I known she wouldn't come to the school no way, cause for one thing it had took her about five years to get those nails on her left hand growed out like they was. When we would be getting to it, she always laid that left hand real soft on a pillow out of the action, like it was eggshells, and I would watch it then, this hand all useless and helpless in the ball of colored nails, while my hands could go do whatever hands will do. I like the way it make me feel. So I known she never would cut those nails and I didn't want her to. She would come by the school though, to see what was happening, such as me getting beat down by D-Trak maybe, when he was twice my size.

That was another thing Devlin didn't know.

A few went up to the Parrot after practice that day. Some from our crew and some from Trig's. Keisha and Tamara and Weez in one booth—Sharmane had left to take that baby home. Pretty soon Weez and Keisha truck off to the ladies' together and when they come back I see Keisha fired up in there and now she fixing to nod off. Weez, she might of snorted some. She say she never put a needle in her arm and I don't see no tracks to prove she lying. I tell her to stay away from that smack altogether but then she get on me cause I smoke a rock sometime. Which it ain't the same thing at all, yo, plus I don't do nothing I can't handle.

First off I was sitting with Boxcar and Kool-whip in the next booth over. Boxcar had clean off all the blood from his face and he say his nose don't hurt him now, don't think it's really broke. So I sat a minute and then I walked up to the bar to get some more Hennessies. Gyp and Mud-dog sitting there, and D-Trak at the end of the bar.

"Yo, Clayvon," D-Trak say. "How you feel?"

"Feel all right," I say.

D-Trak look at me and I look away. That was lame I didn't want to hold his eyes, that was punk stuff. Cause he, like, too close to me or something, like, when he coming across the mats with his big foot swinging for my head, like that. Barmaid come over and I ordered the drinks. Then I stood there looking at D-Trak in the mirror. In the mirror, he shake his head.

"It was y'all wanted to play it rough, yo," D-Trak say. "Kicking down Freon like that and all."

"Ain't Freon able to take care his own punk ass?"

Barmaid bring me the three Hennessies, I drank off the one that was for me. Right then in walk Trig—with Devlin. It make me feel sick in my stomach—them hanging together like they was the two boss dogs.

"How bout you, Clayvon?" D-Trak go. "Ain't you able take care y'own?"

I drank some of the glass that was for Boxcar. When I press up against the barstool where I'm standing, I could feel the shape of my nine where it riding in my waistband, underneath my hoody. Trig sitting up there drinking beer with Devlin like they road dogs from a long way back.

D-Trak reach out and slap me on the arm right where I took a kick and got a bruise.

"Ain't trying to jump on your game, bro," he say. "Like the man say tonight, gotta leave y'outside trouble outside."

I shoulda agreed with him since it was what I thought too. "You outside now, ain't you," I say. "Yay, bro, Freon had that coming anyway and more to go with it."

D-Trak quit smiling. He light him up a Salem and blow some smoke but not exactly in my face. "That what you think? Cause why?"

I finished Boxcar's drink and start on Kool-whip's. "Cause what they say down by the wall—it some little light-skin ma'fucka with short dreads that busted on Stuttz from that car."

"Them lames down by the wall," D-Trak say. "They might seen that and they might seen striped monkeys flying outa they nose."

"If a monkey dropped Stuttz he was yelling '*Poe Homes!*'—what they say."

"At right?" D-Trak start pounding a rhythm on the bar top with the flat of his hand. "What they say about Stuttz dropping Jaynette, then?"

"Don't say nothing," I say. "Cause Stuttz ain't done it."

"At right?" D-Trak's hand still keep slapping down. But I ain't said nothing more. What it is, Stuttz had been turning in short counts and like that and Candyman jacked him up for it. It was Candyman throwing down on Stuttz—Stuttz not even strapped that day. And yo, as far as Jaynette, she must of just stepped in the way somehow. That's how it went down, and some people seen it, but they wasn't nobody talking about it. And Candyman sure didn't want nobody to.

D-Trak hand still beating. "Yo, Clayvon. Ain't nobody know who kill Stuttz. Ain't nobody know who kill Jaynette either one. *Might* be better we leave it that way. Whatchoo think, yo?"

But I don't say nothing. Just walk off from him and the smoke he blowing my way. Damn, that felt lame, letting him talk down to me like I'm some kind of punk kid. I went to the jukebox and thrown on some Snoop. Right when the Dogg Pound start yipping, Devlin pushed back his chair and he's outa there. I could feel that Snoop beat start to pick my feet up then. Weez stood up and we turn around a time or two right there in front of the juke. Boxcar and them say something to me about I drank they Hennessies all up, but I didn't listen, cause I just stepping, feeling that warm spread out my gut all through to my toes and fingers. I'm turning around and hearing that *Whuz my naaaame????*

from the juke and laying my head back to look up at the old mirror ball in the ceiling. When *bang,* D-Trak crash into me with a shoulder from the back and send me half knocking into Weez.

"Uh-oh," D-Trak say with a big step back. "Watch y'self, Clayvon." He grinning, got his hands up flat like he didn't mean nothing, but I know he did. And when I didn't say nothing D-Trak just shrug, walk on into the men's where he headed in the first place.

Weez just roll her head, didn't wanna dance no more, she blowed out, she say. Sat down in that booth again and lit herself a Salem. She shake one out for me but I didn't want it. Back in the other booth Boxcar and the others turned they backs to me, and the men's room door still shut with D-Trak behind it. Here was Keisha zoned in the booth between Weez and Tamara, breathing out through the white of her teeth and eye-white shining up under her lids. I look around, Trig had gone out too. I never seen him go.

Then I went myself, out by the back door. Just for a minute, I told Weez. They a concrete dock out in back there with a rusted pipe rail, and steps go down. I slip a match cover in the lock so I could come back in when I was done. Down by the end of the alley they a Dumpster you can stand there still out of sight of the main street, and out of the wind. So I got my pipe out, fired a rock. Then I'm kicking and rushing and my teeth are grinding like old dinosaurs on the movies—T-Rex, yo! Only I felt that spot on my back where D-Trak had bump me, not a hurt but more like an itch up there. I could still hear the bass beat coming out from back of the bar, then it got louder for a second cause somebody else coming out—motha*fucka* lost my slip from out the latch. I see that match cover fall out the door, turning and fluttering like a wing. And the music damp down when the door click back—motha*fucka* locked me out.

He come down my way and I seen it was D-Trak. So then I shot his ass. He never even seen me draw my strap cause he was looking in my face. It dark back in that alley, and little flames come out the nose of the gat like in the movies and somehow I'm hearing it again in my head, *Whuzz my ma'fucken naaame???* so loud in there I never heard the shots.

I put the strap back in my belt and walk to D-Trak where he lying. Dude was done, yo! One hand in his hoody after his own gat—I bent down to take it but then I stopped. My ears was ringing but nobody was looking out and I didn't hear no siren—just the bass still coming out the back end of the bar.

I took out my nine and put in a new clip and stuck it in my belt again. Then I walked out past the Dumpster to the cross street and back around the corner to the front of the Parrot. They was some people I passed but they didn't look at me to notice. Inside the bar they was playing Tupac loud. Hadn't nobody heard nothing from the alley, I could tell. Mud-dog and Gyp was still sitting at the counter so I step up and drink a beer with them, cool G.

"You see D-Trak?" Gyp jerk a thumb toward the back. "He went out there looking for you, bro."

My strap still warm against my gut, but I ain't trip.

"Naw," I say. "I got locked out, yo—just come back around the corner."

Gyp shrug. I thought him or Mud-dog or both them would head out the back to look for D-Trak but they didn't neither one. So I drank another can, I was that cool. Then I went home.

Momma got that look when I come in, like I been up to trouble and she can smell it. Like she ever look at me some other way no more. My sister she sulling on the couch, got a history book open on her knees but she looking at the TV. I went and hung up my uniform so it can air out and be fresh for next day at Devlin school, and then I took a shower. They saved me some dinner in the oven, fried chicken and macs and cheese. So I ate it watching the news with them, you know, not nobody saying much at all. The news was like usual. Down Eager Street, can't hardly tell if the sirens and shit coming out from the TV or in through the window.

They gone to bed early. I didn't feel like going out no more, guess I must of watched a movie till I come down where I could sleep. Then some time in the night I could tell I was laying in my bed, about to wake up kinda sicky, and I didn't want to get up that way so I was still hanging back in my dream. I seen D-Trak coming to me out the back of the Parrot again only this time I could tell he didn't intend to put no damage on me. *Clayvon,* he say, and he put his hand on my shoulder and give me a shake, not rough you know, but friendly. I hear that bass pounding louder from the bar, and my teeth grinding, but I know all D-Trak gonna say is, it all right with him and me, we ain't got no problem. Only so far he just keep saying my name, *Clayvon, Clayvon,* and that pounding keep on and the bed be rocking . . . it was Momma rocking my mattress with her arm and calling me cause probably she thought that knock on the door was cops.

Which it could of been at that. I felt sick like I known I would when I got out the bed, didn't know whether to shit or throw up. So I got my pants on and sorta shoved past Momma and went to look through the peephole.

Nobody there but Boxcar, so I opened up.

"Man," Boxcar say. "I got trouble. You got to come with me."

Boxcar was sweating. It was shiny all over his face and running down into his collarbones.

"Lemme get my keys," I say.

I locked up and followed him to his crib, which was upstairs. In the front was they two kids Cheese and Nola standing there staring through the bathroom door at the other end. Keisha had fell down in there with her head sorta jammed up between the toilet and the sink.

"Oh God . . ." Boxcar whispering for some reason. "What happen. God, what happen?"

I don't know what his problem was cause it wouldn't of took Columbo to figure out what went down. The spoon was laying right on the floor and the rest of the works was there in the sink. I picked up the cotton piece and smelt it.

"This some that Chinese been coming in," I say. Didn't smell nothing special but I known it already. "Ain't you told her to go slow with that shit?"

"She ain't listen," Boxcar moan.

"We need to get these kids outa here," I say. And I kinda herded them back into the room where they slept at, Cheese and Nola.

Alonzo Cheese real name and he not even two, could walk but not talk yet, not at all. Nola was maybe about a year older. Cheese nose runny with snot caked all over his upper lip and I wished somebody had wiped it but I didn't. The floor in there was all covered over with paper and crayons and little plastic toys like they give away from Mickey D's. The kids was still looking at me in there . . . their eyes felt like the eyes of mice.

I shut the door on them, and went back.

"What am I spose to do?" Boxcar crying. "What am I gonna do?"

I don't know why but I crouched down and felt of one Keisha's feet. She was wearing slippers but they had fell off. My feet was bare too and they was cold on that tile floor, but not as cold as Keisha's feet.

"Ain't nothing you *can* do," I say. "Bitch is dead."

"Yeah," Boxcar tell me. "I can see that."

6

Both the policemen were younger than Devlin, considerably so, which made it difficult for him to take them seriously. Their fresh faces and pink cheeks made them seem inconsequential; they reminded him, weirdly, of television. Their names, they told him, were Curtis and Spencer, but he had instantly forgotten which was which.

Devlin received their visit in the makeshift office in the back room of the downtown school. In their presence he found that he felt silly in his Tae Kwon Do uniform (though normally it suited him as well as skin); he also felt that they looked foolish in their blue uniforms. The ungainly belts, bulging with flashlights and radios and clubs and guns, contributed to this effect. Distracted by such matters, Devlin was having trouble paying attention to what they were talking about, though he knew he had excellent reason to be interested in everything they had to say.

The one with the natty black mustache took out a photograph and smoothed it out on the card table that served as Devlin's desk. Devlin read the image upside down: a color snap, slightly out of focus. A man was seated near a birthday cake and a wine bottle, head thrown slightly back.

"You've seen the guy," said the sandy-haired officer, reversing the photo, right-side-up, for Devlin. "Lincoln T. Hearon, known to his friends as D-Trak."

"I know him," Devlin said. He had been warming up on the bag when the officers strolled in unannounced, and now his chilling sweat glued the uniform fabric patchily to his body. "Knew," he corrected.

"Somebody shot him," said the sandy-haired one.

"Right," said Devlin. "So I heard." He dropped his eyes to the edge of the card table, which was frilled with cigarette burns from some previous owner. Devlin had salvaged the thing from a vacant lot, repaired a sprung leg to make it serviceable.

"Look, Mr. Devlin," said the black mustache. "Doctor?" He waited until Devlin shrugged to show he didn't care which form of address was employed.

"You're a doctor, right?" said the black mustache. "Some kind of shrink? I mean, um . . . this is a *good job* you got, am I right?"

"I make a living," Devlin said.

Black mustache appeared grateful for this admission. He hitched his collar to scratch the back of his neck. "And your address at home, you know—nice neighborhood. One of the nicest in town."

"Call me lucky," Devlin said.

"Question is," said sandy hair, "we can't quite figure out

what you're *doing* down here. I mean, why—" He waved his hand parabolically over his shoulder, toward the square Plexiglas pane that overlooked the main practice floor. Michelle and Rebo and Bigfoot and Clayvon and a few others had already dressed and were warming up on their own, but the cop's gesture seemed to include the street outside, beyond them.

"Well," Devlin said, "I meant to try to do some good."

Black mustache snorted, then looked mildly regretful. Sandy hair squeaked forward in the metal folding chair. He tapped his nail on the snapshot of D-Trak.

"Dude was shot not four doors up from where you sit."

"It's a tough area," Devlin said. "Some people die young. Young men, young women . . . children. You know it better than I do, I expect."

"At least you know something," said black mustache. He glanced down at the loose tails of the belt that cinched Devlin's waist.

"Black belt, huh? Pretty good at this martial art stuff, are you?"

Devlin shrugged. "I'm fair."

"Fast enough to catch a bullet?"

Sandy hair motioned black mustache to back off a little. "Look," he said. "Dr. Devlin. We're wondering if maybe you don't know what's going on."

"Do *we* know what's going on?" said black mustache.

"We haven't had a lot of what you call organized gang activity down here," said sandy hair. "What we do have plenty of is drug dealers." He twirled the photograph under his blunt finger. "Crack."

"I know," Devlin said, picturing D-Trak's hooded figure

overtaking him by Poe Homes. He had subsequently become rather fond of D-Trak.

"You *know* this guy was hustling rock?" said black mustache.

"Not around here," Devlin said.

"Oh, so you know that too. Then I guess you must also know you got two different sets of crack dealers in here to be teaching them karate and everything."

"Tae Kwon Do," Devlin said reflexively. "I didn't put it to myself quite that way."

"Really," said black mustache. "You might want to put it to yourself—these two sets are starting to shoot each other."

"That may be," Devlin said. "What we try for here is to get people in a frame of mind where they don't want to settle things with guns."

"Excuse me," said black mustache, "but so far your score seems kind of low."

"Well," said Devlin. "We're swimming against the stream."

Sandy hair leaned back, turning his head to gaze through the pane toward the street door, which was just swinging open. "Jesus," he said. "*Now* look who's here."

Devlin was already looking in that direction: Trig had just come in, composing his black leather fringes like a crow rearranging its wings.

"The supreme son of a bitch himself," said black mustache, who had, Devlin noticed, a touch of his own West Virginia inflections. Trig took off his shoes and added them to the pile inside the door. He swung his gym bag up and padded barefoot across the mats toward the dressing rooms.

Sandy hair turned back toward Devlin, the folding chair flexing under the shift of his weight. "Fella, I can't quite tell what you think you're up to, but let me tell you what things look like to us. Drugs and gangs go nice together, right? It might be the big gangs are trying to move in on these ones you got here."

"Assho—uh, outsiders—coming in from out of town," said black mustache. "This guy Odell, or whatever they call him."

"He's not from out of town," sandy hair snapped. "He just had a California vacation." He spoke again to Devlin. "Maybe it's just some local hassle, I don't know. But we've had a drive-by shooting, and then, this sorta anonymous whack . . ." He tapped D-Trak's picture. "I mean, we do *not* want this kind of thing to get started around here. And whatever's happening between these sets, it does *not* look healthy to me for them to be mixing on each other's turf."

He looked back onto the practice floor, watching Michelle work out with Trig, who'd put on his uniform and returned. Michelle changed up, smiling, and sent a lazy hook kick that barely missed grazing Trig's nose. Trig followed through with a light palm block—he too was smiling.

Sandy hair picked up D-Trak's photograph and flexed it between his thumb and fingers. "Understand, I'm not gonna miss this guy. Let'm all take each other out is what I say. But when it starts, people gonna get caught in the crossfire. You know what I mean?"

"Oh yes," Devlin said.

"I mean, why do you need this?" said black mustache. "You can't be down here for the money, right? This is more like some kind of a crazy hobby you got. Right?"

"Right," Devlin said. "Whatever."

Black mustache sighed, reached into a pocket, and snapped a business card onto the table. "Well, we do have this murder investigation, sir. If you have *information,* you can call this number."

Sandy hair was watching the practice floor, where Michelle and Trig still sparred in a smooth, subaqueous slow motion. "That's one nice-looking white girl," he said, and cleared his throat. "Now what is *she* doing down here?"

"She's my daughter," Devlin said, with no particular emphasis.

Sandy hair swiveled on the squeaking chair and turned on Devlin a look of disgusted disbelief. After a moment he turned up the flap of his pocket and took out a cigarette and lit it. Devlin waited for his first exhalation, then reached across the table and pinched the cigarette by the head, hard and fast enough to grind out the coal between his thumb and forefinger. Pain from the burn bloomed up and stayed, but Devlin kept his face impassive. Sandy hair looked quizzically at the sprig of tobacco that curled from the torn butt he still held in his hand.

"Man," said black mustache, "you got to be completely crazy. Am I right?"

FIVE MINUTES after they had gone, Michelle called the class to order, as she would do every day, according to the clock. Devlin lingered, seated at the card table. In the photograph, D-Trak's scar did not show, or perhaps the picture had been taken before the wound that made the scar. For a moment, Devlin watched the students through the cloudy

Plexiglas. They stood in their ranks like trees, like living wood, still flexible. They would remain so until a word of his released them.

He walked out and opened the class, still holding his burned thumb and finger pinched on the pain. A moment later, when he made his fist, the pain divided in two points like a pair of eyes. When he punched he screamed his *kyai* among theirs, and the two pains flowed together and then again divided. Again, again, again. The pain focused and burst out in Devlin's *kyai,* and he knew it was happening all over the room, the muted anger at the cops' intrusion, pain at the loss of D-Trak, of Keisha, and other pains and angers that came from everywhere. Devlin worked with them, block for block and kick for kick, basics, without a break, until the purge was perfect. He called them to attention and let them rest—standing again like a grove of trees, as if a wind might sway their trunks. Then he began to talk.

"Gentlemen," he said. "You know statistics are against you. The numbers say you'll go to prison. Numbers say you'll die before you're thirty."

He waited, watching them. The front row: Michelle, Trig, Bigfoot, Kool-whip, Boxcar, Clayvon. In the next rank: Rebo, Freon, Butch, Gyp, Sharmane, Tamara . . . and so on back. At the rear of the room, Froggy tumbled on the floor, careless in the care of Weez. The white narrow space was acrid with sweat. Devlin thought he had them to the point where they wouldn't need to listen but could simply hear.

"I don't believe in statistics," Devlin said. "I believe in individuals. Each one's life is the choice of each. Each *one* has a chance to beat the numbers."

He waited, watching their lidded eyes, focused on the middle distance; he watched the rise and fall of their breathing. Let them breathe in the thing he'd spoken, until it rooted like a germ. Then he judged it long enough.

"*Charyet!*" he called, harshly enough to break the spell. "*Junbi!*"

So it went on.

At the end of practice, when they had all bowed out and been dismissed, Devlin beckoned Trig and Kool-whip. "You two stay."

Kool-whip was blank; Trig nodded, as if he'd been expecting it, or not. It was Michelle who seemed surprised, turning back from the doorway of the women's dressing room.

"Private lesson," Devlin explained. "You're welcome if you want to stay."

"Sparring?" Michelle said.

"Forms," said Devlin.

"I guess I probably should head back," Michelle said. "Homework, you know . . ."

Devlin sat on the floor and did butterfly stretches, waiting for the others to file out. Weez was still on her folding chair, rocking her upper body slightly with Froggy resting against her shoulder; when the infant was asleep she laid him softly belly down on the mat. In a moment Sharmane had come out to relieve her. The door swung and shut and swung again with each departure, injecting short, sharp bursts of the outdoor cold. Passing the doorway, the groups separated as in some chemical process of refinement: Eager Street headed one way and Poe Homes another. A Poe Homes contingent, Gyp, Freon, and Mud-dog, escorted Michelle to her car without particularly appearing to.

Devlin was pleased with that, though the cop's phrase *drive-by shooting* flickered in his mind before he could quite suppress it.

When Michelle's car had pulled away, he turned back to Trig and Kool-whip, spent about half an hour teaching them the next form up. *Tae Guk Sam Jang* . . . They caught on fast, Trig a little faster than the other. Devlin had decided to accelerate their training, bending the usual Tae Kwon Do protocols in order to build cadre faster. Trig was the more talented perhaps, but Kool-whip was not so far behind him, and Devlin thought it politic to choose one from each group, to avoid the appearance of prejudice.

"We need to build up the children's class," he announced when they were done. "Get some of these guys a little younger—eight or ten."

Trig glanced over his shoulder at Froggy, still sleeping on the floor at Sharmane's feet. "You gonna teach it?"

"You are," Devlin said. "When you make black belt, then we start."

"Be a while," Trig said.

"It might be sooner than you think." Devlin turned his head to include Kool-whip in this notion, but Kool-whip had already gone to the dressing room.

Trig headed in that direction too, and after a moment Devlin followed. Usually he waited to change until the others were all gone; the little room was fairly cramped and he preferred all the students clear of the place before he and Michelle locked down. Today, such considerations hardly seemed to matter.

Kool-whip scurried into his clothes and bolted; late for something, Devlin thought, or maybe he didn't want to hit the street at just the same time as Trig. Trig, on the other hand, seemed almost languid, folding each article of his uniform in careful creases before he laid it down. As he stopped over his gym bag, Devlin got his first good look at the healing wound on Trig's left shoulder, straggling letters engraved there: P O E.

"What the hell is that about?" Devlin said.

"It's us," Trig said, stepping into his loose jeans. "Poe Homes." As he tightened his belt, muscle worked smoothly under the crusted pattern of the brand.

"How'd you do it?" Devlin said, pulling up his own trousers.

Trig slipped on a black T-shirt made of some shiny synthetic stuff. "Soldering iron," he grunted, as his head thrust through the collar.

"Good God," Devlin said, involuntarily, for he hadn't meant to seem impressed. "What for?" He cocked his knee and put out a slow roundhouse kick to try his extension, stopping it with a slight pop and holding it there. A habit, to make sure his street pants weren't too confining, that he hadn't tightened up.

Trig peered down at his rigid foot, the toes curled back from the ball. "Freon," he said. "He found the iron . . . He got Tamara to draw it on him. Then he drawn it on Tamara."

"Tamara?" Devlin's support leg wobbled. He caught his balance and neatly retracted the kick.

"You know it," Trig said. "Then everybody in my crew was doing it, yo—so's not to be lame, in front of a woman. Like—"

"You let Freon sucker you into it that way?" Devlin snapped out his other leg and held it. "You?"

"Thass it." Trig shrugged; the T-shirt sleeve rode up to

expose the lower edges of the brand. “Me the same as everybody else. Except Sharmane.”

“What did she have to say about it?”

“ ‘*Hell* no, I ain’t doing any of that’ . . .” Trig had for an instant become Sharmane; then he was Trig again, grinning privately as he bent to retrieve his hoody. Devlin watched how the gun weight dragged at the belly of the garment as he lifted it. He pulled in his kick and began buttoning his shirt.

“What does that tell you?”

“That she got more balls than me?” Trig laughed, then cut it off short. “Thass not all it was to it, though. For me. It was D-Trak, we been dogging together for a long time back. So it’s like what you say . . .” Trig nodded toward the door that opened onto the practice floor. He wormed into the hoody, the hidden gun thumping against his hard, tight stomach. “You take that inside hurt and put it on the outside.”

“With a soldering iron,” Devlin said.

“Like what you say,” Trig said, adjusting the strings of his hood. “They more than one way to get to it.”

“Sure,” Devlin said. “So long as it’s your choice. What else do you plan on letting Freon fool you into?”

“I hear you,” Trig said. “I be giving that some thought.” He swung the fringed jacket around his shoulders, bowed to Devlin, and was gone.

KEISHA’S FUNERAL came on a Wednesday and Devlin, touched to have been asked to go, rescheduled his midday appointments and attended, dressed in the suit he wore to work. He hung back toward the wall of the storefront church on Lexington Street, feeling out of place, though many of the mourners were his students. The waves of emotion that rolled through the room were foreign to him, his own feeling seemed narrower and more dry. From the periphery, he observed. The space was about the same size as the one he'd rented across town, and almost as raw. No permanent pews, only rows of metal folding chairs, CHURCH OF THE REDEEMER stenciled on the back of each. At the bottom of the room stood a low dais with an unimposing wooden altar painted the same bluish white as the walls and ceiling. An electronic keyboard pressed out strains of digitized organ music, while a second player bent notes on an electric guitar. The singing was powerful enough to bring Devlin to the edge of tears, but it seemed allowable to put on his sunglasses; the fluorescent light was sharp and harsh and many of his students were already wearing theirs.

They didn't quite know what to say to him, Devlin could tell, outside the context of the school, but they did lend him company in their way, standing shoulder to shoulder with him, along the wall. Their funeral suits, he noticed, were more expensive and better cut than his own. It was the older people who bore the threadbare look of poverty the neighborhood would have prepared him to expect, but Devlin did not know them. He recognized only Irene Packer, from the television and the newspapers: she sat frailly erect next to Boxcar at the edge of Keisha's family, a black cloth covering her head. After the service she walked cautiously toward the door, others making a respectful way for her, balancing herself with the aid of a rubber-tipped wooden stick. Devlin was introduced to her as master of the school, of which she'd apparently heard some good. He held her matchstick hand for a moment in his own and forced himself to look directly into her eyes, forgetting that his own were masked, behind the sunglasses.

Passing the looming gothic gate of Greenmount Cemetery, the cortege seemed to leave the world itself, for at that moment the uncertain clouds that had sealed the sky pulled apart and let down startling shafts of winter sunlight. The grave itself was a reddish gash in the thin skin of last night's snow. Devlin oversaw the burial from the roadway's edge, standing among several from the school. The wind whipped their ties back over their shoulders, and those without sunglasses were squinting in the mean flicker of the unaccustomed light.

When it was finished, Devlin watched Trig step to Sharmane, take Froggy from her charge, and lift him to his shoulders. Trig walked up the hill, toward another grave. He'd raised his hands and folded them over the small of Froggy's back to hold the child more securely there, while Froggy, delighted with the ride, pulled on his ears to steer. Devlin followed them for no particular reason, his eyes lowered to the slushy tracks Trig was making in the snow. A pair of crows skimmed low over the graying monuments, the wind up their tails. Trig stopped six feet short of Jaynette's headstone and looked down. This grave had not quite settled, so the snow there still expressed the arched shape of new sod. Froggy chortled and pulled Trig's ears, and Devlin kept on watching them from several paces back, knowing that Trig must know that he was there, or that someone was. All down the hill came the slapping of car doors and the churn of motors as others scattered from the burial. When Trig turned away and started back down, a reflection from his wraparounds flashed at Devlin like a wink, and Devlin wondered if Trig could read the repertory of his own useless knowledge. His mouth was sour, as if a bitterness had passed from Trig's tongue to his own.

DEVLIN AND ALICE went out to dinner that night—no particular occasion, just themselves. Adults' night out, a tradition they'd established when Michelle was small; they did it once a week, to keep their sanity. These last few years they no longer had to find a babysitter, of course; in fact, Michelle was out somewhere herself, often as not, on grown-up night. Devlin had changed his shirt and tie out of a sense of ceremony, though he still had on the same suit he'd worn to the office and the cemetery. Alice was dressed up, perfumed, and she looked lovely, but Devlin was having trouble concentrating on her conversation as he drove. The funeral had left him coated with a thin film of depression—that must be what it was.

The restaurant was a favorite of theirs, a converted country house a few miles north of town. A massive wine cellar, excellent French menu, and a prosperous clientele, much like themselves. Each of the small dining rooms was redolent with success and luxury. Before, this had never bothered Devlin. He was anything but overweight, he had a right to an appetite, but somehow he had to force himself to order.

Alice could tell; she could generally tell. She leaned toward him, stem of a crystal wine glass in her hand, her eyes luminous in the simulated candlelight. She wanted to know, what was it? Devlin told her about the funeral, haltingly; the details he could render didn't really convey whatever nebulous emotion the episode had made him feel.

"What did she die of?" Alice said.

"Overdose," Devlin said. "That's what they say. She's got—had—two children with my guy Boxcar, I think. They didn't go to the funeral."

"The neighborhood's not noted for longevity, is it?" Alice said. She paused, smiling politely at a waiter as he lowered an appetizer plate before her. "How far into drugs *are* all these students of yours down there?"

Devlin revolved the ice in his melting drink. "They look pretty healthy," he said. "The ones that work out."

"They're young," said Alice.

"True," Devlin said. "They're straight when they come to practice. Past that . . . it's out of my control."

Alice forked up a morsel from her cylinder of goat cheese; the cheese was decorated with two colors of sauce, fanned to the edges of the plate in a spiral pattern. "Good," she said, and pushed the plate toward Devlin. "Try it?"

Devlin shook his head. He sipped the watery drink, put it down on the tablecloth.

Alice laid her fork aside. "Why?" she said. "Why get involved with people like that?"

"You tell me," Devlin said. He hadn't meant to be antagonistic but it seemed he couldn't stop. "You did, once."

"I was twenty-four," Alice said. "I thought I could make a difference."

"Right," Devlin said.

"You get caught up in it, you get sucked under. Right down with the people you were planning to help," Alice said. "That's what happens. You can't save the world, Mike—not all by yourself."

Now Devlin felt vaguely combative. There were answers

he could have made, all of which would ruin the evening, if he hadn't accomplished that already. He thrust his hand in his pants pocket, past his keys and pocketknife, and fingered the place on his thigh where the bruise from the Camaro had been. It was gone now, with no palpable trace; he had reabsorbed the secret. True, he was leading a secret life. He didn't know why, he didn't know if he wanted to know why, but he did know he didn't want to talk about it.

Alice had caught up a corner of the tablecloth and was kneading it, studying the lace edges as she chewed her lower lip. Devlin reached across and disengaged her hand from the fabric and held it in his own. "Hey, I'm sorry," he said. "I don't need to be dragging funerals to dinner."

Alice looked at him directly, her face close to his. "Truly?" she said. "Sometimes you worry me."

Devlin experienced a moment of disorientation, as if he were seeing the scene from without: the handsome, barely middle-aged couple joined in this moment of tender communion. He let go her hand and sat back. "My condition isn't serious," he declared.

"You swear?" said Alice.

"Honor bright," Devlin said, and gobbled a bit of his slice of terrine, to prove it. Within two minutes they'd found something safe to talk about.

WALTER, who was eight years old, sat in the playroom of Devlin's psychiatric office dismembering little green army men with a pair of scissors. His method was programmatic and unvarying, like an auto-da-fé or some ritualized medieval or Islamic punishment. First the feet were severed, then the hands. A deep vertical snip through the crotch was never omitted; Devlin recognized with a dreary fatigue that he would be obliged to discover the reason for this detail. Decapitation was the final act, accompanied by a slow voluptuous smile on Walter's part. When he was quite done with one soldier he went on to the next. The green men stood to Walter's left, in an orderly single file, like Jews marching to the gas chambers. On his right, the boy neatly sorted their component parts: feet here, hands there, heads over there . . . like Pol Pot used to do it.

"Are you going to kill them all?" Devlin inquired.

Walter looked up at him, across the frozen scissor blades. When startled, the boy would stop moving, as abruptly and entirely as a snake. This trait discouraged Devlin more than he could fathom.

"Am I allowed to?" Walter said.

"Of course," Devlin said. "If you like."

With a trace of a smile fleeting over one corner of his mouth, Walter returned to his work. Seated on the floor across the low table from the boy, Devlin set the soles of his feet together and pressed into a butterfly stretch. Walter was absorbed, oblivious to him, his tongue pressed pinkly from between his thin lips as he made another vertical crotch cut. The boy had been sentenced to therapy for executing and mutilating the family cat in the same style he used with the plastic soldiers. The cat, however, had put up a great deal more resistance, and Walter's injuries were attributed to that. Devlin bought the story as far as the scratches and punctures were concerned, but Walter also had bruises which implied that the cat must have packed a hell of a punch; also Devlin had never yet encountered a cat that smoked cigarettes. He had made the call to social services, whose response had been, not atypically, sluggish. Anyway it was a white, middle-class situation, the address not far from Devlin's own. The mother was in therapy herself, though her various transient boyfriends apparently were not.

Oh, great chain of being, Devlin thought, as he mashed his knees out and down to the floor—there was no such thing as its last link. Not the cat, not the little green army men, not the children whom Walter would doubtless someday engender . . . As for the toy soldiers, they were eminently dispensable. Devlin bought them at the grocery store for forty cents a bagful. Their label designated them as "U.N. Peace-Keeping Troops," which sometimes privately amused him, though not today.

"Does it hurt them?" Devlin finally said in neutral tones.

Walter glanced at him cannily. "Their blood is green," he said.

THERE WAS an unlikely February thaw and the snow was melting to lay bare dismal patches of soggy lawn in the yards along the Devlins' street. No answer to his greeting when he swung in through the kitchen door. Alice would be napping, probably, Michelle in her room. Devlin took his practice bag to the basement, then decided it would cheer things up to build a fire. He shoveled ash, brought in wood and kindling from the garage, and was just kneeling to apply the match to the paper when he heard Alice on the stairs.

"What are you doing?" Her voice was tired and slightly annoyed.

The flare of heat brought pain to Devlin's blistered fingers. He licked them and sat back on his heels.

"I thought a fire might be nice," he said.

There was no lamp turned on in the room and the ascending orange blaze from the fireplace threw Alice's shadow high on the wall behind her. "We're going out," she said.

"Right," said Devlin. "Well . . . Shell might enjoy it."

"You forgot," Alice said flatly. She displeased easily of late, seeming to feel he was too much absent, too preoccupied with the downtown school. They had not discussed the matter directly since their last outing, but Devlin knew he'd smoothed the subject over without really answering her questions, and of course Alice, being no fool, would know that too. Tension had rooted itself in this silence between them; Devlin suspected that something would happen to shatter it soon.

"Besides," Alice went on, "Michelle's got a date. She won't be here either."

Devlin bit his lip and stood up. "It'll burn down. We don't need to leave for an hour. Have a drink . . . a glass of wine, before we go."

"Look at the carpet," Alice said.

Devlin sighed. "I'll clean it up."

"Suit yourself," Alice said, and walked off jerkily toward the kitchen.

Devlin took the vacuum cleaner from the closet, connected hose and wand, and plugged it in. He switched on a lamp and surveyed the litter of bark and ash fanned out in the area of the hearth. From the kitchen came the cushioned closing of the refrigerator door and the sound of a chair scraping over linoleum. Devlin went in and found

Alice seated at the kitchen table; she had in fact poured a glass from the bottle of Chardonnay beside her hand. He moved behind her and began to massage her shoulders.

"Feels good." Alice reached up to touch his hand. "Didn't mean to be cross. I woke up with a headache."

"No big deal." Devlin stooped and kissed her fingers. "Do you feel up to going out?"

"Sure," Alice said. "What movie?"

"Why don't you pick it?" Devlin said. "Wait and I'll get you the paper."

He left Alice scanning the movie ads and went back to do the vacuuming, a two-minute chore. Some other, more obnoxious, noise punctuated the roar of the carpet-cleaning head, and when Devlin switched off the vacuum it went on: a car horn bleating just out front. Upstairs there was a clatter as Michelle presumably sped up her preparations. Devlin thumbed back a front-window blind to take a look. The car was pulled up perpendicular to their front walk, a low dark piscine form, the glare of its headlights breaking over a tree trunk. Devlin's teeth were set on edge. In West Virginia, when a teenager, he had often gone to greet hornblowers at the gate with a shotgun or a rifle casually in hand, as a faint warning.

But he was emptyhanded now as he flicked on the eave light and slipped out the front door. He had not waited to put on a jacket, and the damp air chilled him slightly as he moved over the bricks. The horn stopped for a moment just as he came out, and then resumed its monotonic rhythm, tightening Devlin's jaw. In the radiance of the eave light he could see the car more clearly: a black Camaro, smudged with Bondo patches. Later he would recall his sensation as something like what deranged war veterans had sometimes described to him during the years of his psychiatric training, but at the time he felt only a smooth, floating blankness. He was divested of his personal identity in the way all his martial arts practice was meant to prepare for but rarely attained. His leg swung up in an elegant arabesque and at the height of its arc chopped down in an ax kick, heel striking a deep dent in the driver's side roof. Devlin howled like a wolf and spun, his foot slipping a little in the slush, and dropped two more ax kicks onto the hood. He was closer now. He attacked the windshield and window glass with elbows and hammer fists. The glass starred and buckled but didn't altogether shatter, and Devlin kept screaming like a banshee, watching the driver's face disappear behind the white cobwebby lines of impact. The clutch squealed and the car bucked off the curb and Devlin whirled again and drove another dent into the rear fender as it pulled away. He chased it partway down the block, then stopped, breathless, hands braced on his knees, returning to a frightened awareness of himself.

Michelle and Alice were both on the front doorstep, staring at him aghast as he came panting up the walk. Before he drew very near, Michelle whipped away, her face mostly hidden in her hair, jumped into her own car and shot away with the tires crying.

Devlin sucked wind. He could not quite meet the stony eyes of his wife.

"He . . . he almost killed me," Devlin gasped.

"Really?" Her brittlest tone. "It looked like you were trying to kill him." Alice turned her back and stamped into the house, Devlin following through the door she'd left open.

"It was in the fall. A drive-by—" He corrected himself. "A hit-and-run."

Alice drilled him with her angry eyes, a room's length away. Devlin stumbled on, his tongue thickening with a childishly hopeless guilt.

"I was out running." He touched the muscle of his left thigh. "Remember that bad bruise I had?"

"You told me that was from karate."

"Right," Devlin said, beginning to feel a misplaced glimmer of relief. "Well, what really happened—"

"You want to start explaining things now?" Alice screamed. *"It's TOO LATE!"*

White-ice rage. She ran up to their bedroom and slammed the door. Devlin turned into the living room and crashed into a chair, sat staring into the thrusting red blades of the fire. A feeling in his chest as if some huge hawk's claw had pierced his rib cage, crushed the bones, and fisted itself around his vitals. He sat there for some time but the sensation did not abate. The front door had been left open and he could feel the draft but he could not summon a conscious thought. At last he got up and went out again and shut the door behind him.

Upscale as Devlin's neighborhood was, he needed only a twenty-minute walk to reach another that was almost as menacing as the Eager Street area downtown. Here too he was the only white person foolhardy enough to travel on foot, and he wandered the rough blocks for some time, half hoping someone would offer him some mischief, but at the rate he was ignored he might have been invisible.

The temperature was dropping and slush was freezing in the gutters. Devlin buttonhooked to the west and reentered the wealthier white streets, windows cheerfully well lit, sidewalks empty at this hour. Again, he had come out without a jacket and now his face and arms were numbing despite the lupine energy of his stride. The talons in his chest began to loosen as he tired, but he could not outdistance the thing inside him, and he realized he had no idea what else the thing might decide to do. He came to a small park where leafless dogwood trees stood sentinel over a frozen pool and stood there for a moment watching the wind comb through their thin branches before he walked on. His teeth began to chatter now, sporadically; he could control the response with concentration. As he approached his house he felt his pockets and discovered that by sheer dumb luck he happened to have a key.

The kitchen clock told him he had been out almost three hours. There were signs that Alice had made herself some rudimentary meal, but the house was quiet and the bedroom dark. Devlin was ravenously hungry. He put together a ham sandwich and ate in tasteless chunks. He drank a beer. He sat in the den with the newspaper fanned, unread, across his knees, sometimes glancing at the dull blank face of the switched-off television. Around eleven, Michelle's car pulled in and Devlin went to speak to her if he could. Halfway up the stairs she paused and looked back at him in sad resignation as if she were his disappointed parent, then shook her head and went on climbing. He heard the door to her room close.

Devlin lay on his back on the couch, staring at the newspaper. Presently, he turned off the lamp and began staring at the ceiling. The last embers of his fire had long since burned down, but plenty of ambient light leaked in at the windows; it was never completely dark in a city. At infrequent intervals a car passed along the street outside, refractions of its headlights wheeling lazily around the room, then disappearing. Devlin was trying to recall Bondo patches on the Camaro that had clipped him in the fall, but he couldn't. The failure left a butterfly anxiety trembling in his stomach. It seemed to him as if there were two Devlins: one capable of the act he had performed and another with no understanding of that capability. Yet for that moment there had been only one. Such a sense of unity was very seductive; he might follow it almost anywhere it led.

He woke from an uneasy doze because his back was hurting. With sock-foot stealth he climbed the stairs and slipped into the bedroom. He had avoided all loose boards and the hinges gave no telltale creak, but Alice's whisper filled the room like a gunshot.

"I'm not asleep."

Devlin nodded in the dark, pulled off his clothes and slung them on a chair back. The covers settled over him like a slurry of warm mud. Alice lay on her side, facing the door; after a moment Devlin reached across and spread his hand over the warm place between her shoulderblades. There were times when their quarrels would be purged by angry, frantic sex; anger threw them together like cats in a barrel tossed over a waterfall. But Devlin could feel in his palm that this would not be one of those nights. They knew each other that well, body to body. As Alice rolled onto her back he took his hand away.

"Mike," she said. Her tone was neutral, perhaps not unfriendly. "What's going on?"

Devlin could feel that her eyes, like his, were wide and prying at the ceiling. "Nothing," he said. "I don't know."

"Mike . . ." she said. Her voice hardened slightly in the dark. "You've had two . . . psychotic episodes in, what?—the last four months?"

Devlin was silent. His wife's voice dryly resumed.

"Get help."

"There is no help," Devlin said. "I ought to know. I *am* the help."

He turned his head. The darkness in this room was much more perfect because the blinds were drawn; he could not see her.

"You're scaring me," Alice said. "You're scaring me, Dev."

"I'm scaring myself," Devlin said.

Alice rolled back on her side, curling up inside herself, away from him. There was nothing more to say. Devlin knew that she had never been enthusiastic about the company of crazy people; it was why she'd changed her job. In the long run, she was quite skilled at protecting herself, perhaps more so than he. But Devlin knew he wasn't crazy, not in his own eyes.

How should I spend my life? he thought. That had become the question. Dribble it out in a dole of days? Or spend it right up?

"*Koryo.*"

Michelle dipped to her right and slowly drew herself erect, half-tension, her paired arc-hands moving like the lens of a gunsight, sweeping over the flags and coming to focus on her father's face, with a slight forward thrust, a click. The space between her hands framed him, as she knew it would frame her for him, in the shape of a playing-card spade or an inverted heart. She looked through him, her eyes proceeding out and out, concentration dropping from the mind into the body, that point just below the navel. *Chi.* The commanding voice was no longer his but came from nowhere, everywhere.

"Si chak!"

For the next forty seconds she was aware of almost nothing but the flat snap of her uniform popping on each block and kick. Only at the concluding arc strike all her confusions and frustrations burst from her in a *kyai* strong enough to shake the walls of the room and leave her airless, ideally frozen, planted to the floor.

Michelle and Devlin bowed profoundly to each other; she turned smartly and walked off the floor and took her seat among the others. The ritual form of Tae Kwon Do was like a cast, she thought, which would allow the fracture of the other things between them to set and finally heal.

Outside, the wind tore back her hair, chilled the sweat still clinging to her skin. Gusts chipped at her face, making her eyes watery. She smiled amiably, vacantly, at the cluster of guys who always managed, tactfully, to cover her departure, and ducked into her car. Door lock, seatbelt, ignition. She sat back. The thrust of acceleration drove her deeper into her seat.

She drove west, her mind reluctantly restarting. Because she didn't really feel like going home, she stopped in a coffee shop near Lexington Market, ordered a Diet Coke, and sat in a formica booth, sipping from a straw and turning the pages of a history book she had taken out of her schoolbag. The letters scrambled and ran together senselessly. She was bored. School, high school, was done for her. Her applications were all in: Vassar, Williams, Yale, Mount Holyoke. Michelle's grades were good enough that she hadn't bothered with a safety school.

She crunched ice, gazing dully out the plate-glass window over the sloping sidewalk crowded now with people coming off work. This slight ennui, as her old life was ending and the new, unknown life not yet begun. If she would confess it, she was also beginning to be bored with her high school friends, her dates. Even Frank, the boy driving the Camaro, no longer interested her very much—which was just as well. Whenever they ran into each other now he made a great mocking demonstration of fear and avoidance, but behind all that it was quite definite he would no longer speak to her. As for her father's outburst, she still had not found any way to think about it.

She finished her Coke, dropped the book into her bag, and went outside, passing her parked car and walking down into the great concrete barn of the indoor market. At different stalls she bought fruit and imported cheeses, a whim, a surprise for her mother. The market was crowded mostly with black people, hurriedly shopping before suppertime. Michelle walked through and out the western doors of the building and crossed the street to the outdoor pedestrian mall on the other side.

The brick walkway was lined on either side with cheap clothing and shoe stores, jewelry and electronics and pawnshops, record stores blaring from their outdoor speakers. Everyone on this stroll was black, but Michelle knew it was safe enough. In the notch between the buildings at the end of the mall, a couple of project towers rose; over there it was much more dangerous, like Eager Street, but the expressway between the mall and the projects made a fairly secure border. She walked, looking idly into store windows. Her schoolbag, bulging now with the cheese and fruit, bounced on her hip with her steps. About halfway down the mall, two boys in sweats and warmup jackets and gold chains picked up her trail and followed her, a few paces back, hooting and catcalling and beginning to raise their voices with louder and lewder invitations. Michelle ducked into a record store. They didn't follow her inside, but though she browsed for a good ten minutes, they reappeared when she came out, and dogged her as before.

She kept walking toward the expressway, careful not to hasten her pace; she realized she should have turned back in the direction she'd come from. The winter twilight was fading quickly now. She felt no genuine sense of danger, only annoyance swelling into anger. *Don't strike in anger* . . . it was her father's voice. *Anger only confuses you.* True, but they both also knew that if you got outside your anger, it could be focused and used as a weapon. Now and then she glanced back to mark their positions. It might be simple. Quick stop, spin and back kick to the solar plexus would take out the first, and the second should be lined up then for a follow-through roundhouse kick to the face. Break his nose . . . but she couldn't picture what would happen next. Run. The mall was crowded with strangers all ignoring her predicament, and she imagined they might easily turn hostile when she moved.

She was running out of mall, and the sidewalks on the streets beyond would be comparatively deserted. Time to do something. Double back. She looked over her shoulder again and saw both boys shrivel suddenly as if they'd been struck by silent deadly rays; both sheered off quickly in the opposite direction. Puzzled, Michelle turned toward the expressway again. The black Lexus was pulled up across the mouth of the mall and Trig stood by its trunk with his thumb and forefinger cocked and aimed like a pistol. As Michelle saw him he dropped his hand.

"You want a ride?" Trig said.

"Sure," Michelle told him. "Okay."

He indicated the passenger door without opening it; Michelle slid in while he walked to the other side of the car. She picked up a couple of CD cases from the seat and sat holding them uncertainly against her jeaned knee. Trig stroked the gear shift and the car flowed smoothly into the multiple lanes of traffic on Martin Luther King Drive. Music began as the car rolled out, sledgehammer single-beat bass and voices aggressively thrusting like the voices of the boys on the mall. As if he'd read her mind, Trig shut off the stereo, then took the CD boxes from her hand and filed them in a soft leather pocket of the car.

"Thanks," Michelle said. "I could have handled it."

"You would of," Trig said. He hesitated. "Just don't cross the road."

"I know that," Michelle said, at once regretting the sharpness of her tone. She thought of telling him where her car was parked, but didn't.

Trig took a side street a few blocks north and piloted the car through the gates of Druid Hill Park. Michelle looked across at him but he was inscrutable, the wraparounds a black wedge crossing his brown cheekbone. He said nothing, looked straight ahead. Michelle held herself poised, slightly away from the leather cushion of her seat. A smell of goat cheese wafting from the bag between her feet embarrassed her slightly, but if Trig noticed it he made no comment. The car was silent as a submarine.

He turned away from the zoo and the arboretum, and drove around the high side of the lake. The wooded slopes rolled back to the right of the car, the trees all bare-branched but for a few evergreens among them, the park deserted now because of the cold. A telephone mounted between the car seats rang; Trig answered, muttered something brief and terse, and replaced it on its mount. When it rang again, he pressed a switch that stopped the ringing.

They parked on an asphalt fan at the top of a hillock above the Jones Falls Expressway. To one side was a model town designed to demonstrate traffic laws to children, enclosed behind a waist-high storm fence; on the other stood a small concrete structure which replicated a medieval turret. Below, the lake was partially frozen, the fountain toward the western end shut off for the winter. Trig seemed to be looking through the windshield at the inert metal mass of the fountain. Michelle could hear her watch ticking, over the barely detectable hum of the engine. It was dark enough now that the cars on the road bordering the park were beginning to turn on their lights. After what felt like a very long time, she reached into a side pocket of her bag and came out with a pin-rolled joint in her palm; she turned to show her hand to Trig.

Trig began laughing and didn't stop. He shoveled down in his seat, beat his hands on the steering wheel, took off his sunglasses to dash tears from his eyes.

"What's with you?" Michelle said, beginning to laugh a little too. "You didn't even smoke it yet."

Trig seemed to be unable to reply. Michelle shrugged, dug for her lighter. They smoked the joint, talked for an hour, then ate the fruit and cheese.

WHATEVER IT WAS, it wasn't boring, Michelle thought. A taste of the forbidden maybe, though no one had explicitly forbidden it to either of them. Still they were, if not secretive, discreet. There was no question of bringing Trig home to her house, she knew that. As for Trig, he also seemed concerned to protect the privacy of their . . . friendship. Why, certainly they both must have known it was more than that, but neither had expressed it. There was more physical contact between them within the school than outside it; at practice their movements together seemed increasingly like dance, but maybe it had always been that way, she thought. Outside, they had not ever touched, except for fingertips, passing a joint or a glass. It was that that wasn't boring, the balance on the cusp.

They never left the school together, but Michelle would drive her car somewhere it could be safely parked, then wait for the black Lexus. Sometimes she'd stay late for Trig's extra lessons, to facilitate the timing; not every day, but once or twice a week. Or there'd be nights she'd leave the house, armed with some cover story about plans with friends—if she was asked, which she usually was not, since her parents trusted her enough not to pry into her movements.

By unspoken mutual agreement they kept clear of places where either was likely to be known. Her high school hangouts were unlikely to appeal to Trig. He took her clubbing with him once but she was uncomfortable in the crowd, which seemed to contain too many of his business contacts she didn't want to know about, and when she asked to be taken away he was quick enough to oblige her. They sought out quieter venues, restaurants neither had ever been, little bars out of the way. Sometimes, cautiously, they'd try a movie at one of the malls, or music at the Haven or Spike and Charlie's.

They went to Hammerjack's once on a lark; the place had been taken over for a rap and rhyming contest, open mike, and Trig thought it would be a laugh. He should have known, Michelle thought later, that it would draw people they knew from both Eager Street and Poe Homes, but then she should have known herself. It was Freon she noticed first. Somehow it always seemed to be Freon because he always seemed on the verge of making a fool of himself.

Freon had shed his jacket and was wearing a red sleeveless shirt, to show off the muscle he'd built up at Tae Kwon Do, Michelle suspected. Anyway he looked pleased with himself and with his arms. But the tank top also disclosed a mark on his left shoulder, straggling letters in warping lines of burn scar: P O E. Clayvon and Butch, angling toward Freon through the crowd, seemed to have been struck by this too. Butch was sweating alcohol—she could smell it—and Clayvon looked high on something she had never tried.

Butch jabbed a blunt finger into Freon's brand. "Poe Homes, huh, nigga? You like that sound?"

Whatever Freon said in reply was lost in a squeal of feedback from the stage. But Michelle could feel that Trig's attention, though he wore his wraparounds, had also swerved to Freon.

"Poe Homes," Clayvon was saying. "Nigga, you like to holler that out car windows, yo?"

"Sometimes," Freon said. "Sometimes I might."

Butch prodded his finger into the scar again, and Freon slid back, rolling his forward arm up in an oily movement to sweep the probing hand from his shoulder. Yes, Michelle could see and acknowledge, Freon had learned some things these last few months, but then Butch and Clayvon had too, and it might be they weren't just playing now.

Clayvon slurred something quite a lot louder, crowding toward Freon along with Butch—something loud enough to bring the bouncers: big guys, whose overbuilt bodies closed off most of the scene. After a couple minutes of heated explanation, it seemed to be over, whatever it had been. Butch and Clayvon cut away through the crowd, and Freon shook his head and raked his fingers through his locks, then grinned to greet Tamara and Sharmane, who had just shown up.

Michelle tried a smile on Sharmane, who stared back at her with undiluted distaste for a moment, then drew her lips mockingly back from her teeth. On the stage the first band had kicked in, and Michelle was glad of the distraction. She moved to Trig's other side and looked at him a little unhappily.

"Might oughta stick it out," Trig said. A muscle worked smoothly in the corner of his jaw. Hips swaying lightly to the music, he looked toward the stage.

Michelle stuck it for about an hour, but she couldn't focus on the rhymes, and she had the feeling Trig couldn't either. They danced a little, without much joy; she had the feeling of being watched, though she didn't check to see who was watching. It wasn't so much that she felt uncomfortable as that being here wasn't the point. The band went on break, and in the lull before the canned music started, Michelle curled her fingers into the crook of Trig's elbow.

"Take me home."

He pushed back his sunglasses to see her clear.

"With you," Michelle said.

Trig nodded slowly. "Where's Freon?" he said then, but Freon had disappeared, along with the girls. Michelle didn't ask why Trig wanted to find him.

THE PARTY at Hammerjack's had started in the afternoon, so it was still full daylight when they left the building, blinking with the surprise of the sun. Trig piloted the Lexus out of the maze of overpasses where the club was tucked, then north past the harbor mall and into the projects. Michelle reclined on the fat leather cushion of her seatback, her face toward the window. The unfamiliar landscape scrolling by beyond the glass did not seem entirely real to her, even when Trig glided down a street of burnouts and parked the car beside Poe Homes.

Another day of false spring, delusively warm. Earlier there'd been some rain, and the air was sweet when they got out of the car. Trig led her quickly across a small square courtyard and undid several locks on a ground-level door and brought her in.

For some reason she wanted to check the refrigerator first. Almost empty, as she'd have thought: a bottle of Asti Spumante, four cans of malt liquor, cheese, mustard, and a box of baking soda. She let the door fall shut and walked back into the living room. It was very clean and neat, all black leather and glass and chrome, with the slightly unreal look of a set in a furniture store. Michelle kicked off her shoes and worked her toes in the angora-like hairs of the white carpet. Trig swallowed.

"Want something to drink?"

"No."

"Music?" He waved toward the sleek entertainment consoles that occupied most of one wall.

Michelle shook her head. Trig seemed to have run out of things to say. The miniblinds were lowered, slitted, and cast zebra stripes of shadow and light across the space between them.

"Trig," Michelle said. "I crossed the road already."

She took off her blouse; she was not wearing a bra. There was a snap of static electricity as they came together; it made them both smile. The hardness in his waistband was unnatural.

"Wait a minute—" Trig turned his back to pull off his shirt. She watched the glossy movement of columns of muscle along his spine. He laid the shirt carefully on a chair seat instead of tossing it; something was bundled inside, concealed from her. When they joined again there was no obstruction.

IN HER DREAM there was a rattling noise, like dry beans dropped into an empty can. She woke to the sound of Gyp pounding the window frame and shouting for Trig. A dizziness swam over her as she sat up too quickly, gathering the sheet to her collarbone. Trig had jumped into his pants already. Through the doorway to the living room she saw him snatch the pistol from the bundle of his shirt, then he sprinted out the door, leaving it swinging.

It was eerily quiet then, except for bird song that came through the windows from the courtyard. Michelle threw on her jeans and shirt and went out, dithering a moment to see if the door would swing locked behind her. Finally she propped it with a shoe. The beans-in-a-can sound came again, louder, then a brake squeal and the crunch of a collision. She ran barefoot to the mouth of the courtyard and peered out. Halfway down the sidewalk someone was lying on his side in the midst of a pooling substance that looked like tar or motor oil, his short dreads gumming to the concrete as the pool enlarged. Something lay out of his reach near the building wall; it took her a moment to read this as a gun. At the corner, a rusting gray van had skidded over the curb and slapped into a lamppost. Trig and Gyp swarmed around it like sharks on the carcass of a whale, the pistols in their hands going crack-crack-crack, but the van was still alive, its back wheels spinning and burning rubber. The van thumped down from the curb and plowed to the west, leaving Trig in a half-crouch, still squeezing his spent pistol.

Michelle ducked back into the courtyard. It wasn't like a movie, she thought inanely, no close-ups, they didn't make sure you saw the things that would help you make sense of it all. The pebbled concrete now felt very cold to her bare feet. The courtyard was empty except for things: a couple of saplings planted in brick rings penetrating the concrete; a small pipe jungle gym; and, near it, a lopsided Big Wheel, its plastic abraded from hard use. Michelle felt a mute attention from the blinded windows surrounding the court although she could see no one looking out.

The door had remained propped on the shoe. She went in and finished dressing speedily, found her keys and purse, and even brushed her hair. Trig blew in the door, panting, his bare chest streaming sweat. Gyp, a half-step behind him, froze in the doorway and stared at her with raw disbelief.

"Yo," Gyp said. "Got to get her out of here."

"You know it," Trig gasped. "You gonna drive her, man. I can't—" he hissed in air—"can't use my car. Cops gonna turn me over anyway, and I got to lose this heat a while." He held up the guns basketed in his hands—three of them now.

Michelle thought of the pistol she'd seen lying near Freon's body. Freon.

Trig went to the kitchen and came back with the guns swinging heavily in a blue plastic grocery bag. He set the bag on a table and came to Michelle, his warm hands framing her by her upper arms. She glanced at the P O E scar on his shoulder; her lips had been there an hour before. His eyes were the same, still belonged to him.

"You all right," Trig said. It was a statement, not a question. "You ain't seen nothing. You weren't never here."

"Yes," Michelle said. "No. I wasn't." She dipped her head to swing her hair across her face.

"Hey," Trig said. "I'm sorry."

"What for?" She looked up; her voice didn't break. "You know. Nothing happened."

"All right, girl." Trig gave her arms a little shake. "Better get going."

Her car was parked in the lot behind Lexington Market.

Gyp drove her there through the thickening twilight. It occurred to Michelle that she would even be home in time for supper. When they arrived at the lot, Gyp slapped the dashboard and opened his mouth to say something, then shook his head and remained silent. He waited, watching through the side window, until she was safely in her car and under way. Some one of them was always showing her this courtesy.

She made it as far as Northern Parkway, then pulled into a side street, parked carefully, set the brake, and cried half-hysterically, hunched over the wheel with her shoulders pumping. It went on for about five minutes, then she spent another five putting herself back together. The hair again, a touch of makeup for the chapped look of her skin, eyedrops (she carried the drops to counteract the side effects of smoking dope). The rearview mirror, when she twisted it down, showed that she would pass a light inspection.

She pulled up at the house in the last whisper of daylight. The strongest stars were already showing in the darkening blue of the sky, and a couple of doves called to each other from the eaves. The kitchen window framed her mother's head and arms as she worked on something over the sink, holding her in the orangey glow of the socketed light above her.

Alice looked up as Michelle came in. "How was it?"

"Fine." A bolt of panic shot through Michelle's stomach. She couldn't remember her cover story, whatever it had been. "It was terrific, really."

She forced a thin smile, but her mother wasn't paying any real attention, and didn't follow up. Alice held an eggplant up to the light, then went on peeling it.

Her father stood up abruptly when Michelle came into the living room, twitching a folded newspaper against his leg. It was still awkward between them when they met outside of Tae Kwon Do. Michelle drew a long breath and fell on his neck. She was almost taller than he, but it didn't matter. She tucked her face into his collarbone and let her hair cover her. His hands came up and calmingly stroked her back.

"Hey, hey now. Everything's all right," Devlin said, knowing that he didn't know if it was all right or not.

5

SHARMANE

I COULD OF danced at that party, if Gyp shown up, I was ready. It wasn't like we had no date, though, more just *See you there?* and Gyp smiling. That lazy way he hope would melt you through the hips like butter in the pan. Like he half seeing me and half not. But I got myself done up, that afternoon. New hair, cut short in the back but with a long flip forward hanging down on one side, and new nails and makeup and these high-heel sandals with straps that criss-cross over the ankle and this gold stretchy cat suit Tamara help me pick. She got herself some new stuff too. So, like, it wouldn't be Gyp's choice if he notice me or not—cept for he didn't show.

Instead it was Freon, then Trig and the Devlin girl, looking real miserable to get caught together, and trying to hide theyself in the crowd. So after while I left Freon trying to make up to Tamara and I go outside to the pay phone to where you might could hear yourself think and called Gyp on his car phone. He answered the third ring and I hung up. That let me know he was in the car but I still didn't know where the car was at. Did I?

Back to the party. Here was Clayvon and Butch getting up some kind of a beef with Freon, which I just as happy to keep away from cause, you know, things was more tenser than they had been and we didn't see much of that Eager Street crew no more, outside of Devlin's classes. So me'n Tamara danced with each other, and here come some stranger dudes wanting to dance, which we did, only not more than just one dance, not letting'm move in or buy us no drinks. *Got to get back to my girlfriend,* you know.

Told me I was dressed for success, that much. I slip off and called that car phone another time. It been about an hour. Gyp answer and I hung up like before. Didn't say one single word.

I had smoke some with Tamara on the way down but now it just making me woozy and worried and I was getting a headache to go with it. It was local groups so far and not all that good with they rhymes and the bass just hammering on my head when I got back inside. Clayvon and Butch wanted to make a play then and they being pushy, almost nasty, so I thought then I wanted to leave. Give it up. I told Tamara she didn't need to come if she didn't want to but she came along with me. And Freon left with us, which I didn't care anything about, but he did.

We always could go back, Tamara say, cause we did have our stamps. But I didn't much think I would. It wasn't hardly happening down there noway.

Back at Poe Homes, here was Gyp down on the corner,

by himself and just hanging loose, the car parked not too far away. Just making himself available, you know, if anybody want to cop. I give him the eye-roll when he first call to me, but then seem like I couldn't stay mad. Wasn't like I caught him slipping with some other girl. More like he waiting on me almost. And he did say he been meaning to come down. Said it was early yet, which was the truth. We hadn't fixed up no certain time.

We stood there talking on the corner. I saw how Gyp keep looking at my shoes. Thinking how it would be like to undo them straps . . . maybe leave'm on instead. Then we fixed it up to get something to eat and go back to the party after that, or somewhere . . . or nowhere. Gyp naming off different restaurants we could go but what I thought was take-out Chinese. I liked the thought of sitting up in Gyp apartment, watching each other eat with chopsticks, maybe not going out at all. If we could of just shook Freon . . . and Tamara even. But they was there, so Tamara came down to the Chinese with me, and Freon went off to the liquor store.

It was one of those fool-you springlike days you get in the middle of a Baltimore winter—fool the buttercups out the ground, like Gramma Reen would say. Not that we had no buttercups to get fooled, not now. But warm wind was blowing and the sky coming clear. Crows was flying low all over the vacant lots and calling at each other, big old raggedy black crows. It made me laugh to look at them cause I starting to feel good.

On the way down here was Cherry and one of her girlfriends hanging out the window to they place so we step in a minute to finish off that blunt we started earlier. It made us a little late coming back with the Chinese, or else it was time getting all stretchy like it will when you smoke that good dope. We come back a different street than what we went down on, headed straight for Gyp's place, not passing by Poe Homes. The sun had drop down by then and some clouds was blowing up and the big old crows blowing along with'm what it seem like, still making a lot of noise.

Then we leaning on Gyp buzzer for what seem like about twenty minutes—no answer. Rentacop at the security shack say he ain't seen him come or go . . . not that you could count on him to be awake to see it. I wished I had a key but I hadn't never got Gyp to give me one. We went outside to look around. Gyp car not parked nowhere in sight and no sign of Freon either. That dope we smoked went wrong on me another time and I felt down, so hard let down, with them food bags dragging on my hands. It just starting to get dark.

Then, here come somebody, over from Poe, and I saw the fringes swinging from the coat so I known it was Trig. Only when he come up near I saw he didn't have no shirt on under it, and he was barefoot too which struck me strange—hell it wasn't *that* warm. Look like he just jump outa bed in a hurry *and who with?* I was wondering only I could tell it ain't the time to ask that question.

He didn't stop to say nothing either but just blew by us, cutting toward the back side of Gyp building where it all sealed up. He holding something cupped up under that coat but it didn't hide it any too good—I could see the greeny plastic grip of that pistol of Freon between the buttons. I seen where Tamara saw that too.

"What up?" Tamara say, but Trig don't answer, just blow on by with his feet *slapping* on the concrete. Then we was half jogging to stay up with him, my ankles wobbling over them heels, food bags knocking on my legs.

"Whussup," I say. "What happen, Trig?" But he don't want to look at me, so when he come to the tear in the fence at the back of the building, I reached and twisted my hand up in his coat fringes so he can't get through. "Trig," I say. "You got to tell us."

"Shit, then, they shot Freon," Trig say. He saw my face. "Gyp all right, he just . . ." Trig sweating and half outa breath. "Just gone somewhere."

"Freon?" Tamara say.

"Gone to the boneyard," Trig say. He holding the guns against his gut with one elbow and prying loose my fingers of his coat with his other hand. Tamara set down her food bags on the ground so careful and gentle so nothing gonna spill and she wrap her fingers through that chain link and start screaming.

"Goddamn," Trig say. "I can't be standing here."

Then I heard it, sirens, must of been hearing it for a while already but then was when I noticed. Sound like they coming from all directions too. I let loose of Trig and he slip through that fence and swung back that sheet of plywood on the trick nail and was gone into the building out of sight. I known he had his dead-drop up in there on the sealed side and I known if he got caught up there with all that rock they was slanging he gonna go down for ten years probably, not even counting that apronload of hot guns he was hauling.

"Tamara," I say. "You got to get yoself together, *right now.*" Cause cop car was right then rolling up to where we at. One of them diddly little new cars they got now, the Taurus.

Cop roll down the window and cut back the siren so we could hear. One the same two cops that had been hassling

Devlin at the school a while before, I thought, not that I could call his name. Cop roll down the window and put his hand on the door latch. Didn't quite get out the car but look like he thinking about it. Tamara had quiet down and she wasn't tangling with that fence no more, but she still got her back to the car, crouching down over them food bags.

Cop want to know did we see anything, hear any shots, see anybody run, like the usual. I told him no. I make myself look right in his face, not cutting my eyes to where Trig gone. Hoped Tamara she doing the same.

Cop ask me the same questions all over again the way they love to do. And I tell him another time we ain't done nothing and ain't seen nothing cause we ain't been here more'n a minute or two cause we was four blocks down picking up the Chinese.

"Chinese?" cop say, and he squint on them bags and he pop the latch and set a foot out the car like he want to step over and see was we lying. Which he was welcome to have it all if he wanted it cause it was all cold and gummy by that time and we wasn't gonna eat it noway now. Something turned over inside of one bag and the plastic filling up with gluey old hot and sour soup.

Tamara stood up and turned around. Her eyes was dry and her face look like flint and she got something in her hands.

"Chinese is right," Tamara say. "Now don't you want a motherfucking egg roll?"

WHAT A LOT of work it is to make a person. I guess to a man maybe it ain't. Just *slip-slide—splat!* and then the man gone. Long gone, if he want to be. But if you a woman, that when you start work, making that other body out of little bits of your own I guess, and split yourself about in half getting it out of you when the time come. But you ain't done yet, got to nurse it and feed it and wipe its ass and try to keep it from running out in the street. Only it ain't like that for a man I don't guess. You can get rid of a person just that quick. *Boom, splat!* He done now.

So this what I'm thinking, looking into Freon box. Odell like they call him in the paper, under that coat-and-tie picture from eight-grade graduation which is far as the dumbass ever got. Odell Gavins. The picture all fuzzy and he ain't got his dreads yet but there in the coffin he got the dreads, and he got this powder-blue suit on that was kind of hairy. His skin didn't look right and his mouth sewed shut I guess and his eyes closed, but he didn't look like he was sick and he didn't look like he was sleeping—dead folks just mostly look dead to me, what it is. Froggy was climbing on me, going back and forth from me to Gramma Reen who setting there in the front row with her eyes half-lidded like a turtle in a tank. I was thinking Froggy already been to a whole lot of funerals for somebody not even two years old yet. And I love Froggy but I was feeling glad I ain't made no babies of my own and I was thinking if a doctor was to walk in with his knife I like him to cut out my woman parts right there in the church if he wanted to. Cause it ain't worth it. Sixteen years to make a person and you end up with this thing in a box.

Tamara crying and hollering all over the church. Sweet for Freon all that time she pretending to treat him like dirt, all that time they got they side thing going and nobody didn't know. I felt bad for Tamara, understand, but it wasn't like I was gonna exactly miss Freon. I was sorry about him being a fool and all that, but fools ain't harmless, yo. It was him more'n anybody had touched off all the trouble, and I thought now he was out the way, trouble might stop.

IT THE Wednesday afternoon after the funeral Gramma Reen start putting on her Sunday clothes. Her church dress and stockings and good shoes and that little round hat she pin to her hair to keep it riding straight. I was wondering where was she planning to go, cause they wasn't no church meetings Wednesdays. She caught my eye in the mirror right when she got done jamming that pin through her hat, and it was like she read my mind.

"With you," she say. "Going with you this afternoon. I wants to see that white man."

"White man?" I say. I known she had to mean Devlin though, cause it was practice time.

"White man does that ring dang doo," say Gramma Reen. "Whatever you call it. You *know* who I mean."

Ring dang doo was because she always made out she couldn't say Tae Kwon Do. I might of give myself a smile over that, cept I was groaning inside too, cause it meant humping over there on the bus. We been catching rides with Gyp most days, but Gramma Reen wouldn't ride in no drug-money car.

Seem like it take us half an hour just to drag our way down to the bus stop. I got Froggy stroller to push but I still felt like I wanted to run circles around Gramma Reen—like I some kind of a jackass dog. Then a big chunk of time for that bus to heave and snort itself across town, and creeping back up from the stop over there. Gramma Reen had just got herself a new walking stick, a metal one that came down to a little square with four rubber feet instead of just one. Spose to help her balance some but it didn't do nothing for her speed. I was thinking we gonna be late, not late exactly but I like to have ten minutes or so to stretch and warm up before class—I had got hooked on that. I'm all aggravated with how slow we going and kicking myself at the same time cause all Gramma Reen done for me in her life and she don't hardly ask me for nothing.

Sooner or later we did get there, not all that late really either. I got Gramma Reen settled down in a chair by the door. Weez was there to help with Froggy, and Michelle came over, in her uniform already, to make over Froggy like she usually do. She introduce herself to Gramma Reen with them nice white-girl manners, and Gramma Reen she just simper right back at her.

But none of that bother me no more once Devlin clap his hands and started the class. Any bad thoughts just wash out of me once we knelt down for that *mun yom.* Like the whole rest of my life was gone, and I could stand up clean and clear. Michelle and Trig stood side by side at the front of the class cause that was the way the ranks went, but it didn't bother me none like it would of to see them together anywheres else. They wasn't no outside things could really get into here. Like Devlin would say it, it was another world.

But today, cause Gramma Reen was there, like I saw it from the inside and the outside too. Her in the back and Devlin in front. I thought how it might look to her *and* him. The group was thinned out from what it had been. Butch and Clayvon ain't show up to practice since that weekend

Freon killed, and then the others . . . I saw how people been going down like birds shot off a wire—Jaynette, Stuttz, D-Trak, Keisha. Each one gone down left a hole like through Swiss cheese, so Devlin and Gramma Reen could look through them holes and see each other.

My mind would go off loose like that sometimes the first few minutes of practice. Then it just stop, and nothing left at all cept what we doing then and there. It was better'n blunts or sex or dreaming or sleep. Devlin would talk about it sometimes, getting to that place. But you couldn't understand what he was talking about unless you already been there yourself; it was a place words couldn't reach.

Then practice over. I went to get dressed. When I come out in my street clothes, I seen where Gramma Reen leaning over and pulling off her shoes, real slow. She noticed how everbody piled up they shoes at the door and come into the school barefooted. You wouldn't need to tell her her manners, even if the place was strange to her. But she still got to have that stick, and the rubber feet made little circles on the mats as she went limping long in her stockings toward Devlin office in the back.

I had been wondering all along if she meant she just wanted to look at him or talk to him too. So I followed along after her to see what she gonna say.

Devlin set her chair back in that little room without nothing in it. Took her a long time to lower herself down. Then she said what her name was and who she related to.

"Yes, ma'am," Devlin said. "I'm glad to meet you."

I looked at him from where I was standing in the door and I seen he meant what he said. It was like when he looked at Gramma Reen's face he could see something of what I saw there. I notice him noticing her shoes was off too.

Gramma Reen fold her knotty old hands on the crook of her stick and look across to talk to him. "Mister Devlin," she say. "I see where you got a handle on these boys. They comes in here and they acts like folks. But outside of here, they shooting and killing each other, Mister Devlin. I know you knows it cause I seen you at the graveyard."

"Yes, ma'am," Devlin say.

"You got a handle on'm," say Gramma Reen. "I want you to stop'm from killing each other, now. They's been enough people dead already. That boy Odell might of needed killing but he ought to be the last one."

She looked at him for a minute or more. I known that look when I was a kid, you couldn't lie to her if she looked like that.

"Yes, ma'am," Devlin said. "I'll do all I can."

Gramma Reen nodded at him and she started getting up. This didn't take her quite so long as it did to sit down but still it was like them two parts was longer than the conversation. I looked back at Devlin one time while I was helping her through the door. They wasn't nothing different about his face you could really say, it was blank like it would be in practice, but like it got a crack straight down the middle. I known he hadn't planned on saying what he did, but it was like he didn't have no choice.

TRIG WAITING for us when we made it back out to the street. This surprised me cause I thought he be slip off to one of his secret meets with the Devlin girl they both thought nobody didn't know about.

"I'ma ride y'all home," Trig say.

He pop open the back door of the Lexus and I seen Tamara already setting in there. Gramma Reen mostly won't ride in Trig car neither, but this time, she look one way and then the other and she never quite look at Trig but finally she shuffle on over and let him help her in. I was happy to see her do it cause the weather had turn cold again since Freon got shot and during the class it had start raining and icing and like that.

I got in the front then, and held Froggy in my lap. Most the way across town he sleeping, it a lot smoother ride than the bus. Didn't nobody say nothing all that way, and Trig kept the radio off, and the phone too. I could tell Gramma Reen would of like to take her regular stand about the car but she just too tired out for it. If I look over the seatback I could see her head slipping over to the side when she nodded off and then pop back up neat like a bird head do.

When we pull up at Poe Homes I let Tamara help Gramma Reen inside the house and let her take Froggy in there too, him still sleep. The car standing there humming and Trig drumming his fingers on the dash, only I wouldn't get out the car.

"I got to be heading," Trig finally say.

"Believe I'll ride with you," I told him.

Trig shake his head. "I don't think you want to."

Flump-flump go the wipers, pulling sleet off the glass.

"Trig," I say, and I light me a Kool, though I don't be smoking half so much since I start Devlin school, just when I party or if I get nervous. "What good you think gonna come of you running with this white girl?"

"You don't know nothing about that," Trig say.

"Nigga, you think nobody don't know?" I say, and I just about blown smoke in his face. "*Everbody* know, cept maybe her daddy. And what you think happen when *he* find out?"

"You think I'm afraid of him?" Trig say.

"What I'm spose to think?" I say. "You bow down to him. You *yassuh* and all like that with him."

Trig turn his look on me like it would freeze a hole on through you. I known it wasn't right what I said. Wasn't no Uncle Tom type of thing between him and Devlin, between Devlin and anybody else neither. It was a different thing.

Another cat would have popped me one probably—or tried to. I was set up and ready for that. Knifehand block to crack his wrist and then arm lock above the elbow with the other hand . . . Cause I learn the shit from Devlin, same like everybody else. But when Trig did move all he did was put the car in gear and so we rolling. After a minute he put on the radio and it playing Marvin Gaye. "What's Going On"—seem strange to me later it would be that song.

I eased back on that black leather and start thinking about what *was* gonna happen when Devlin find out about them two. Wondered how dumb he could be he didn't know about it yet. Then I thought maybe he do already know. Maybe he thought it was *irrelevant.* That was a big Devlin word. You don't never look in the other dude face when you fighting with him, cause it *irrelevant.* Right up there with *unnecessary,* in Devlin book. Nobody ever hit you with they face, Devlin did say.

We was headed back across town the way we come, toward where the school was. Didn't make no sense to me cause I didn't see how Miss Michelle gonna hang in this neighborhood by herself, and after dark too. But I didn't say nothing. Trig drove up McDonogh, pass by the school where they just one light lit up behind the gate, shining on that heavy bag hanging there still and empty. He drive by the Parrot Bar. We hadn't gone there no more since Freon, and Michelle wouldn't of set foot there noway I didn't think. But Trig pull around the corner and park the car about halfway down the block.

"Whussup?" I say. "You not meeting Michelle over here."

Trig look at me. "I ain't meeting her nowhere tonight."

"Shit," I say. "Why ain't you told me that?"

"You wouldna believed me," Trig say. I didn't say nothing back to that cause he was right.

Trig killed the lights and shut off the car. There wasn't hardly nobody walking on the street cause of that nasty sleety rain. I was curious what we doing here but I didn't ask.

Trig pull stuff out the pocket of his hoody and start screwing this finger-size something onto the other part, which was a pistol a little bit smaller than what Freon had.

"Jesus," I said. "Whatchoo doing?"

Trig finished with the silencer and laid the gun down in the space between the seats. He looked over to the mouth of that alley that run behind the Parrot. A Dumpster was there at the end so you can't see too far.

"Remember D-Trak?" Trig say.

I nod to him when he look at me.

"Clayvon like to step out behind there to fire up, you know," Trig say. He look back at the alley. "I come to find out, he just gone out there about ten minutes before D-Trak did. And guess which one of'm never come back?"

"Trig, I don't wanna—"

"Don't wanna *what?*" Trig voice cut sharp. "What *I* wanted was leave you home."

The gun was between us. I could of snatched it but I didn't. There was something rising up in me and I didn't know did I *want* it to stop.

"Clayvon was in that van shot Freon," Trig say, laying his hand down over the gun. "It was him and Butch—I don't know how we miss both of them. I need to count one off, Sharmane. They can't keep killing us and me let it go."

"He won't be out there," I say then. Hard for me to talk clear through this thick tingly place that fill up my throat. "It raining this way."

"Shit," Trig say. I seen his teeth for a second in the flare of a streetlamp. "Don't make no difference to a junky."

He turned up his hood and step out the car. When he cross the street I seen he not wearing that jacket with the fringe, but some cheap nylon thing, dark blue. Didn't take no genius to figure out why that was. When he good inside the alley I got out and followed. Don't know yet if it was cause I wanted to or cause I thought it would be worse not.

My legs stiff and I wet my foot stumbling into the gutter, that water so ice-cold it shot pain to my hip. Time I peep around the gutter I already heard *whump!* Trig kicking Clayvon—I guessed it was Clayvon underneath that wool hat. Something flew out his hand and broke tinkling . . . crack pipe, I thought. Clayvon reaching for something in his pants but Trig kick him again and he couldn't get it. Trig hit him a backfist that snap his face back into the light and I seen his lips was bleeding. Trig just only using his left hand—pistol floating in the other one. Clayvon reach again and Trig kick him the same place to drive the arm deep into the body. I thought I heard a bone snap that time. Clayvon laid back into the wall, not doing much of nothing no more—he had the crack eyes but his body wouldn't do for him. Trig pistol didn't make no more noise than a sneeze. Rain coming down on the roofs was louder. It sneezed onto Clayvon about six or eight times I think, and then Trig clicked it and went to put in another clip.

So I ducked back around the Dumpster and headed for the car cause I needed to get back there before Trig ever known I left. My wet foot felt so off beat with my dry one I thought about stepping in the gutter again on purpose so at least they would match.

Not as long as a minute to get rid of a person. He made it look easy. But you know it ain't.

4

"WHERE'S CLAYVON?" Devlin finally said, after three days of his absence from the school. No answer. He studied the faces arrayed before him in the room, all smoothed blank of any expression, like windblown sand in a desert. Butch swallowed once and that was all. There was a desert silence too.

He had taught them this, so he might have been pleased. And in fact he was satisfied in a way, in some area other than his curiosity. His concern. But maybe the question, answered or not, had touched off something.

Butch and Gyp. Devlin didn't see how it began, didn't see the moment it crossed the line. The first he noticed was Gyp's bleeding lip, then Gyp spun into a reverse turn and cracked a backfist onto Butch's cheekbone—a technique illegal during practice, though Devlin taught them such things for the street. Devlin shouted something that nobody heard and darted toward the center. For a moment it looked like becoming a general melee, but then Trig twisted Gyp out of the action with an armlock and Devlin ran Butch into a corner. That was enough to finish it. Butch had learned enough by now not to risk Devlin hitting him.

Unconsciously Devlin wiped his forehead with his sleeve and walked to the front of the room to call the class to order. Done for the day. He gave Butch and Gyp a hundred pushups, and as the others knelt for the concluding meditation, he saw that the two policemen had slipped into the rear of the room, unnoticed . . . probably during the brawl. That thought robbed Devlin of any words of wisdom he might have had to say.

Curtis and Spencer—Devlin remembered their names now, though he didn't remember which went with which. Black mustache strummed a rolled newspaper against his thigh, while sandy hair twiddled an unlit cigarette with a certain ostentation. Devlin dismissed the class and reluctantly invited the officers into the back.

"Business good?" said black mustache. "I mean, like, the karate business."

"Tae Kwon Do," Devlin said. "It's fair."

"Seen the paper?" said sandy hair.

Devlin shrugged. "I expect I'm going to see it again."

Sandy hair nodded and black mustache sat down at the card table, unfurling the front page of the local section. Devlin, who remained standing, looked at the date first—it was yesterday's, but it all looked unfamiliar. He must have skipped to the funny pages.

"You know the guy," said black mustache, and now Devlin looked at the three-column photo: a body tossed against the side of a Dumpster in the alley behind the Parrot, behind a sagging crime-scene tape. There was no face to recognize, just a jawbone thrown back.

"Not much of a likeness," Devlin said.

Black mustache thumbed his forefinger on a name circled in the text: Clayvon Lipscomb, age nineteen. Bruises, contusions, multiple gunshot wounds . . . Devlin scanned a little farther: the deaths of Lincoln Hearon and Odell Washington were also mentioned and there was some speculation about an incipient gang war, perhaps caused by a dispute over drug territory.

"Now this guy," said sandy hair, "this guy was about half beaten to death at the same time he was shot. Somebody was really wailing on him, you know?"

Devlin didn't know. He rocked on his feet, looking at the picture. Clayvon. Sandy hair stuck the cigarette still unlit into the corner of his mouth.

"So we wondered," black mustache said, "if this could have anything to do with your . . . activities."

"I didn't do it," Devlin said.

"Come on, Doc," said sandy hair. "Look what we got—two guys shot in the same exact spot and both of them come from two different sets and both of them also come to this operation you got here. And Odell Washington went here too, which we know because we saw his sorry ass the last time we stopped by."

"What are you saying?" Devlin said.

Black mustache looked up at him. "We're thinking maybe you're not exactly pacifying this situation, Doc." He seemed proud of that word . . . *pacifying.*

"Suggestions?" Devlin said.

"Shut up shop," sandy hair said. "You're just confusing things down here anyway. Clear out before it gets any worse."

"I don't think so," Devlin said.

Sandy hair sighed profoundly and shifted his feet, looking down at the cigarette which was now in his hand again. "Buddy," he said, "you are in the middle of a problem here. Whether you want to see it or not."

"Yes," Devlin said, "I'll take care of it."

Black mustache shook his head and stood up, leaving the paper where it lay. Sandy hair stuck his cigarette in his mouth again and took a lighter from his pocket. "Relax, I'm not gonna light it in here," he said to Devlin. "*I* wouldn't die for a cigarette."

THE SCHOOL HAD emptied out by the time Devlin came from the back room. No after-class lesson because Trig and Kool-whip were already gone—shunning the cops, possibly. Michelle had left too. Padding barefoot across the matted floor, Devlin noticed for the first time that one of the mirrors was cracked. Probably someone had been slammed against it during the brawl. He stood and faced his cracked reflection, shifting his weight so that the ill-matched halves of his face and body sawed and fretted against each other.

Daylight was lingering on the street when he came out and locked up; the days were gradually growing longer. He climbed into his car and drove, turning downtown instead of toward home. An aimless choice; his mind was blank and he could not bring it to bear on the situation the police had meant to rub his nose in. It would come home to him, he knew that, but as long as his car kept drifting through the downtown traffic the moment could be deferred.

A block or so north of the harbor, he passed a green Corolla parked on a side street, and reflexively checked it in the mirror when he had gone by. The string of license-plate characters reversed on the mirror glass—it *was* Michelle's car. He had turned another corner before he stopped his own car and got out.

It was dark now, and Devlin walked from pool to pool of streetlight, zipping his jacket and tucking his head against the wind. His wife's voice chimed inside his head: *Don't be a cop, Mike.* For the moment that seemed very good advice, and he stopped on the corner, foot raised to turn back, but then the image from the newspaper appeared to him, where the cops had left it spread on the card table in his makeshift office. It now seemed to him that if he returned to the car he would find Clayvon's blood-drained body sprawled across the back seat.

On the opposite side of the street was parked a low-slung black car. Devlin tightened at the sight of it, then made himself relax with a long forced exhalation and an effort of will. It was the Camaro—he had been thinking of the Camaro—but this was a fancy black Lexus instead, and little resemblance between them apart from the color. Through the rear glass of the Lexus, Devlin thought he saw two heads joined across the gap between the front seats, but when he got closer it seemed to have been a trick of the uneven light, for the car's interior was empty.

He put his hands in his pockets and looked over the roof of the Lexus, past Michelle's car to the opposite side of the street. There were a couple of shops there, and a deli-style lunch place, but all these were already shuttered for the night. At the corner was the awning of a second-class hotel, and between the awning and Michelle's car stood a couple twined in a luxurious lover's embrace. Devlin felt a twitch of middle-aged envy, watching them. They held the kiss for a long, rapt time, before they separated and began to walk toward Devlin, swinging their locked hands together. They stepped into a globe of streetlight, and then he saw their faces.

He was halfway across the street before they noticed him, registering him first as undifferentiated threat, a fast-moving something headed their way. Michelle let go of Trig's hand and slipped toward the wall, away from the light, while Trig made a half-turn toward the street and paused with his hands loosely rising. Devlin stopped short of the curb and flipped back the hood of his sweatshirt. If Trig was surprised to recognize him he showed it only by the tightening of a muscle in his jaw.

"Dad . . ." Michelle stepped forward into the light, swinging her hair back.

Devlin looked at her. "Seems like your allergies are clearing up," he said, and regretted it instantly.

"Well, what the hell did you expect?" Michelle burst out. "After you drive everybody else away—nobody I know anymore's got the nerve to even park in front of the house."

Devlin swallowed and put his hands in his pockets again, feeling a band of tension clenching his neck and shoulders.

"Anyway, you practically set us *up!*" Michelle glanced briefly at Trig, who was watching Devlin. "You get me all involved in—you *wanted* me to be. What do you expect me to do, anyway?"

"I didn't say anything," Devlin said.

"You didn't have to." Michelle slammed into her car and fired down the street with her tires squalling.

Devlin didn't turn his head to follow her because he was still watching Trig, thinking of things he knew that he hadn't taught Trig yet. His position wasn't very good because he was standing in the street, a full step down from Trig on the sidewalk, but if he faked Trig into coming forward, Trig might stumble on the curb . . .

"Relax," Devlin said. "I'm not going to jump you."

"All right." Trig let down, just perceptibly; his large brown hands moved in the yellow light ambiguously, like fish. *Now,* Devlin thought, now was the chance—

"Take a walk?" Trig said, looking at him sidelong.

"Sure," said Devlin.

He stepped up onto the curb and fell into step beside Trig, who dipped into the side pocket of his fringed jacket and took out cigarettes and a lighter. It was *now* again, an even better opportunity, but Devlin didn't want to anymore; maybe he never had. Trig exhaled menthol smoke and dropped the lighter back into his pocket and stepped out toward the harbor with the cigarette's coal glowing at the corner of his mouth. Devlin went with him, taking quicker steps to match Trig's longer stride.

It was windy and sharply cold along the wide, brick esplanades of the harborfront mall, and people scurried past with their heads bowed under the wind, hurrying for the enclosed shops and the restaurants. A garbage boat growled and snuffled along the concrete piers, gates clasping and unclasping to gather debris onto the metal belt that conveyed it up from the water and dropped it into the hull.

"What do you think of me?" Trig said.

"Inside the school," Devlin said, "you're as good as they come."

"All right," Trig said. "We outside now."

"I don't know so much about what goes on outside," Devlin said.

Trig glanced at him, pulled on his cigarette, shot a column of smoke from the side of his mouth, away from Devlin.

"They say you sell drugs," Devlin said. "You carry guns, you and all your crowd. People are dropping dead all around you. Of nonnatural causes, I've noticed that."

"All right," Trig said. He was leading them down past the lightship and the submarine, toward the dark bulk of the aquarium.

"Why do you ask?" Devlin said. "Are you working up to a marriage proposal?"

Trig stopped by the ticket booth and called for two.

"You aren't gonna have much time in there," the ticket man said. "It's almost closing."

"That's all right," Trig said, and turned toward Devlin. "I just want to show you one thing."

They rode the escalator to the top of the building, then Trig led the way down the spiraling ramp. There were only a few tourists still poking their way down through the shark tank, and Trig steered Devlin away from them, into a side gallery where bright fish swam in small, illuminated dioramas in the wall. They stopped in front of a Plexiglas cube that stood on a chest-high pedestal, like a sculpture of some kind.

"There," Trig said. "Check it out."

What it looked like was a cube of swamp: driftwood and stone and algae and moss, with a few minnows circulating through it. Near the edge of the glass a small, wormlike something wriggled alluringly inside what seemed to be a cleft of rock.

"There," Trig said. "That's me."

Devlin stared into the tank, not comprehending, until after a moment his eyes resolved what he saw there. What looked very much like a big driftwood snag was mostly made out of snapping turtle, its beaked jaws stretched wide and pressed against the inner glass. That squirming, wormlike thing was actually a filament of the turtle's tongue.

"See, he don't do nothing," Trig said. "He don't ask no questions, he don't make no pitch. He don't go looking for nobody. If somebody come along and think that thing look good in there, well, that's them." Trig snapped his fingers against his palm, the sound of one hand clapping.

The longer Devlin looked into the case, the more of the turtle became apparent to him. The snapper itself was strung all over with algae and moss, which made its turtle contour hard to read and made it more resemble a lump of decaying underwater wood. It possessed an enviable stillness; nothing of it moved at all except the lure of its tongue. The webbed claws were spread obscurely on the still surface of the water, motionless. The open eyes were small and tiger-striped with spokes of black and cat-yellow, more like bright sunken shells than living eyes returning Devlin's look.

"You understand why they still turtles, yo?"

"What?" Devlin said. He saw Trig's face uncertainly reflected from the case, superimposed on the still form of the turtle.

"Them dudes, they crawl up on the beach and lay they eggs, right? Dig a hole in the sand and cover'm up, then they scoot back in the ocean"—Trig whistled softly—"they gone. Ain't coming back. Then, if nothing get the eggs, the little turtles hatch out all by theyself and they ain't no bigger'n that." Trig displayed his large thumbnail. "They start making it down the beach to the water. They got to figure out which way to go, don't get no help from nobody. And hawks eats'm and bears and wolves and snakes eats'm, and then if they make it in the water, it's crabs and big fishes and sharks and everthing eats'm, and even big turtles'll eat'm too. So how is they any more turtles left, yo?"

"You don't need that many," Devlin said quietly. "Not so many to get through."

Trig had scrambled snappers and sea turtles, for one thing, but in principle it still made a kind of sense. During his West Virginia boyhood Devlin had sometimes caught snappers in ponds or streams, and he knew that if you picked up a snapper by its tail, it couldn't turn to bite you (if you held on tight). Or if you offered it a good stick you could lift it that way once it took hold, because when a snapping turtle once got hold of something it wouldn't let go till it thundered. So they say. Devlin realized that Trig had probably never seen a turtle outside of the aquarium or programs on TV. "Maybe just one," he said.

"Right," said Trig, in a tone that suggested he was still surprised by this answer even though he had been leading Devlin toward it all along.

"They say you kill people," Devlin said to Trig's reflection.

"Yo," Trig said softly. "I might if they was trying to kill me."

DEVLIN WAS barely able to feel relief at seeing the Corolla parked in the driveway when he got home. He was late, quite late, and had certainly missed dinner. The kitchen was dark except for a small shaft of light above the sink, and a red dot that glared at him from the oven's control panel, like the turtle's faintly luminescent eye.

Alice was sitting in the living room when he went in, reading a paperback novel. She looked up when Devlin entered, but without great curiosity.

"Sorry I'm late," Devlin began. "I had an emergency call, and there wasn't time—" He ratcheted back through the mental roster of his patients, but he lacked the energy to elaborate the excuse much further, and the truth was that Alice didn't seem very interested in hearing any more of it anyway.

"I left something for you in the oven," Alice said.

"Thanks," Devlin said.

Alice went back to her book. Devlin sat down on the sofa, which seemed rather far, across a fairway of expensive carpet, from the armchair where she sat. The reading lamp softened the contours of her face, and although a thready line or two appeared around her throat, she was still very pretty. Still. She turned a page of her book and then looked up at him, her expression only neutral.

"What?" she said.

Devlin swallowed. There was, he supposed, the interesting situation of their daughter, but he could think of no way to raise this subject. His mind scraped over it without finding a purchase—like scrabbling to dislodge a rock that didn't have an edge. The surface of his secret life was polished and unbreachable, and now it seemed he'd gone so far inside it, he couldn't get back out. Too late—as Alice had screamed at him after he trashed the black Camaro. If he'd become a stranger in the house, it was his own doing.

"Nothing," he said. "Nothing at all."

He pushed himself up from the sofa and went into the kitchen and ate his supper, without much tasting it. When he had finished he washed the dishes, took out the trash, hung his Tae Kwon Do uniform out to air for the next day. The living room was dark when he passed through it; Alice had apparently gone up to bed.

Devlin checked the door locks and the downstairs windows, then climbed the steps with reflexive stealth. A blade of light outlined the lower edge of Michelle's door. He knocked lightly and at the answering murmur pushed it inward.

Michelle reclined on a mound of pillows and cushions at the far end of her bed, which looked too small for her somehow, or she too large for it. She was framed by an oversized floppy stuffed lion on one side and an oversized shaggy unidentifiable something on the other. A magazine was unfolded on her lap but she didn't really seem to be reading it.

Devlin held the door open an inch and listened for some sign of Alice's whereabouts, but heard nothing. He pushed the door into the frame until he heard the latch click shut.

"So?" Michelle said.

Devlin shrugged and moved toward the bed. Michelle drew up her blue-jeaned legs to make room for him to sit.

"Did you tell Mom?" Michelle said.

"No," Devlin said. The corner of the bed gave down under his weight. "Did you?"

Michelle gave a weak smile, tossing her hair back and looking at the ceiling. An old poster was tacked up there of an actor bestriding a motorcycle; one of the tacks had fallen out so a corner of the poster dangled.

"You want me to stop seeing him," Michelle said.

Devlin opened his mouth, but no words came out.

"Is it because he's black?"

"Oh, give me a break," Devlin said. "You know better than that." The flick of irritation freed his tongue. "He deals drugs, he carries a gun—where do you think that car came from? The clothes? He's already got a kid. Whose mother's dead. Shot dead. You're going to college in the fall—I hope. Trig is not exactly college material."

"He's very intelligent," Michelle said.

"Sure," said Devlin. "I can see that."

"You know all this stuff—it doesn't stop *you* being his friend."

Friend? Devlin didn't say anything. He had not exactly thought of Trig as his *friend,* but to deny the term seemed a dishonest quibble.

"Go on, tell me it's different with me," Michelle said. "Go ahead and say it."

"Well," Devlin said, "why is it you haven't brought him home to meet your mother?"

This low blow was enough of a success that Michelle flinched and turned her face toward the wall. Devlin swallowed and put his hand on her knee. When she was born, his two palms could have covered almost all of her. Now he found her tense against the gesture, or maybe it was him; he took his hand away and put it on the coverlet.

"Shell," he said, "I—" He meant to say that he had not intended to frighten away her other suitors, but then he didn't know if that was really true.

"I want you happy," he said. "And I want you alive."

Michelle looked at him, her eyes filmed over.

"Would you give it some thought?" Devlin patted her knee and got up and left the room.

He undressed quietly in the dark, laying his clothes across the bureau. The bedroom radiator clanked and hissed as he slid under the covers. From the quality of Alice's stillness he knew that she was not asleep, and after a moment he reached across and took her hand. He was grateful when his pressure was returned. Alice's hand was smaller than his, and lightly callused—Devlin wondered why this should be so, since neither of them did much manual work. It seemed a friendly hand, and it anchored him for the few minutes they lay linked so, not turning further toward each other.

Presently, Alice disengaged her fingers and turned to the other side. Her breathing lengthened into sleep. Cut loose, Devlin experienced free fall. He tried to stabilize himself by counting turtles, new-hatched turtles filing neatly into the sea, but their progress was interrupted by so many predators, Trig's impossible bears and wolves . . . Then the turtles were dream turtles, each one bigger than the one before, and the last and largest of them all seemed to wear the ancient, wizened face of Irene Packer.

DEVLIN DIDN'T ATTEND Clayvon's funeral, but his Eager Street students all went, and they never came back.

Their absence cut the school in half. Michelle had stopped attending too, so that Trig now stood in the senior position at the upper right-hand corner of the class formation, making the various ritual pronouncements that were assigned to the top student at the beginning and end of each session. Every time Devlin watched Trig performing those functions he thought of asking him where Michelle was spending these hours now. A funny idea, in its own bleak way, but he didn't put it into practice.

Class now took place with a cold sobriety, no loose talk, no conversation whatsoever. Froggy no longer came with his minders, and the Eager Street girls had disappeared with their men. No one seemed to be dropping into the Parrot after practice. The Poe Homes contingent came and went in a tight block, the two women in the center and the men with hands in their belly pockets, watching all directions on the street as they passed the door.

Devlin let it ride for a week, then left them kneeling after a closing meditation. He knelt himself, sitting on his heels, facing them.

"We've been missing a few people," Devlin said. "I wonder where they went?"

There was no answer, none at first. Devlin didn't search their faces. He kept his head bowed, studying a crack between a pair of the vinyl mats; the crack was unremarkable.

"Candyman's back."

It was Trig's voice, but when Devlin looked Trig was mute. He seemed to be carved from some dark glossy wood, his eyes half-lidded and downcast, his body still. Devlin waited but nobody added anything to this remark. Finally he stood up and dismissed the class. Without invitation,

Trig followed him toward the room in the back, and so did Gyp and Mud-dog.

"Lonely around here lately," Devlin said, and sat down in one of the folding chairs beside the card table. "Don't you think?" He turned the newspaper around on the table so they could read it if they wanted to. The paper had lain there untouched since the visit of the cops, its edges curling. Of the three of them, only Mud-dog reacted visibly, shuffling his feet. Mud-dog was slightly older than the others and seemed somewhat less brash, less confident. He was missing some top front teeth and, though he normally wore a bridge, he always took it out for practice—maybe that's what made him seem comparatively shy.

"Gentlemen," Devlin said, "the cat has got your tongue."

He looked through the Plexiglas pane to the practice floor. Tamara was sitting on the mats, doing the butterfly stretch, while Sharmane cooled down with a slow set of crescent kicks in front of the cracked mirror. Mud-dog shuffled his feet again and clicked his tongue against his palate. Devlin brought his gaze back within the space of the little room.

"Cops think you've got a gang war going," he said. "What's the deal?"

Trig smiled without pleasure. "We keeping it on the outside, like you say."

"Is that right?" Devlin stood up, as none of the others had seated themselves. "That approach doesn't really seem to be working so well anymore."

No one spoke; Gyp, Trig, and Mud-dog all looked into different corners of the room.

"So who's Candyman?" Devlin said. "Where'd he come back *from?*"

"Brooklyn," Gyp said. "Candyman run that Eager Street crew, he the one start all this sh—this trouble."

"It was that Freon, yo," Mud-dog said. "Hadn'tna been for him—"

"Quiet," Trig said. "Let me tell it."

Devlin waited, the others were silent. On the practice floor, Sharmane changed up and began sweeping slow, in-to-out crescent kicks with her other leg.

"Jaynette was a accident," Trig said. He shaded his eyes briefly. Devlin thought he could feel the wave of weariness pass over him and recede.

"Froggy's mama, you didn't know her," Trig went on. "She got herself shot by accident, just taking a walk. You might remember it was on the news a lot. Candyman trying to pop one his own guys over something and he miss and hit Jaynette. Then with all the hassle he was . . . Candyman went and laid up in Brooklyn, cause he got his connection there or something, I don't know."

"Then Freon—" Mud-dog said.

"I'll tell it," Trig said. "Yeah, Freon, he shot one Candyman dudes to get back for Jaynette. What he thought. Then one of them shot D-Trak, I think. One of them shot Freon. And then . . ." Trig stopped and inspected the yellowed surface of the Plexiglas.

"Then somebody shot Clayvon," Devlin said. "Does that make it their turn, or what?"

"Don't know about that," Trig said. "Look to me like they got more guys left then we do."

"But all their guys have disappeared," Devlin said.

"From here," Trig said. "That's Candyman. He the one took'm outa here, yo. I know him. Now he back, he don't want them out from under his hand."

"Terrific," Devlin said. "Now what?"

Trig shrugged, looking absently at the Plexiglas. Tamara had left the floor a few minutes before and now returned in her street clothes. She stopped to inspect herself in the row of mirrors, beside Sharmane, who was still doing stretch kicks, cooling off.

"Listen," Devlin said, "do you think I brought you all in here just to teach you better ways to kill each other? You were supposed to learn something else than that. It's not supposed to be *us and them.* It's supposed to be just *us.* When you train with people, they become your family. Your brothers. Sisters. You take care of each other. You quit fighting each other. This place is a sanctuary that you share. If I meant to teach you anything, it was that. Next to that, what you can do with your body doesn't matter."

"Ain't your fault, Devlin," Trig said. "You done what you could."

Devlin could not have imagined anything more embittering, though he thought that Trig wouldn't have meant it that way. For a moment he had difficulty speaking.

"A lady came by to see me the other day," he said. "Miz Packer—she's your grandmother, is that right?"

"All right," Trig said. "I seen her in here."

"She wanted to know if I could stop all this trouble," Devlin said. "She seemed to think it was up to me."

"Well, it ain't," Trig said. "Ain't a lot you can do."

"Maybe not," Devlin said. "But *you* can do something."

"Beyond what we been doing?" Trig said. "I don't see it."

"You can clean your own house," Devlin said. "Put your guns down."

The others watched him with mild curiosity. He spread his open palms before them.

"Empty hand." Adrenaline began to jump in his veins as he listened to himself. "*That's* the point. You ought not to be needing guns by this time."

"You saying we spose to go over there and whack'm with Tae Kwon Do?" Mud-dog said.

"I'm saying, go over there empty-handed and show you don't mean any harm," Devlin said. "You all know each other. You train together. From what you just told me, it was all a misunderstanding straight from the start. Think there's enough people dead already? If you talk to them, you can probably work it out. You know, it might not be easy, but it's not impossible."

Trig and Mud-dog and Gyp all looked at each other.

"You've been here quite a while now," Devlin said. "You know what's right."

All three of them looked at Devlin, who picked up the curling newspaper from the table, folded it over once, and slapped it into a plastic wastebasket.

"The time does come," Devlin said. "Are you going to do what you know is right, or are you going to just wish you were?"

OVER THE NEXT FEW DAYS, Devlin seemed to drift in a cloud of supercharged intention. For once, his private practice seemed to take care of itself, not mechanically, but without apparent effort on his part. Without strain. His failure to do what he thought was enough for his patients did not torment him they way it often had of late. At home, Michelle seemed to be avoiding him again, and Alice was reserved and distant, as she had been for quite some time, but the ghostliness of Devlin's home life no longer bothered him. It seemed to him inevitable that ordinary life must go pale beside the sparkling thrill of what they were expecting.

That Devlin would actually go along on the venture was not a foregone conclusion, it turned out. There were arguments.

"Ain't your problem," Trig said. "I'd say you need to stay out of it."

"My idea, though," Devlin said. "So how can I send you into it and me stay behind?"

"Yo," Trig said, "you expecting me to take Gramma Reen along too?"

Devlin laughed. "They're not her students," he said.

So finally Trig gave up. Devlin asked himself what the Korean masters would have done in his place and answered they never would have let themselves *get* into his place . . . but he no longer cared.

They'd set the approach for Saturday, after the noon class. It was Trig's theory that around midday the opposite parties would less likely be drinking or doped up. Practice as usual on Saturday morning, everything normal except for the size of the class. Tamara and Sharmane didn't show (Devlin assumed Trig would have told them to stay away), so Devlin was down to just three students, the number he'd had the first day he opened the place. He saw a certain symmetry in that.

Symmetry was what it was all about, Devlin explained that day. A light workout would do it, he'd decided, so after basics they worked slowly for the rest of the hour on the fine points of their forms. Devlin put Mud-dog and Gyp through their rudimentary paces, several times at different speeds with different goals. Try it as fast as you possibly can, all speed, no power. Then muscle your way through every move—high tension. Then do it just completely relaxed, fluid as a swimmer. Imagine yourself swimming in the air, so that your body has no weight. Then maybe you begin to feel how every movement that you make is balanced by another, Devlin said. When Mud-dog and Gyp were finished with what they knew, he went through the higher-level forms in unison with Trig, to demonstrate. It's the balance of the steps you take and the moves you make, Devlin explained, that creates a balance inside of you, an inner order that runs like a gyroscope—you can carry it with you everywhere you go.

Nothing strenuous today, no sparring. They meditated and left the floor quietly, and Devlin went to the dressing room with the others instead of waiting for them all to finish and leave as he usually did. He could tell from the absence of weights and sags as they lifted their street clothes that they really had come without their guns today.

Outdoors it was surprisingly sunny, almost warm. Devlin left the front of his jacket unzipped; he hardly needed the sweatshirt underneath it, but he kept the hood turned up to make himself less conspicuous, as always. The scraggly cherry trees standing in islands of mud down the center of Broadway had just begun to bud, and the breeze felt fresh and flavorful, like spring.

Walking distance, Trig had said. They turned north on Broadway, into the light, friendly wind that inflated Devlin's hood but didn't chill his face. He felt a sort of effervescent urge to chatter, but no one spoke, and he held it in.

Two blocks north they turned into a side street and walked west. This was the block, Trig had said, and now Devlin began to notice the expensive, late-model cars with curlicue antennas, parked along the curb—likely sign of a drug enclave. On the opposite side of the street somebody was just getting out of a maroon BMW. Kool-whip. And from the driver's seat came Butch.

"Yo!" Was it Gyp who'd called to them, or Trig? Devlin thought he saw Kool-whip's hand go to a pocket, but Kool-whip had stepped onto the sidewalk behind another car, so that now he was visible only from the chest up. Butch had also quickly moved to the far side of the BMW. Someone else was getting out of the front passenger door—green field jacket, close-cropped hair.

"Yo, brotherman . . ." Gyp stepped between two parked cars into the street. "We wondering where you been keeping yo-self."

They were straggling apart now, and Devlin didn't like that. They had walked this far in a tight compact group, but now Gyp was alone out in front and Mud-dog was definitely lagging well behind—their positions might look suspicious to the others across the way. Devlin moved out into the street, closer to Gyp, and felt Trig coming up behind him. The man in the field jacket had straightened up, facing them. Reddish hair and the pockmarked face.

"Yo, Candyman," Trig called. "It cool—we just come up to talk."

Devlin saw Dutch and Kool-whip let down a little as they exchanged a glance with one another, and with a flash of something, relief maybe, he thought, *We're in.* The breeze jumped up, blowing loose scraps of newspaper from the gutter; a dented malt liquor can turned over loudly on the pavement. Gyp was in the middle of the street.

"Cee-man, we ain't carrying, yo," Gyp said. He raised his empty hands and seemed to smile.

"That's funny," Candyman said. "Don't you know it's a war?"

Candyman fired two times and Gyp took two steps backward and sat down gently against the door of a parked car, arranging his hands delicately across his chest. Symmetry. Devlin hadn't seen the draw but now Candyman shifted the gun to cover him, and he saw the gun's dark eye, and Candyman's eyes the same way he had seen them when the girl was shot. Jaynette. He saw Candyman's strange hesitation but he himself wasn't able to move either. Then somebody pulled his leg out from under him and he was lying next to Trig underneath another car.

From around the wheel he lay behind, Devlin watched Gyp slowly, slowly leaning over, then stretching himself facedown in an expanding pool of blood. Whine of a couple of ricochets, shriek of a child or a woman from an apartment somewhere above the street. Devlin rolled over toward the curb. Trig was up and crouching on the sidewalk, while Mud-dog, bent low, scuttled toward the corner that they'd come from.

"Yo, Devlin," Trig hissed at him, his face contorted. "Next time you get a smart idea, whyn't you keep it to yo-self?"

3

SHARMANE

BLUE TIMES for a good while, after Freon got dusted. Never did see Tamara so low. She sleepwalking through her days, won't look at you, and dead eyes if she do. You couldn't talk to her about it. She had took it all to herself. Didn't see much of her noway cause she be mostly hanging somewhere else. I got to worry was she doing some serious dosing.

Then one day up she shown again thumping on the door like she used, and when I unlock she look like herself again, my homegirl Tamara. Funny thing is, what she want to do is cooking. You know, cooking nothing I never much wanted to know about, and Tamara neither one. Cause I rather just be cruising into some restaurant, pick up Chinese . . . even Mickey-D cook better than I do most days.

Why you want to sweat for an hour just to get a biscuit? And then you still got the dishes to wash. But today, if she want to, I'ma do it.

Tamara start working on me all about Gramma Reen gumbo. That Nawlins recipe she ain't made in a long time. Been a while Gramma Reen ain't felt like cooking like she use to. Knees got the arthritis and hips hurt her too much to be standing there in front of the stove. "My hands don't do right neither," she say. And mostly she just sit by the TV. I kept the place clean, I do that much. But cook . . . I rather bring in that carryout. Frozen dinners. Wasn't nothing like that when we coming up as kids. Gramma Reen she cook from scratch, and they wasn't no money to buy that other type of shit noway. Now with the money Trig always throw us we could get whatever. Trig give us a microwave too, which Gramma Reen say she despised it, but she eat out of it just the same.

That gumbo, couldn't carry that out from nowhere, wasn't no restaurant in town could make it neither. "And can't you just smell it?" Tamara say. "That good smell run right down the back of yo throat. Girl, you *know* you gonna want to fix yourself some of that one of these days. Wait too long and you ain't gonna have nobody you can ask how you spose to do it."

And that be enough to get me going. Cause they still mornings I wake up with some little thing in my head to ask Jaynette. Some nothing just she and me would of known about. And till I get the sleep shook out my head I couldn't remember Jaynette not coming around to answer no more questions.

So I put it up to Gramma Reen and I got her to say she

show me the moves if I go and buy what she needed. Which I known I would do it anyway. Gramma Reen been sticking close by the house almost since that trip we made to Devlin's school. Not even going to church like she use. The church ladies sometime come and have a meeting there in the front room at our house. Or Gramma Reen watch the church on the TV.

It boosted her up when I ask about that gumbo. She made me beg her some, but I could see her smiling. Not smiling to me but back down the years of her memories.

Then she gimme a list as long as your arm and we head over to Lexington Market to get it filled, me'n Froggy and Tamara. I drug Tamara along with us cause it was her started the whole thing anyway and I needed some help with Froggy. He could walk pretty good by this time and he didn't like to stay in the stroller and sometime he run away from you if he was out. Funny to see him try'n run. Trig bought him new clothes at Christmas—I bought'm with Trig money, that was. Little red coat with gold buttons and red rubber boots and a stripe knitted hat with a pointy top and a little woolly ball hanging off by a string of yarn. And Froggy would strut around in that stuff like he think he just the coolest.

It was a Saturday we went to the market, and not quite as cold as it had been. So we just walked on over there instead of catching a ride or taking the bus—wasn't all that far noway. We went around all the little booths inside the building, bought up the shrimp and the fish and the sausage and celery and onions and okra, plus about five kind of ground pepper Gramma Reen say we got to have. When we done, we got cups of draft beer and a box of chicken livers and carried it to a table upstairs to eat it. Bought Froggy a big old sticky donut and laughed to see him rubbing the chocolate on his face.

Then back at the house me'n Tamara just chopping—you got to chop for hours to make this thing—clean shrimp and bone fish and slice sausage and okra. Gramma Reen not doing no work but she walk in the kitchen and check to see we doing like she want it done. She had turn off the TV and start telling stories about old times with her Nawlins friend the gumbo come from, and even drank a little jelly glass from the forty of Colt 45 me'n Tamara pulling on to keep us happy doing all this work. Froggy trolling all around the kitchen floor and us just trying not to step on him and I got a little bit of a beer buzz going from the afternoon so I feeling fine.

Time then to make the roux in Gramma Reen's old thirty-pound iron skillet she cook cornbread in cause she say we can't use nothing else for that job, which she say the most important part. Spose to cook flour in butter till it turn black, only you ain't spose to burn it, which I didn't understand how they expect you to know the difference. By when everthing was chopped and I had everthing laid out by the skillet, turn around to ask what we do next and Gramma Reen gone to sleep.

Two little jelly glasses of beer did that. Or maybe not. She been taking naps anyhow this last few weeks, sometime in the afternoon. And she look so small, curl up in that stuff chair, head laying on the arm and a sweet little snore like a kitten.

I didn't want to wake her up. Me'n Tamara thought we just keep going. Sun going down through the kitchen window and you know we be hungry time we get done. I melted down that butter and thrown in the flour and stir as hard as I knew how to do it, cause skillet was hot. My hand cramping by the time it start to turn color, and sweat on my face from standing over the stove.

"Work that spoon, girlfriend," Tamara say. "I want to see it turn black."

"Like yo ass," I say.

"And don't get no flecks," Tamara say. "You hear what she say about flecks."

"I'll fleck you one," I say.

Then the doorbell bong and next thing I hear key in the lock so I know it Trig. Hope so, anyway. The shit in the skillet just starting to get a nice red color, like a brick, when Trig and Mud-dog come dragging in the kitchen. Froggy put up his hands so Trig pick him up but Trig ain't paid him no mind. Trig face don't show nothing but you could tell by one look at Mud-dog that something ain't gone right wherever it was they come from. Only I didn't want to hear about it right then cause I didn't plan on messing up that sauce. I kept stirring and stirring in the skillet fast as I can pump my arm. Froggy start fussing so Tamara pick him up. That roux turn chocolate brown and then it turn like bittersweet chocolate so I figure it black enough for me and I pull it off the fire. Give it a few more stirs, while it cool down. It wasn't flecked none neither. Then I could look at Trig . . . he just then took off his wraparounds and was rubbing fingers where the nosepiece pinch him. But I still not gonna ask him what was it.

"Gyp gone down," Trig say. "Candyman shot him."

I stuck my finger in that roux, to taste was it all right

and hadn't burnt, but it did burn *me,* stuck to my finger like glue and kept on cooking. I knocked Trig out of the way rushing the sink to get some cold water on it. Could feel that burn pain to my elbow and glad to feel it too cause it gimme time to think what I needed to. What I thought before—Gyp ain't never gonna be around for no long term. He don't end up dead or back at the Cut, he be gone with some other woman I know. Get you can when you can and that's it—that's me. How a man think, ain't it? And that why Sharmane ain't popped no babies.

I stuck a piece of ice over my finger and I took Froggy out of Tamara's arms and handed him to Trig. "Take care your son," I say to Trig, which he took him in the other room and park him in front of cartoons, is what. I made Tamara get behind that stove and help me finish that gumbo. Cause we hadn't fucked up the gumbo yet and I didn't intend we gonna. And don't be intending to cry in it neither.

But after the cartoons got going Trig come back in the kitchen and we got to listen to the whole dumb-ass story, Trig telling and Mud-dog throwing in a grunt now and then. Now that was where I could of cried—Trig going for something like that, or Gyp either one. Devlin rules work good inside of the school where it all agreed on in advance or else, but you get it on the street it don't mean nothing no more. Cept maybe for Devlin himself. Cause Trig told how Candyman held the gun on Devlin and didn't shoot before Trig had time to jerk him down. I could of asked him, yo, could you of reached Gyp instead? But what did it matter. Gyp already blowed away and I ain't even been there but I could still read the thought right out of Candyman brain—

better not shoot this *white* ma'fucka or the heat gonna be all over my ass for sure.

Then Gramma Reen finally did wake up and Trig got to shut up then cause she won't stand to listen about no dope dealings. Gumbo was done good by then with the shrimp throwed in last to cook just tender. We all sat down and ate it together, Trig and Mud-dog too. They ate more than you would of thought, coming off a killing. Men is that way, I don't know. It good gumbo how it turn out and smelled like it sposed and I ate me a couple of bowls myself. Live long enough you learn that much, heart might be hurting you but you can still eat.

COUPLE WEEKS after Gyp funeral, we took Froggy to the zoo. Funeral was, you know, about like the rest of'm. Only Devlin didn't show up, which I wouldn't either if I been him.

I been after Trig to do something with Froggy. Do it for Trig as much as for Froggy, cause Trig had been sulled up since that last shooting. Didn't come around our house hardly at all no more. Not going to Devlin school neither—we had all quit, what was left of us. Trig just lay up in his apartment—less he have to be out slanging. Ain't none his crew left but Mud-dog, so Trig got to handle the shit himself which he about had quit doing, before.

Zoo was Trig idea and it all right with me. So long as he come up with something, that all right. Friday morning and a nice clear day—starting to warm up for spring. Even Gramma Reenie got a little green in her that morning. Put on her street shoes and say she going out shopping and up to the bank. When Trig pull up that Lexus he want to take her where she need to go, but today Gramma Reen got enough salt back in her she ain't gonna ride in his car.

So me'n Froggy pile in the Lexus and Trig gun us up into Druid Hill Park, some dope tunes playing on Trig CD and hammering with that big bass speaker in the trunk. White bitches and baby-sitters all giving us the eyeball when we pull up in zoo parking lot, from the noise we making, I spose. Don't like to see niggaz driving no Lexus noway. And I give'm the eye right back—the Tae Kwon Do look we all learn from Devlin, smooth and shiny and hard as a knife.

Zoo time. Sun warm on the back of my neck—not quite enough I took off my jacket. Trig haul out his big G money roll at the gate and buy a year membership without I say nothing about it. They redone the entrance since last I gone up there. Got all these bricks on the floor with people names carved on'm, like a graveyard only I ain't known who none of'm was.

Froggy laughing and clapping his hands. He want to get out of the stroller and scramble. We going along, me pushing the empty stroller, looking at bears and cats and some kind of long-tail hairy-ass monkeys in the old iron cages by the front. Hyenas what it was Froggy like so well before. Trig and I thought they was funny too—Trig say hyenas is like God trying to make dogs and fuck it up. Hyenas gone, though, time we get to where they spose to be at. That round cage all empty, sawdust and dog shit all swept out. Only here by the cage is Michelle White Bitch Devlin, all smiling and acting surprised like it some kind of accident she just happen to run into us here.

Trig and her kinda reach for each other fingers but then

they check me and stop. Like they thinking I somehow ain't on to they shit. Then Michelle toss back her long shiny Miss Natural White Bitch hair and give me a straight look in the eye, only I put on my shades so I hope it bounce right back in her face.

"Sharmane," she say, "I'm sorry about Gyp."

Now where was she coming from with that shit? Michelle ain't got much way to know I hanging with Gyp—mean Trig been talking my business to her, which I blamed on her. Could of slapped her face right then, I could of. Course she mighta raise up her little Tae Kwon Do foot and kicked my head down into the duck pond cept I didn't think she'd do it. I looked at her eyes and I seen she didn't even know herself Devlin had went and got Gyp killed with some more of his eastern philosophy bullshit. Don't know what Trig did tell her but I could see he ain't told her that. Michelle didn't mean no harm, no more than Devlin. They done it, but they didn't mean it. Ain't no excuse and don't make no difference. But seem like I couldn't hate her as hard as I wanted to.

Then Michelle sorta wrap her arm around my shoulder. And I sorta let it stay there. Just a second or two before I shake it off. I might of give her a little squeeze back.

Then we go ahead and look at the rest of the zoo and shit. Ate some hotdogs, took Froggy on the merry-go-round and the train. We might of stayed there two or three hours. Till Froggy got tired and acting up a little.

Michelle want to lift Froggy into the car. "Oh," she say, when she pick him up from the stroller, "you got so heavy." He grown a good deal since she seen him last, cause she quit coming around Devlin school before we did. And he heavy too, for real. Like was more of him pressed in the same space it needs for somebody else. Darker than Trig or Jaynette either one, and that heavy and thick, like his bones was the stone bones of dinosaurs.

I let Michelle put him in the car this time. Then when we leaving I see her pass a look with Trig so I know they meaning to hook up later. Didn't bother me so much though, like it might of another day. Michelle so sweet with Froggy, like it was something natural between them. That one thing I could like about her, she didn't just only want the man all by himself.

Trig drove us back to the house then. Michelle had got in her own car and went off wherever. Trig pull up the Lexus in front of Poe Homes. I was bent over pulling out the stroller and lifting out Froggy and digging on the floor for some little plastic zebras and monkeys Trig buy him at the gift shop. So I ain't see it, not at first.

"Shit goddamn," Trig say, like he just breathe it out. Not loud at all but I dropped the toys on the car seat and turn around.

Nothing to see, only the door to our house open like it never was. Not open more than half a foot. You couldn't see inside it but they was trouble and death just curling around the edge of the crack like smoke.

Trig go up the steps like a tiger hopping on a rock in the zoo, big and muscley but not making no sound. He gimme a wave to stay back when he go in, but I just sling Froggy back in the car and I slam the locks and follow in after him.

Front room like normal, don't see nothing wrong. TV still there, and the stereo. Gramma Reen white china praying hands knock off a table but they land on the carpet and ain't even broke—I didn't find them till later noway. Didn't see Trig and didn't hear nothing. Start to call him but I stop myself. Tap dripping in the kitchen sink and that was all. I cross the room tiptoe and just peep in there.

First thing I see it Trig coming in the other kitchen door, halfway crouch and holding his gun in that two-hand cop grip. Gun barrel aiming right my way so I froze till he see who I is and let it down. Gramma Reen flopped out on the floor between us, Trig by her head and me by her feet.

Never took a dead person for nothing but dead. Trig drop on his knees and listening to her chest and feeling her wrists and holding his fingers under her nose. Wasn't much mark on her that you could see but still I known he wasting his time.

Place wasn't really tore up like you might of thought. Little wire hamper Gramma Reen use to two-wheel her groceries home been dumped across the kitchen door and the sacks spill out. Couple eggs broke and couple more rolling around the floor—sad-looking little brown eggs. Bottle of juice dump out too but it ain't broke. I picked it up and set it on the counter.

Right there by the sink her purse all shook out. All the funny old shit you find in a purse, broke combs and old Kleenex and keys don't open nothing no more. Yellowy plastic accordion job with pictures of me and Trig and Jaynette when we small, plus the one of my gone-missing mama I use to whine to see when I little. They some blood speckles on the plastic and on the counter too. I wipe it off the pictures without thinking much and fold the pictures up to put back in the wallet—old red leather wallet with the finish crack off that she use to hold shut with a rubber band. The cash all gone out of it of course.

"Ma'fucka follow her home from the bank," Trig say. I

didn't say nothing cause I known he was right. We been seeing that deal round here before. And Gramma Reen always draw out a lot when she go to the bank. We try and tell her not to do it but she don't want to listen.

When Trig stand up from the kitchen floor he holding a bloody-looking kitchen knife in his hand. I looked and seen it was ours—only knife we had that would cut. Bought it myself over to the Giant and I remember I washed it that morning with some other dishes from the night before, and stuck it in the drainer.

"Jesus," I say. I wanted to puke. But Trig shake his head.

"Ain't no cut on her," Trig say. "She ain't cut nowhere."

"What you saying?"

Then I seen Trig teeth. He twanged the knife blade by the point.

"What do you know but she got in one lick," he say. "Might be more'n one."

Then Trig lay down the knife and he shovel his arms underneath Gramma Reen and raise her up. Her head rolled back long way too far cause that's where her neck broke, and I reached over to raise it but Trig already catch it in the bend of his elbow. He carry her that way in her bedroom where she already make up the bed like she do ever morning—tight so you can bounce a quarter off the sheet. And laid her down and straighten her legs and pull down her dress where it rucked up. Never seen Trig so gentle. He fold her hands up on her chest and smooth her hair down on the pillow . . . old white hair come loose from the pins she put in it. Then Trig stand up and look at me.

"Where Froggy?"

"In the car."

Trig went by me with that same tiger step, like he was honey pouring out of a jar. Like, you know, I wasn't minding Froggy, but I didn't care. Let him run after Froggy one time. I shut the door to her bedroom, went to the kitchen and start cleaning up. Mop up the broke eggs and put up the whole ones. I put up all the groceries she bought, can beans and dry beans and spaghettis and rice and some hamburger and chicken to freeze, a little sack full of ham hocks. Funny, you think, you gone eat a dead person groceries, but I tell it to Gramma Reen through that shut bedroom door, ever bite I put in my mouth I bless your name. They was blood spots and handprints on the counter by her purse and I didn't know if I ought to wipe that up or not.

"Go on and clean it," Trig say from behind me. "We ain't gone be leaving this lame for the cops."

So I went ahead and scrub down the counter. But that knife . . . I didn't want to touch it. Wasn't nothing special about the knife, just a strip of steel and not even stainless. Gramma Reen would sharpen it up on the edge of a plate. I was just looking at the thing when I hear Froggy talking in her bedroom: "Wee . . . Wee!"

He had push open the door someway and pulled himself up by the cover on the end of the bed. Reaching across and grab the lace of that old lady shoe she always wear when she go out—give that foot a little shake. "Wee" close as Froggy can come to "Reen." He wasn't crying or scared or nothing. Just curious, and a little bit puzzled maybe. How come he couldn't get Wee to wake up.

"Let her rest, Frogman." Trig pick him up. Just that gentle, like before.

Froggy still hanging to Gramma Reen shoelace, floating the dead foot up in the air. He had a big hand for a baby that size. I had to peel his fingers off one by one.

Trig carry him in the front room and I stuck a tape in the box. Bugs Bunny, Disney, I don't know what. Time he get settled, Trig gone to the kitchen, and I follow him back in there. That when I notice the praying hands fell down—I picked them up and put them back on the table. Trig done rinse the blood off that knife and he standing there twanging the tip and looking out the kitchen window over the sink.

I pass by and step in the door to her bedroom. She laying there easy as you please—how it look. Had live a long time, anyway. Didn't just know how old she was herself. Her own gramma born in slavery, so she say. Bet she didn't weigh no more'n a box of Rice Krispies. For just a minute I wish I been the one to pick her up and lay her out.

How they do, they stalk you right to the door from the bank and then once you unlocked they jump right in behind you—nobody don't see what happen that way. She had one good run left in her anyhow, wouldn't of thought it but she did. Must of knocked them praying hands down herself, breaking for the kitchen. Then trip him up with that grocery cart dumped across the kitchen door and snatch that knife out of the drainer where I left it. Dude would get cut where? In the face maybe. Or in the hand, grabbing the knife away. She kept it sharp, on the edge of that plate. I believe he got cut both places maybe. Funny thing to be glad about but I was glad.

"*Now* I'm gonna start killing some these ma'fuckas," Trig say.

I turn around in the door. Trig still snapping that knife blade and looking out the window. All my life long I never seen Trig cry. On the next kitchen window over the way lady had put her out a little geranium on the sill.

"Wasn't more'n one did this." I say.

"Shit, ain't what I'm talking about," Trig say. "Dude won't last the night."

Which I known anyhow. Right then Trig ain't carry the weight on the street he had cause all his crew get shot but still that dude done wasted the wrong grandmother. Cuts on him and pocket full of money . . . he ain't gone be finding no place to hide.

Trig twang the knife blade. "Candyman crew," he say. "Oh, Candyman . . ." He singing it a little that time, but his face stiff up.

"Whuffo," I say. "They ain't have nothing to do with this."

"Shit, I know that." I seen Trig teeth. "But they *available,* don't you know?"

And I did know how he felt. Could have felt the same, some time. I wouldn't of said it was a bad idea. Trouble was, he had it too late.

2

DEVLIN KNELT, sitting on his heels, his hands placed palm down on his knees, head half-bowed, eyes half-lidded, facing the Korean flag. His nostrils slightly flaring, he inhaled down the back of his throat into his diaphragm, then opened his mouth for the exhalation as the band of belly muscle compressed—but he was not consciously aware of these procedures; it was as if the air did the work of inflating him from outside and then sucked itself away. Through the lashes of his partly closed eyes he stared at the yin-yang symbol on the flag, searching for its center, but the center was nowhere to be found; it shifted and ran away along the wavy line where the red teardrop mated with the blue one, until the whole disc began to shimmer and spin and lose itself in a haze of golden dots before Devlin's exhausted vision (he had been sleeping poorly these last couple of weeks) and then snapped back, sharp and crisp and clearly divided. Devlin stood up and bowed to the flag, saying nothing to the empty room behind him, and began.

He had no students now. The old ones stopped coming after Gyp was killed, and Devlin was not interested in attracting new ones anymore, though he kept to his regular class schedule. Every day, when he had finished his appointments, he would park on McDonogh Street and slip unobtrusively into the storefront, pulling the gates shut behind him so no one would be likely to come to the door. The lengthening hours of daylight meant that he could practice without turning on the lights.

The emptiness of the shadowy room seemed justified, correct, symmetrical. It seemed to him that the school had expanded and contracted on a smooth, orderly rhythm as well proportioned as the dilation and compression of his lungs, its members appearing and then vanishing inevitably like ninety-nine bottles of beer on the wall, birds on a wire, tin targets carried in a shrinking ellipse by a shooting-gallery belt. Anywhere else, he suffered nightmares and chagrin and private agonies of guilt. But this was sanctuary. Each day when he infiltrated the gate he slipped out of his whole prior history as if from a smothering winter coat. Sanctuary . . . he remembered saying that to Trig. But now when he was practicing, he no longer thought of Trig, or anyone.

He did full basics without a pause, hand techniques and kicks and combinations. It warmed him but scarcely tired or winded him. Afterward, he sat in butterfly position on the floor for about two minutes, fanning his knees gently and breathing in and out. When he rose again his limbs were clothed in a slick new suit of sweat. Then he practiced all the forms he had ever learned from start to finish—it took him half an hour or forty minutes to get through them all. Forms had become the elusive center to his hour of sanctuary, like the slipping center of the yin-yang. When he was done with forms, he felt a distant sense of oppression or anxiety, suspecting that soon, when he left the building, the story of his life would again close over his head. Since he was alone, there could be no sparring, so to defer the moment when he'd have to step outside his shelter, he wore himself senseless with drills on the bag.

Sometimes he could cling to the sensation for hours, at least for an hour, after he had locked himself out of the school. Sometimes the feeling would spontaneously wash over him during his workday, while he saw his patients. He felt himself becoming less of a talker, but a better listener with them, as his conviction grew that nothing he could do or say much mattered. Do no harm: that was the first covenant. If he could sustain his state of stillness, it might be possible for him to exist without injuring anyone.

"THEY DON'T really need me to tell them anything," he said, attempting normal conversation with Alice over dinner, a little shoptalk about his patients. "They don't even need me to ask any questions."

"What do you mean?" Alice asked, a forkful of wine-stewed chicken halfway to her lips.

"Nobody needs to talk to *me,*" Devlin said. "I'm just a backboard, so people can talk to themselves."

Alice returned her fork to her plate, the bite untasted. For a moment Devlin thought she might burst into tears, and he found himself oddly hoping for that to happen. The candles flickered—they were dining by candlelight, alone, an effort to shore something up, they thought. Michelle was out, they didn't know just where, though Devlin might have hazarded a guess. Then the candles drew themselves erect, and Alice composed herself and seemed to look at him across the deep and orderly array of her defenses.

"You know this is depression talking," she said calmly. "You should know you're going into a really deep trough."

Devlin swallowed and said nothing, and Alice continued talking, reasonably and distantly, about bipolar disorder and the new medications. Devlin waved the proposition away.

"Forget it," he said. "Let's say I'm just playing devil's advocate." Even in his own ears it sounded like a lame retreat.

Still, their lovemaking took place as foreseen, or hoped for, and was even surprisingly successful. Yet for Devlin, at least, it had a tragic quality, which reminded him of his last time, years before his marriage, with another love, one that had failed. They must have both known or at least suspected that it would be the last time, so that their touches and their movements were shot through with despairing urgency. An excellent performance, from the technical standpoint at least, but it had left him feeling shattered and unwilling to reach her.

It wasn't the happiest memory to go to sleep on, but Devlin did sleep, as Alice also seemed to do, for an hour or two or three, until he woke to the swish of tires and a dying engine in the driveway, the semisurreptitious click of Michelle's car door. He didn't bother to look at the clock.

Michelle was being moderately stealthy, but the weather was warm enough by this time that they left their bedroom window open, and he could hear the whisper of her shoe soles on the asphalt, and the slight grating of her key in the lock. She might as well be reckoned an adult, he reminded himself, listening to the tumblers turning in the kitchen door she locked behind her. This time next year they would not be listening for her return.

There were a couple of plumbing noises, a shaft of light cutting briefly across the upstairs hall from the bathroom and then extinguishing. Then the semisilence of the darkened house. Alice shifted her position and Devlin sensed she was awake. He felt that they both stiffened slightly, as if the consciousness of each was an intrusion to the other. She reached across the sheet and found his hand.

"Mike . . ." Light pressure on his palm. "I don't want to let you drown . . ."

"I know that," Devlin whispered.

". . . but I won't let you drag me under."

He knew that too, and was even grateful for it, but this was not a response he could make. Her hand remained in his for a short time, and he might have been asleep already by the time she let him go.

AT THE SCHOOL he need not remember moments of this character; it was the only place he could successfully evade them. And it cost him no effort; everything simply fell away from him as soon as he walked in the door. That simple. He had stood defeated before that simplicity every day of his life. But defeat and victory were not distinguishable, once you had managed to let go. The simplest things were the hardest to master. Apparently he had known this always, but it seemed he had not been able to practice the knowledge before now. Now there was only now, and no Devlin at all, when he practiced *Kum Gan*, the image of the Korean mountain he would never see, only bone and muscle and air moving in perfect concert together. A dim shadow figure followed him in the mirrors to his left, but he never glanced to check the rectitude of his positions. Three palm strikes forward and three knifehand strikes retreating, the uniform snapping audibly with each. Then he pulled up in tortuous slow motion into a crane stance, the move where previously he'd always faltered and lost his balance, now focusing toward the flag's yin-yang as his right knee straightened and his left knee slowly rose, the blocking arms crossed and divided slowly—then turning sharply to the left as the blocks snapped into locked position. A wave of *chi* erupted from the bottom of his belly and shot from his eyes like a flamethrower. Now he faced the other in the mirror, and maybe this was the ghost that had to bear the curse of Devlin's past and future for this time, but now he was not aware of that thought or of any other.

MICHELLE STROLLED through the covered brick arcade of Hollins Market, glancing inattentively at the stalls: meat and fish and cheese and flowers . . . She thought of buying something to bolster her cover story, but meat or fish wouldn't keep in her parked car—besides, her parents had long since stopped being nosy. She came out of the far end of the building onto the street and doubled back along the narrow sidewalk, swinging her empty hands. It was a little past four o'clock, and lukewarm sunlight spilled down the western end of the street, where a gull came wheeling up above the low brick row houses, cried, and dropped away behind them. She carried no purse, just her driver's license and a couple of bills fastened with a paper clip, buttoned in the left breast pocket of the jean jacket she wore. Hollins Market was a sort of honky oasis in the midst of the projects, a two-block strip where it was safe enough for her to park and walk and wait, though it was also very near the crack corners, and conveniently close to Poe Homes.

She went into a Mexican place, chose a bar stool and ordered a Corona. A fake ID rode in her right jacket pocket, separate from her real credentials so she wouldn't mix them up if the police should stop her car. But the barmaid served her without asking for proof. Funny, but ever since she'd been with Trig she'd hardly ever been carded, whether he was along or not, as if his company had somehow aged her.

She poured about half the beer into her glass and began watching it evaporate. Beer buzz had never appealed to her much—she preferred pot—but the phony ID was a social requirement, and it was more comfortable to sit in a place like this with a beer in front of her than a Coke. She tapped the glass with her fingernail and watched the sliver of lime swim in the foam. It was class time, just about. Across town, her father would have opened, they would all be warming up. Michelle didn't know that everyone had stopped attending—Trig had never mentioned it to her. If she stayed away herself it was from embarrassment, not anger; she didn't want Devlin to see her together with Trig in any circumstance whatever.

Getting caught by her father had been a major anticlimax, and Michelle couldn't quite decide if she was relieved or disappointed. At home, it was all as if nothing had happened, and Devlin treated her with nervous affection, and didn't ask her any questions. The trouble was, though, that something *had* happened and both of them knew it. What was it exactly that had happened? If her mother had been involved, the whole thing would have gone very differently, Michelle knew that, but she also knew that Devlin's notion of the trust between them meant that he'd never tell her mother. So here they all were in the Twilight Zone. Michelle caught herself up, glancing at her reflection in the mirror behind the bar and pulling a strand of hair behind her ear; she had almost uttered that last thought aloud.

For the look of the thing, she lifted her glass and took a flattened sip of it. Down the counter, the barmaid was wrapped up in a conversation with a thirtyish man with a goatee, while passersby glancing at the plate-glass window of the place would see their own reflections, not Michelle. Twilight Zone. She would leave Baltimore in the fall, entering Williams with an academic scholarship and half a year's worth of advanced-placement credits. That departure date put a bracket around her whole thing with Trig—as her father had said, *he* wouldn't be going off to college. It was real on one side of the bracket and unreal on the other, though it depended on the time of day which side she thought was which. Most times she felt sealed up with Trig in a sort of magic bubble where she was secure and untouchable. She knew that the bubble might be perforated at any time but most times she didn't believe it would be.

A hand smoothed her hair down the nape of her neck, pressing and probing the tendons; she looked in the mirror and found Trig's face reflected there above her own. They kissed, Michelle stretching up to meet him, raising herself from the bar stool. Still a spark of illicit thrill to kiss in a public place like this, black man and white woman, though no one paid them any attention. Trig broke contact and sat down on the stool beside hers.

"Smell like burritos in here," he said. "You hungry?"

"No," Michelle said. "Not for that."

Trig smiled. The barmaid appeared and looked at him inquiringly.

"Let's go over to Gyp's," Michelle said.

They had been using Gyp's apartment for the last little while, because Trig's place in Poe Homes was prone to telephone calls or drop-ins, from Mud-dog who was nervous working so many corners by himself, or maybe from Sharmane. No one expected anyone to be at Gyp's anymore since Gyp was dead, which might have given Michelle the creeps but didn't.

When Trig had parked the car on Lexington, she got out and walked beside him across the patch of ragged, littered grass to the security shack, where the guard no longer looked surprised to see the two of them. The elevator was still broken; they walked up. When they stepped onto the storm-fenced catwalk, the lowering sun cast distorted diamond shadows over them from the wire. Raising her shirttail with the hem of her jacket, Trig put his warm hand on the bare skin of her back, and she felt the warmth spread meltingly as they passed through the queer shadows. She touched her upper lip delicately with her tongue, and leaned into him, hip and shoulder, as he unlocked the door.

With the shades drawn, it was completely dark inside. Trig turned in the shaft of light from the open door, groping for the light switch. The lamps came on, the way Gyp had wired them—Michelle sucked in her breath and took a step back, startled at the sight of Butch, who was pressed against the wall by the door hinge. He seemed equally dismayed to see her. For a moment she thought he would bow to her, but he didn't. Then she noticed he was holding a sawed-off double-barreled shotgun in his hands; he didn't seem to know which way to point it.

Kool-whip was there too, holding a dull-colored automatic pistol to the back of Trig's skull. Trig had frozen, expressionless, his open hands hanging in the air above his hips. Butch stepped through the open doorway, holding the shotgun vertically. He looked both ways down the catwalk, then came inside and flipped the dead bolt shut.

"Yo." It was a third man speaking, someone Michelle had never seen before. He looked older than the others, with a short natural haircut and a meaty, pockmarked face. "We been waiting on you to come up."

"Candyman," Trig said.

Candyman stepped forward and felt under Trig's arms and down his legs, finally removing a pistol from the back of his waistband. He ejected the clip and looked at it, and then slapped it back into the gun butt. Kool-whip lowered his weapon and stepped back. Trig glanced at him over his shoulder and smiled enigmatically.

"Let's not have no karate bullshit, yo," Candyman said. He walked to the stereo cabinet and laid Trig's pistol on a shelf. He was thick through the chest, with a bit of a belly; a gold medallion swung out from the throat of his maroon turtleneck when he turned to face the room again.

"Fucked up," Trig said. "You ain't got no beef with me."

"It fucked up, yo," Candyman agreed. "You oughta stayed on your own side of town."

Michelle noticed that the sawed-off shotgun was more or less aimed at her waist—Butch pointing it toward her from his hip. She walked gingerly across the room, passing between Candyman and Trig, and sat down on the edge of a white leather couch. The eyes of the shotgun didn't track her. On a chrome-and-glass end table near her elbow was a telephone.

"You out of business, Trig," Candyman said. "I like to see where you keep your shit."

"People in hell want ice cream cones." Trig laughed. "Think I'm gonna give up my good?"

"Give it time," Candyman said. "How long before Mud-dog come up here?"

"Ain't coming," Trig said.

"Well," said Candyman. "Let's wait and see."

Trig took off his fringed leather jacket and hung it over one arm so that his left hand was concealed.

"You can throw that down anywhere," Candyman said. "Have yourself a seat."

"I'm cool," Trig said, remaining where he was.

Candyman looked at Kool-whip. "Shoot his ass, then."

Trig waved at Kool-whip, deprecatingly, and tossed the jacket toward the couch; it struck the arm opposite Michelle and slid into a crumpled heap on the white hair of the carpet. Trig sat down on a spring-back chair with leather cushions.

Butch sneezed and wiped his nose with the back of his free hand. Michelle glanced at the telephone, which was made of clear lucite, to show all of its inner workings. She stood up and went to the door without interference and was touching the knob of the dead bolt when she heard Candyman's voice.

"Where you plan on going, white girl?"

Michelle withdrew her hand from the latch and turned. "I thought I'd leave you gentlemen to settle your business in private."

Candyman smiled and shook his head. "Nice."

He crossed the room and put his hand politely under her elbow and guided her back toward the white couch. At the point when he was between her and the others' guns, Michelle felt her adrenaline surge and she glanced at Trig, but he shook his head almost imperceptibly—just a slight jerk of his chin.

Michelle sat on the couch where she had been before. She still couldn't believe that anyone here would harm her, although she knew she really should believe it. Candyman looked down at her ruefully, then turned toward Trig.

"You ought not to brought her up here today."

Trig slouched down in his chair and exhaled toward the ceiling. Candyman looked at Michelle again; she felt his genuine regret.

"Too bad, yo," Candyman said.

SHARMANE WAS walking slowly back into slanting sunlight, returning from Lexington Market, looking down at her shoes and the stroller wheels turning. A quarter-full plastic shopping bag hung by its loops from the stroller handles, balanced that way. She hadn't bought much, hadn't really needed anything at all, but the apartment was spooky with Gramma Reen gone, the way she'd gone, and Sharmane was in a place where she'd walk two miles to buy a pack of cigarettes or a carton of milk. No other way to get out of herself—Tamara had gone to see cousins in Norfolk, and most of the rest of her friends were dead.

She was leaning into the stroller a little, shoving up the grade toward Gyp's old building, when she saw the black Lexus float to the curb and stop. Michelle got out and started toward the entrance, and then Trig joined her, turning back for a couple of seconds to zap the power locks with his high-tech remote-control key ring. Sharmane flared. She fished in the pocket of her satin jacket and found a cigarette to light, then threw it down after a couple of drags. They hadn't seen her, the two of them—didn't have eyes to see anything.

That explained a thing or two—where Trig had been keeping himself lately, claiming it was business pressures when all the time he was spreading the white girl across the bed where Sharmane had been with Gyp. She scrubbed her toe over the smoldering Kool until it tore into pale shreds, then thrust the stroller up toward the security shack.

"Watch this for me," Sharmane snapped at the half-dozing guard, and scooped Froggy out of the stroller without waiting for an answer. Froggy was sleeping, one fist clasped around a ring of bright-colored, rattling, oversized plastic keys. Sharmane tried to pry them loose and leave them behind, but his grip was too tight and she let him hold on so as not to wake him. He grumbled and stirred, then slept again, damp mouth slurred against the satin fabric on her shoulder.

Heavy. Sharmane started up the steps, knees creaking under Froggy's weight. Glad she had a ground-floor place at Poe. Graffiti were scribbled on the cinderblock walls, a few threats, a few Valentines. The Poe Homes tag had probably been left there by Freon. Sharmane's footfalls made an echo, but there were other footsteps too, a flight or so above her, and she thought she heard Trig say something, then Michelle's husky laugh. She paused then, not meaning to overtake them all that quickly. Give them time to get inside and maybe even get some of their clothes off, before she busted in to tell them what she thought about it all.

She waited, rocking the sleeping child with the circular sway of the hips that had become her second nature, until she heard the stairwell door click shut overhead. Then she quickly finished the climb. At the sixth floor, she carefully cracked the door to the catwalk and peered out, but there was no one, only the warped fishnet shadows the wire cast over the empty passage. She walked down, hugging close to the wall, until she saw a man step out of Gyp's apartment. Immediately she turned into the nearest doorway, pretending to be reaching for a key. After a second, she peeped again and saw it wasn't Trig but Butch, holding a sawed-off shotgun carelessly in his meaty hand, looking first in her direction, then away.

She shrank herself entirely into the doorway, trying to erase herself within it. She didn't know if she'd been noticed and her heart was going too loud for her to hear if anyone was coming. Then a crash, like an explosion at her feet, and she looked down to see that Froggy had dropped the ring of plastic keys outside the doorway, where they could be seen. Sharmane stopped breathing and waited to die. Nothing happened. When she looked out, Gyp's door was shut, and she snatched up the toy keys and scuttled for the stairwell.

Tumbling down the steps, her mind tumbled too, jangling together scraps of thought—no cops, out of the question, not Mud-dog cause she didn't know where to find him, and anyway, he was likely to choke. Then Freon, D-Trak, Gyp—every card in her hand was marked with a death's-head. They wouldn't have expected to see Michelle up there. Shit, Michelle. Now she was on the street, standing beside the Lexus, Froggy nuzzling at her satin shoulder in his sleep. She looked at the useless toy keys in her hand and tossed them irritably over her shoulder, then crouched and felt under the fender for the magnetic keyholder Trig had told her about, in case, some time, he couldn't help her and the car could. Open the back door, strap Froggy in, still sleeping deeply, start the car. She saw the toy keys lying on the torn grass near a candy wrapper and got out to retrieve them because she knew Froggy would cry for them when he woke up.

Seat up—where was that button for the seat? She could just reach the pedals with her toes, but she was under way already, eastbound, already cursing the traffic. A lot more car than she was used to driving. The radio was blurting out something, or maybe it was a tape, and Sharmane lunged to snap it off. At a red light she punched in the lighter, but her mouth was much too parched and cottony to smoke. Double-parked in front of the school on McDonogh, though it was dark, looked closed—the gate was shut but not quite all the way, and the padlock hanging loose, unhasped. Her mind ran back to the open door of the Poe Homes place, dead Gramma Reen behind it, but she pushed on the Lexus's flasher and jumped out.

The gate scraped back with a howl of rust, but the glass

door was locked behind it, key in the cylinder, on the inside. Sharmane slapped her palms on the glass and peered through her own reflection. No lights, but someone was doing something in there. Yes, Devlin. Sharmane drew in her breath to shout, but then the old routines came back, old rituals. You couldn't interrupt a form, had to wait till it was done. He wouldn't hear her anyway, not now. Exhaling into an eerie calm, she watched him draw up lightly, slowly, into a crane stance, limbs moving with a syrupy languor—then the quick turn and snap to the focus point. He was almost finished anyway. U-punch, spinning U-punch, down and lock. When Devlin relaxed from the final back stance, Sharmane pounded on the glass and began to call his name.

Devlin was suspended, peaceful although half blown out from his exertions; he stood facing the flags, not seeing them, his feet together and his hands hanging open by his sides, listening to the suck and release of his lungs. His breathing seemed so loud he didn't hear anything else at first, and when he did notice the noise at the door he only flapped his hand to wave whoever it was away. *Closed.* He mouthed the words, big pantomime: *Out of business.* It was some woman pressing against the glass, he thought, but she stood in the shadow of the doorway so that he couldn't see her face. She wouldn't leave, and Devlin, irritated, started toward the back. A smashing sound made him look again, and he saw her stepping out of the doorway to launch a sidekick at the thick glass panel—nice form on the kick. When she backed up, the light fell on her and Devlin recognized Sharmane.

The door didn't unlock easily from the inside; it required a delicate push-pull of the key to turn the cylinder, and Sharmane rattling the outside handle didn't help. The glass hadn't shattered under her kick, though it was starred from top to bottom, and Devlin could hear her voice, but not what she was saying, through the glass. As if she were underwater, in some other element beyond the barrier. He remembered the sharks circling at the aquarium, Trig's turtle, only it would be he who was in the tank now; Devlin had become the fish. Then the lock gave and Sharmane came toppling in.

"—jacked up Trig, yo," she was saying. "Michelle too," and Devlin followed her tug on his loose white sleeve. When he stepped onto the sidewalk, he felt the cold on his bare feet, on his sweaty skin, and he looked down and saw what he was wearing.

"One second," Devlin said. He had already undone the knot in his black belt and, racing toward the back, he let it fall in a loose swirl across the mats.

In the office he tore off his top and tossed it in a corner, threw on his jacket without bothering with a shirt, rolled up his street pants to contain his wallet and keys. Sharmane was revving the Lexus at the curb. Devlin leaped in and slammed the door. "What the hell?" he said.

Sharmane, gunning across Eager Street, pulled back her foot from the gas pedal.

"Who's got who, now?" Devlin said.

"Candyman," said Sharmane, and Devlin saw him instantly, not his face but the heavy hand and the automatic flaring from inside the field jacket. Then the dead girl by the stroller, Froggy's mother.

"Gonna smoke'm up at Gyp's," Sharmane said. "Cause it the dope drop."

"Michelle," Devlin said. "What did you say about Michelle?"

"She up there too, yo," Sharmane said. "Her'n Trig, they be *shack* up over there. For, like, they *privacy*."

"Oh Christ . . ." Devlin shook his head. "What is she *doing* up there?"

"Cause you *let her go*." Sharmane was practically screaming. "You ain't done nothing to stop it—you just let the shit happen, Devlin, whyn't *you* tell me whuffo? You could of kept your business up in North Baltimore—why you come down here and mess in our shit?"

Devlin thought about the question, watching cars streaming by on the opposite side of the street, not really seeing them. "I thought I could save people," he said.

Sharmane snorted, half of a bitter laugh. "They past saving now, most of'm. Can't you see that?"

"I overreached myself," Devlin admitted. "It didn't work out like I had in mind."

Sharmane made the same snort again. "Well," she said. "Here's where you might get one more chance."

They crossed Martin Luther King into the projects—less traffic here, and in the silence Devlin looked over the back of his seat and discovered Froggy, still asleep, his slack mouth warped against the expensive leather cushions.

"Police," he said, looking back at Sharmane.

"Uh-unh, no," Sharmane said, eye on the road. "Cause it the dope-drop—they be busting Trig."

Devlin glanced at the car phone riding on the mount between the seats. He had always eschewed such things as an affectation, though Alice would have liked to be able to reach him in the car. He thought of Curtis and Spencer, their faces, then SWAT teams. Hostage negotiators.

"All right," Devlin said.

Sharmane pulled up on the south side of Gyp's building, halting so sharply that Devlin had to brace himself on the padded dash.

"I can get you in," she said. "Just you."

Devlin looked across at the building. On this side every aperture was sealed with plywood, and the yard was enclosed in an eight-foot storm fence—no gate visible. Where Sharmane had stopped was a triangular tear in the wire about three feet from the ground. Inside the enclosure, an old newspaper fluttered in the wind, discarding one sheet after another as it turned across the gray-green lawn. Sharmane was leaning across Devlin's lap, fumbling in the glove compartment. She sat back in the driver's seat, holding up a grubby envelope that had once been pink.

"You go through the break in the fence there," she said. "See that board with the Z-tag on it? It just swinging on one nail—you get through that and go on up to 6-D."

She reached into the envelope and pulled out a Medeco key.

"It padlocked from the outside," she said. "Go in and look in the bedroom closet—it's a trapdoor go through to Gyp's from there."

"What?" Devlin said.

"Cause it the *dope-drop,*" Sharmane said, exasperated. "Two ways in and two ways out—gotta be."

"I don't get it," Devlin said. "They sell out of there or what?"

"*No,*" Sharmane said. "Cut and store, that's it. Listen, two sides of this building is everything separate, two different addresses, yo. Six-D on this side back up to Gyp apartment on the front side and they cut'm a hole in between there in case of . . . whatever."

"Candyman knows this?" Devlin said.

"You better hope he don't," Sharmane said. "S'what he be trying to find out."

"All right." Devlin took the key from her and looked at it, then hitched up his hip to stick it in his watch pocket, but he was still wearing his loose white uniform trousers, and there was no pocket in those.

"Far as I go." Sharmane looked into the backseat and Devlin followed her glance. Froggy turned and mumbled in his sleep, his thick-fingered hand jostling a ring of colored plastic keys on the seat beside him.

"How many of them are up there?" Devlin said.

"Don't know," Sharmane said. "Maybe two—at least."

Devlin nodded and got out of the car, walked around the hood to the sidewalk and the fence. The concrete was chilly on the bare soles of his feet; he had run out of the school without stopping for his shoes. Two crows sat on the fence, watching his approach; they didn't fly until he'd put his hand on the wire. He folded back the stiff metal, ducked and swung through. As he passed, a cut end of the wire gouged into the gap between his jacket and his trousers, scoring a bloodless white line on his skin. He straightened on the inside of the fence and looked back. Sharmane had rolled down the window of the Lexus.

"Devlin," she said.

Devlin looked at her, framed in the window—the crazy conical hair style with stiff curlicues plastered to her cheeks, the slant of her vaguely Oriental eyes.

"Don't fuck up," Sharmane said.

When he smiled at her, the thumbs-up smile that he intended, his cheeks felt tight and shriveled. He turned and walked across the lawn toward the building, setting his feet down carefully because there was broken glass scattered with the rags and dented cans and paper trash. The plywood panel Sharmane had indicated was marked with a large, ornate *Z* done in black spray paint. Devlin stuck the padlock key between his teeth and used both hands to take the wood by the edges. The board swung easily to the left. Devlin slipped through and let it drop behind him.

Dark. Dark and musty-smelling. Devlin waited, poised, until his eyes adjusted. The key spread a brassy taste across his tongue; he took it from his mouth and held it in his palm. Some light leaked in through chinks around the boards, and after a minute he could see his way.

He padded down the littered corridor. The elevator doors were open, revealing the car wedged crookedly in the shaft, halfway to the basement, cables severed. Devlin looked up the empty shaft but there was no light to see anything. He groped along the wall and found a door that wouldn't open and one that would.

It was lighter here because the panes of frosted glass that lined the stairwell had not been boarded over. Some were broken, and a pigeon startled by Devlin's approach flew out through a jagged hole. More graffiti covered the walls, and there were other signs of occasional use: crumpled cans, empty crack vials, pockets of urine smell, and a small, drab pile of dried feces. Devlin went cautiously, stopping now and then to listen, but there was nothing to hear but the echo of his own movements.

Still light on the sixth-floor hallway; one of the boards had fallen off the windows. Many of the apartment doors hung open, and some didn't have any doors at all, but at 6-D the door was steel and secured with a massive padlock.

Devlin opened it with no difficulty and stuck the lock in his jacket pocket with the key still inserted. He went in, using the hasp of the padlock to prop the door open and admit a couple of inches of dim light.

A one-bedroom apartment, strictly empty except for a layer of dust on the bare wooden floor. The dust was tracked, and Devlin could recognize the waffle-prints of the Timberland boots some of Trig's crew had favored. Thick iron burglar bars were bolted across all the windows, inside the plywood sheets that sealed the building's face. In the kitchen alcove, a scale and two jumbo boxes of baking soda stood on the counter, along with several neat rows of the little black-capped crack vials, ready for service. Also a large flashlight, with a fluorescent tube.

Devlin snapped it on and walked into the bedroom, which was completely empty except for a cheaply framed print nailed to the wall—purple-robed Jesus kneeling by a rock, face upturned into a shaft of lurid orange light. Devlin opened the closet door and pulled out some empty cartons that were stacked inside. A shallow depression in the rear wall was lined with a sheet of cardboard unfolded from another one of the boxes. When Devlin laid his ear against it, he could hear an indistinct murmur of voices on the other side.

He backed out of the closet, ducking under the hanger bar. The jacket seemed to bind his arms so he took it off and dropped it in a corner. A muffled clunk when the padlock struck the floor through the leather. His bare torso was coated with a thin rime of dried sweat, but it wasn't so cold inside the building, and he still felt loose and flexible from the exercise earlier. From where he stood, he could no longer hear the voices muttering.

He switched off the flashlight and stepped back into the closet, pulling the door shut so there'd be no light behind him. Again, the mumble was audible . . . The top edge of the cardboard was just lower than his chin. He pulled back the corner, and heard Trig's voice clearly.

"What I tell you, bro," Trig said. "You wasting your time."

The palm of Devlin's hand was striped with light from the next apartment. He stooped and peered through the grille beneath the cardboard. Candyman, wearing a maroon turtleneck, was standing opposite him in the other room, posed just in front of some black lacquer bookshelves.

"I got all the time in the world, baby," Candyman said. "It's you the one running out of time."

The cardboard was attached to the grille with mounting squares. Devlin worked the balls of his fingers around the edges, careful to make no noise as he peeled it away. When the cardboard came completely free he folded it in half and shoved it out of the way, sideways down the inner closet wall. The light from the grille now barred his body from shoulder to knee. On the other side, it must appear to be a heater or an air-conditioning vent.

He squatted on his heels and peered through the tiny slits of the grille, turning his head this way and that. His heart bulged when he saw Michelle, sitting at the end of a white leather couch—though she certainly seemed unhurt, almost unruffled. There was some strain in her face, a tense set of her jawline, that he could remember seeing, for instance, on the morning when she left her house to take the SATs.

Calm down, Devlin said to himself; it's what he would

have said to Michelle before the test. He turned his face against the grille and saw Trig, sitting in a chair beyond the far end of the couch. Near him, Devlin saw someone else's hand, and he mashed his cheek into the grille to better his angle. It was Kool-whip, standing just to Trig's left, holding a small, sleek-looking automatic pistol. Devlin wasn't a gun expert, but he supposed it might be one of those nine-millimeter handguns that were said to be so popular on the street.

That made the two Sharmane had predicted. Devlin breathed deep into his belly, and touched his hand to where the grille had creased his cheek. Looking straight through the grille he could still see Candyman, who collected another, slightly larger pistol from the bookshelf and walked across the room toward Michelle. There was a strange stiffness to his back, as if his discs were fused. He laid the gun muzzle against her temple, lazily—the movement was almost without any appearance of aggression. Devlin looked at Michelle's left hand on her knee, measured the distance between its edge and Candyman's wrist. *Don't try it,* he thought. He heard Trig laugh.

"Give it up, Trig," Candyman said.

"Go ahead and shoot her." Trig's voice. "Then you ain't got no more leverage. Just a major murder beef."

Candyman shook his head and withdrew the gun. His stiff back tilted slightly forward from his hips as he moved, so that the gold medallion he wore swung out from his breastbone. He put the gun back on the shelf, glanced toward Trig and shrugged.

"Always other stuff to do," he said. "You could watch, Trig. What you think?"

"That ain't you, Candyman," Trig said. "You don't want to be doing that shit. White girl, connected? They bury your ass underneath the jail."

Devlin breathed in. He was calm now—his mind was cold, even, though his body felt properly warm and electric. This was it. He squinted to see that Kool-whip hadn't moved. One gun in play. He could pop Kool-whip the instant he came through and then reach Candyman before he could get to the other gun. With the surprise advantage it was definitely doable. Cowboy bullshit, Devlin knew, but he felt light and clear, free as an untethered balloon. It was what he'd spent so long preparing for—you take your whole life in your hands and pour it out. He took a short step backward and kicked out the grille.

Screaming out of the wall, Devlin cut straight for his first target, but Trig, half-rising from his seat, had already armlocked Kool-whip onto the floor and had control of his pistol, so Devlin zagged toward target two. It was working. Candyman was pulling flies out of his mouth and hadn't yet reached for the gun on the shelf. But something caught the corner of Devlin's eye and he froze in the middle of the room.

Shotgun to his left, sawed-off shotgun. Devlin didn't turn his head, just rolled his eyes, and there was Butch with a sawed-off shotgun, standing against the wall to the left of the grille. No way Devlin ever could have seen him. The barrels were cut so short that now he could see the crimp on the shells inside—if the thing went off, it would hit everybody in the room, but it was pointed roughly at Michelle.

Devlin relaxed. Michelle was up on one knee on the

couch, a hand braced on the armrest; she hadn't moved any farther than that. Candyman had snatched the other handgun and was aiming at Devlin's midsection with both hands. Kool-whip lay facedown on the floor with Trig's foot planted on the back of his neck, while Trig aimed Kool-whip's gun at Candyman. Butch was pointing the other gun in Michelle's direction, but you couldn't quite say he was aiming it; he looked so deep in shock it was almost as if he'd forgotten he had the gun at all. Plan A might have worked, Devlin thought, but it was too late now.

"Gentlemen," Devlin said.

"What the fuck?" said Candyman.

Trig laughed. Devlin didn't move.

"It's over," Devlin said. Deep voice, reassuring . . . one of his shrink tones. "Let's put down the guns."

Nobody seemed to move a hair. Michelle was staring palely at Devlin but he didn't want to be distracted by looking at her face.

"We can all walk away from it, gentlemen," Devlin said. "Just drop it and walk away. If not, we're probably all going to die. Let's put down the guns."

No movement.

"It doesn't matter who goes first," Devlin said. Without shifting any other part of his body, he turned his head to look at Butch.

"Hey," he said, a bit sharply now. "What do you think you're doing? Put it down."

Butch's face twisted. He clicked something on the back of the shotgun and Devlin's heart stopped. Then he saw that Butch had broken the piece and was removing both of the shells. Butch stooped and gently laid the empty weapon on the carpet.

"That's the way," Devlin said. He felt a stinging sweat sliding down his neck, pooling in the hollow of his collarbones. "Now Trig."

"Shit," Trig said.

"It doesn't matter who goes first." Devlin was facing Candyman, about three yards away. Trig appeared as a shadow at the edge of his peripheral vision.

"Just do it," Devlin said. Trig sighed and tossed his pistol over behind the couch.

"That's the way," Devlin said, elated. It was working again.

"Fuck this, yo," Candyman said. "I ain't playing."

"Game's over," Devlin said. He took a step forward, gently, reversing his stance. Two yards. He could see nothing but Candyman now. That odd stoop brought his head and the gun a bit closer than it would have been otherwise. Candyman worked the slide on the pistol, slamming a round into the chamber.

"One more step, asshole," Candyman said. "Whoever you are. One more step and you done."

"No winners," Devlin said. "No losers." He opened his forward hand, the left one. "Give me the gun."

His voice was steady; so was the gun barrel. Devlin shrank his focus so that he saw only Candyman's hands and the pistol. He waggled the fingers of his left hand and began another soft step forward but Candyman's hand revealed its intention and Devlin changed his mind. He sprang into the air with a flying side kick and heard a ragged explosion at almost the same instant he felt his heel smash into the other man's larynx and through. He fell in an untidy heap on the floor.

Michelle had bailed over the back of the couch as soon

as Devlin moved, scooping up the phone on the way, and now he heard her giving the address to 911. He felt proud of her. Sharmane's warning about the police had slipped his mind. He got up onto one knee. Candyman lay on his back, not breathing. Devlin didn't see where the pistol had fallen.

Michelle hung up the phone and raised her head above the back of the couch.

"Good girl," Devlin said. Something was wrong with her face. "You're all right," he said.

He touched his bare chest and his hand came away thick and sticky. Remembering how upset she would be at the sight of blood, he felt foolish and embarrassed. He got to his feet, swaying and then righting himself. Something was wrong with Trig's face too. The apartment door was open, where Butch had fled; Kool-whip, still under Trig's heel, looked at the opening longingly. Devlin turned his back on them all and strolled out onto the catwalk.

Nothing hurt him anywhere at all. The wind that blew in through the wire was neither warm nor cold, and Devlin was washed in the crimson sunset light that flooded the walkway from the west. Another storm-fenced barrier between him and the open air, six floors above the grubby street. A seagull swooped toward the fencing, crying harshly, and then sheered away. Devlin felt a little dizzy now, and he hooked his fingers through the wire to gain support. There were sirens, but what Devlin saw arriving was the black Camaro, coughing and shuddering just on the far side of the wire, except the wire was gone. A star of reflected sunset blazed out over him from the shimmering windshield. The Camaro unfurled a long warm velvet wing and drew him gently in.

1

TRIG

SHELL COME BY to see me sometime. We ain't like what we was, ain't no *thang* between us no more. No touch visit. Make more sense that way when she gone one direction and I gone another one. She halfway through college now and doing fine. So most the time she off to school and can't come here so much. Except summer. Then she do come more, sometime by herself and sometime with Sharmane and Froggy.

I make sure I ax about her grades and shit ever time she come. For practice, maybe, or something. Froggy up walking and talking now, be starting school time I get out from here, if I don't lose my good time. You get pissed at him now like Sharmane sometime do, you calls him by his real name—Je-ROME!

Shell will bring me a book or two when she come. And

send me letters from school too about what she studying. Some of the shit I can get in here—get Sharmane to find it. I be doing more of this reading than what I use—that way the time don't go for nothing like it do with the TV. I be taking some classes over the school wing along with it. Might try this studying bit for real when I once get out. Sharmane be taking a class or two. So maybe she can hook me up when the time come.

Keep your head to yo-self in here, you get time to think, and the way I think, if you can run one business you can run another one cause they all put together the same way. So get out, get some school, and get started with something that don't land you up in the Cut if it bust up and where you don't have to worry all your employees probably gonna get killed.

Once it all come down, Michelle say to me how she just want to be my friend. This hurt me at the first—can't say it didn't. Seem everybody left me then. But later I thought, well, a friend. Not a bitch or a trick or road-dog or a sucker but a friend. Maybe I could get down with that, yo. And she *has* live up to her end of it so far.

This all a little shaky at the start though cause at first Shell have to beat up on herself like it was her fault I went to the walls, cause of her phoning the cops and all. Which it made me tired to listen to cause it never been that simple. Like, I still had time to jet if I wanted to, instead of laying there blowing my breath into Devlin mouth and watching it bubble back out the holes Candyman shot in his chest. Coulda been right behind Butch and Kool-whip, back on the bricks.

I thought about it too. I known what was going to happen.

The whole thing just a big tangled-up knot and if you once got all the strings undone, one thing you gonna find out is that if Michelle hadn't been up there Devlin wouldna been neither. So Devlin might still be alive some way if not for what she done. But what was the use of her having to think that? Best to just leave it stay tangled up. Let it alone. So what I tell her, she had no way of knowing what was gonna come down, and once it did drop she done the best she know how. Which wasn't so bad really.

Then I got Devlin telling me, *The truth will set you free.* Everbody else think this dude is dead, only I still got to argue with his ass, inside my mind.

Then of course Shell have to testify at the trial and shit. Cause she they only eyewitness alive. And she be beating on herself how she gonna get me in deeper shit with that, and she want to try to lie me out of it—but here me'n Devlin agree for once, let her just keep to the truth. What she know of it. If Sharmane been sitting where she was, different deal maybe, but nobody ever could put Sharmane in a mile of that building, not that afternoon. And it like, I ain't born to go off to college, and Michelle ain't born to lie to the cops and the courts.

So keep it simple, just tell what she seen. She never known what was in that next apartment noway. Only lie she did tell was she stonewalled it on Butch and Kool-whip. I mean she said they was two other guys there cause it wouldn't made no sense otherwise but she played like she didn't know who they was. Which I thought was best. Even Devlin was cool with that, cause of *brotherhood of the do-jang* and shit. And them two wasn't gonna get up to no more nasty now Candyman was smoked, especially if nobody drug'm back into it.

So that was it. They'd of like to give me at least one of the murders, but wasn't no way. All they could hit me with was the dope, and jury didn't even like that as well as they hoped. So I be out of the Cut about the time Michelle graduate from college maybe. If she keep up her grades and I don't lose my good time.

Call it a fucking holiday. I didn't even bother to file no appeal. Partly cause it was just the lawyers wanting to drain off some more my good and partly I'm thinking I could really use some time off the street. Once it all come down, seem like I been tired for a long long time. Wore out and didn't know what I was doing no more and didn't have no idea what I should do next.

But. Same in here as it is on the street, and sometime worse. Here I sit with this Poe Homes bullshit torched on my arm, which if I never let Freon talk me into it we all been a lot better off. Gang I down with ain't got no members no more. But they some serious gangbanging over here, yo, with guys all looking at my P-tag wondering what do it signify cause they ain't ever seen one like it before.

Nothing. I ain't on no gang program no more. Out the dope business too, even though it run real good in here—never took the shit myself noway. Hard to get this over at first, how Trig stand for hisself and that's all. Devlin help me there. I bust a couple noses, cracked a few ribs—kept all this down to the minimum, though. Just enough to make the point. Till people get persuaded to leave me some walking room.

Only next after that, once I shown my arm, what I knew was niggaz slipping around with, *Show me how you done that, yo* . . . So after while I got my own little Tae Kwon Do show running in here just like I was a baby Devlin. Same way I wasn't gonna get down with no one group either. I take whoever will follow the rule, and don't even tell me about no gangbanging. Some niggaz didn't like it that way but I make it stick. It all have to be done in secret anyhow cause the hacks don't like it.

You'd think this would made Devlin happy but all he do is gimme shit. Like how I'm following his mistakes, gone get myself in a hole someway. I say, yo, I'm just only carrying on your flag so what have you got to bitch about? But he keep rumbling and grumbling all the time at the backside of my head.

He right too. In one way, this time he right.

See, I fix it all straight with all the niggaz no problem—not much problem anyway. I got my respect: this is Trig and I just want to do my time and read my books and practice my exercise, which the last part you can do with me if that what you want but don't be hanging me up with nobody else's program. All right. With the brothers, once I make myself clear, this fine. But then you got the white motherfuckers across that line, what they see is Trig generaling up some kind of a niggaz martial-art army. Let that get started with them and here come Charlie Alcorn with his nail run through that dowel.

SO THIS what I got to think about, laying up at the infirmary waiting to get back my strength and try to remember not to scratch around that nail-hole where it itch while it healing and try not to breathe too deep so I don't inhale none of this drug-resisting TB. Listen to Clearwater radio, listen to Clearwater telling me what be happening on back in the blocks. Listen to Clearwater guess when they might send me back there to see for myself. I known he want to ax, "Whatchoo gonna do, Trig?" cause he be thinking some bad shit gonna break once I land back in general population. But he ain't ax me. Known I wouldn't tell him noway.

Nothing to tell. I lay on the rack, nights I can't sleep, and keep on thinking about Rosa Parks. Don't know why can't let that rest. The story fell off the radio after the first day. Just another old lady get jump in her apartment, so what is the big news of that anyhow? Least she live through it. Maybe she might get back somehow. What, she must be eighty-something years old. Ax Clearwater for the newspaper on it, but they just some little story down in the back, and don't show no picture. I must of seen a picture of her sometime in a schoolbook or whatever but that would of been from back in the sixties, don't know what she look like now.

Nights I keep looking for her face up there on the ceiling. Glasses all I can remember—black cat-eye glasses like the women all wearing back then. Gramma Reen never wore no glasses, even though she blind as a bat the last few years—find her way back and forth from the store by memory, I guess.

I never was scared that I could remember. Not one time like this. Even when Candyman had us treed up in Gyp apartment, I ain't scared then neither. I didn't see no way out or nothing but all I known was we ain't sitting through no torture games. Come to that, then we gonna break and if they kill us then that's it. That's all.

Nights I come sucking back out of the dark, wake up sweating and breathing shallow. First thing I think is Rosa

Parks. Man, what that show is the shit ain't going nowhere. One step forward and two step back. Think about Devlin, wanting to save people. I got to admit he did fuck it up. But what I tell him: Once you done lower your *expectation,* get it down to where you just want to save the *one* person, well, you can say you done that all right. Cause you save Michelle. That much you did pull off.

Then Devlin want to tell me, Michelle don't count on his program. The way he got it all figured is it don't matter if you save somebody from trouble you got her into to begin with, so the way he see it if not for him bringing her down to the school then she wouldna hook up with me and then she wouldna been up at Gyp apartment that afternoon at the start—so Michelle don't count for nothing, in his book.

You rather leave her dead, then? I say. Cause when it come down to this I can't any more hold back from screaming at his ass, almost. Why you got make everything so hard, Devlin? Why the *fuck* you can't ever leave it be simple? Then I got the AIDS guys yelling at me to shut up—like they don't make enough noise theyself with coughing and choking and hollering in they sleep.

So I lay quiet and do Tae Kwon Do forms in my head to hold myself back from thinking. They moves in them forms which they don't have no point, they don't have no usefulness really. Only reason they in there at all is cause they hard to do. And these moves I keep coming back to, over and over inside my head.

SO ONE MORNING in they comes and take out my stitches. Ain't but three or four stitches to pull cause it only a little hole. I get in the bathroom and look at the mirror.

Little scar ain't no bigger than a buttonhole, like maybe spose to button my head back on my neck.

And that voice—*You thrown away one life already, do you plan to throw away two?*

That what scare me. What it is.

YOU GET this feeling all the time when shit fixing to go down. Everybody feel it same as you. Like summer storms when they roll up from the bay downtown, the air just get thicker and heavier till you can't draw it in . . . only here it don't never break. No rain.

So I go to eat my slops and I go to work and I go to class in the school wing and I go teach my little Tae Kwon Do sneaky-sneaky out in the yard. All the time it feel like spiders walking up and down my back. Everbody looking at me wondering what I gone do but they don't never ax cause they already know. You got to get back one way or the other.

So I spose to take out Charlie Alcorn, what it is. Which the way it look now, probably gonna touch off a race riot and shit. Then I got a couple lifetimes tack onto my bit, probably, if I live. But everbody know that shit gonna come down cause ain't nobody thought of no other way to play it.

And if I don't do nothing at all . . . If I just stay *centered in myself,* how Devlin say it and how I like to be, then sooner or later Aryan Brotherhood got to hit me again. Cause they don't know no other way to play it. And if they get the job done right this time, race riot anyway, only it over my dead body so I don't have to worry what they add onto my bit.

So what the fuck?

Nights in my rack, if I don't sleep good, I try to make it all up in my head. See it before, how it gonna be. I talk to dead Devlin I use to say, *You know what y'problem is? Live too much in y'mind, yo. All the time you just walking in a dream, but thinking be one thing and doing another.*

More lately though, I ain't that sure. How you gonna do anything you can't dream it first?

All I can do is fix it with the hacks to let me onto the Brotherhood block. They know what coming same as anybody, so I just got to know who to grease. I'm walking the catwalk, metal saying *doom, doom, doom,* under my feet. Walking slow and straight down the middle, setting my feet down hard—I *want* the ma'fuckas to see me coming. They expecting me to strike out of nowhere, but yo, that ain't what they get. Ain't nobody make no move on me even though the tier is all unlock. I ain't bring nobody to watch my back neither. But all the oversize guys from the iron pile they just look and slide inside they cells. Drop the blankets down the bars and lay back listening, peeping through the cracks. Just about as lonely as when I made that other walk to the infirmary, trying to hold my blood back inside my neck. I want to put my hand up over that scar now, where I feel the pulse, but I don't do it. Let my hands go swinging, light and sweet.

Clean your own house, Devlin say.

Alcorn cell gonna be open and him sitting in there with the chessboard laid out. Ma'fucka ain't got no education but he sit around and play chess with himself just about all day. He some kind of master of it, they say. Can't hardly read the newspaper but he can read a chess book. He ain't got no blanket dropped but take him a minute to look up when I come to the gate.

He don't even try to get up from the card table, once he see me there. Both hands flat by the chessboard, ain't reaching for no shank. I raise up my own hands and let my fingers float.

"I ain't holding, yo," I say. I see this don't mean nothing to him cause he believe I can take him off barehand anyway if I want to.

"I ain't gonna do nothing," I say. "I ain't come over here to hurt nobody. All I want is talk the shit over."

Then he looking at me across the chessmen. Alcorn don't bulk up like them other meats down on the iron pile. He put in his time but he don't add no weight, just do more reps to stay stringy and faster that way. Be more better I think myself. He got like always his Manson hairstyle with instead of the swastika the Aryan dagger in that jailhouse purple—point right between his eyes.

I let him look at me a minute before I step inside the cell. Ain't wait to ax his permission and shit. He don't show nothing, but I can see it. I can even understand it. What do you know but the motherfucker is helpless now? Yo, he already killed me, so he ain't got nothing left he can do.

This the point I can't get past. What happen now? What he gonna do? I won't know that till I get there for real. Find out when the time come.

But it don't take so many, like Devlin say, don't need that many to get through. Was it him say that or was it me? Don't matter now. Just need one.